JET XVIII

†

Ignition

Russell Blake

First edition.

Books@RussellBlake.com

ISBN: 979-8376702123

Published by

Reprobatio Limited

CHAPTER 1

Eilat, Israel

The popular domestic tourist destination's waterfront boulevard was buzzing with activity on a balmy night, the scorching arid daytime blast off the Negev desert now replaced by a gentle breeze from the Red Sea, whose waves gently kissed the shore with a barely audible lapping, its surface a mirror barely dented by the wind's stirring. Faint lights twinkled in the distance from Haql, Saudi Arabia, across the Gulf of Eilat, a literal world away from the modern beachfront developments that jutted from along the beachfront promenade.

A spotlight swept the dark sky from the roof of a towering new resort, where a host of glittering beautiful people sipped French champagne and toasted each other while a DJ bobbed and nodded to a pulsing bass beat. The long holiday weekend would see endless such revelry, as the wealthy and privileged from Tel Aviv and Jerusalem mingled in self-congratulatory splendor, the welcome respite from responsibilities to be savored as deeply as possible.

Throngs of scantily clad young women ambled directionless from the hotels along the strand, no special destination in mind relatively early in the evening, the dance clubs and bars not yet packed. Their male counterparts admired them with barely concealed lust, hair slicked back, their expressions equally predatory and hopeful, their body language nonchalant, hours of drinking and banter ahead of them. The air was perfumed by their mingled cologne and perfume, vanilla and jasmine and musk thick as fog. Music from the waterside bistros and the marina yacht club competed with the grinding whine of cranes from the port to the south, its important work never paused, sun-bleached shipping containers lined up in neat rows like troops awaiting battle with an enemy from the sea.

An elderly man made his way down the sidewalk, plodding with the careful steps of someone for whom time is not a friend, and took a seat at an outdoor table in front of a seafood restaurant. Colorful tablecloths and nets and iron diving helmets and sundry fishing gear mounted to the interior walls were visible through the plate-glass window, as was a dark mahogany bar with a shining array of bottles. A shapely hostess materialized with a menu, and a few minutes later a waitress arrived to take his order and place a glass ashtray on the table.

The director ordered the catch of the day and a bottle of mineral water and, when the girl had scurried away, lit a cigarette and took in the lively scene on the promenade. He exhaled heavily, the plume of smoke like a dragon's breath, and considered the series of events that had led him to a forced vacation in a tourist town at the edge of nothing rather than in his customary place, defending his nation against enemies internal and foreign.

The prime minister had summoned him like a schoolboy and informed him that by executive directive, the Mossad would be making changes – the first being one of leadership. The smarmy politician had thanked the director for his decades of loyal service with the fake sincerity of a Bangkok stripper and announced that a new director was to be selected by committee and that the director would be expected to ensure a smooth transition within the month.

The director had been shocked, but not surprised.

"You're throwing me under the bus because you took some heat over headlines that turned out to be false?" he sputtered.

"Not entirely true," the prime minister admonished. "We both know you've been in the saddle for a long time. I feel like we need new blood to keep up with changing times, that's all. And surely you've grown tired of living in your office."

"Our enemies don't rest. This is what it takes to keep up with them. I've never complained. I do what's necessary."

"Yes, and again, you have the gratitude of a nation – which a generous pension should go a long way to demonstrate." The prime minister held up his hands. "But the decision's been made. I'm telling you because I wanted you to hear it from me first."

The director grunted. "So you've made up your mind. What about our ongoing operations? You can't just plug in some bureaucrat and expect him to play catch-up. That's not how things work."

"We've narrowed our candidates down to Noah Greenberg, the head of your Eastern Europe desk. He'll be replacing you, and he's more than versed in operational protocols, is he not?"

The director frowned. "Noah's too young for the job. He doesn't have the experience yet. Smart kid, but you're gambling the nation's safety on a rookie?"

"He's been with you for fifteen years. He's forty-three. I'd say that's seasoned enough." The prime minister paused. "Weren't you about that age when you took the helm?"

The director snorted. "I'd led troops into battle on countless occasions and been a field operative for ten years by then. He's a desk jockey. Like I said, smart, but not street savvy. More book learned than anything. Graduated from Oxford, didn't he?"

The prime minister's eyes narrowed. "Do you have an objection to someone with a doctorate running things? Or is your reluctance limited to Noah?"

"My reluctance is being put out to pasture when the world's never been more dangerous. We have public opinion running against us on the Palestine issue, we're seeing increasing friction from the American Congress, we have new terrorist groups targeting us daily…this seems a poor time to change horses, is my point."

"We're always going to be under pressure. Again, the decision's been made. Your objections are noted, but they won't have any effect." The prime minister strode to the one-way glass window of his office and stared outside for a beat before turning back to the director. "How long do you need to bring Noah up to speed?"

The director thought for a moment. "At least two months. Minimum. We'll also have to worry about filling his chair on the Eastern European desk."

The prime minister didn't move from the window. "You have three weeks."

The director shook his head. "That's not nearly enough time."

"It's what you have."

"Then why ask?"

The prime minister turned and fixed the director with a cold stare. "As a courtesy." His expression softened. "Look, this isn't personal. But I can see you're upset. So take a few days off. You've got a year's vacation you haven't used. Go somewhere. Smell the flowers. Think about what you want the next chapter of your life to look like. Make up for lost time – write a spy novel, chase women, drink too much. All the things you haven't done in forever and have always wanted to."

The director stood. "I appreciate the life counsel, but it's unnecessary."

"It isn't a suggestion. We're headed into a long weekend. I don't want to hear about you back in the office until Monday. I can have your access card revoked if you won't agree voluntarily."

The director's eyebrows twitched. "You're serious," he said.

"I want you to take the time required to cool down and consider what needs to be done. We can spare you for a few days."

"Your first mistake is believing that. Or maybe that's your second. I've lost count."

The prime minister scowled. "Let's regroup on Monday, shall we? This meeting's over."

Now, sitting beachside on his impromptu vacation, the entire discussion seemed surreal and even more infuriating than when it had taken place the prior day. That the fate of the intelligence service was to be decided by a strutting peacock with no germane experience was a slap in the face the director would never get over. That the politician felt he was competent to dismiss the director out of hand and choose his successor without consultation was the final straw.

"Stupid bastard is going to destroy us without even realizing it," he muttered under his breath, and stubbed out his smoldering butt as he shook another smoke from the pack with his free hand. "With leaders like this, who needs enemies?"

A pair of nymphets barely old enough to drive strutted by in high heels, their long, tanned legs straining their miniskirts to the limits, and threw him a disgusted look. He ignored them and lit the next cigarette, his bad habits his business, not anyone else's. He'd resisted the urge to order something stronger than water, his mind racing over possible tactics to stymie the prime minister's directive, and he couldn't afford to blunt his faculties with alcohol, tempting as it was to numb himself to everything for at least one night.

His fish arrived, and he chewed methodically, the dish metallic to his taste, his thoughts elsewhere. He mentally cataloged his supporters in the administration and resolved to make calls the following day to remind them that he knew where all the bodies were buried and that allowing a transitory figurehead to force his retirement might not be in all of their best interests. It wasn't so much that he wanted to keep the job as he feared for a hasty transition, and that his replacement lacked the battle scars to make the correct decisions in impossible situations. Noah had never been tested when things were collapsing, always kicking the final call up to the director, as was the protocol. Which the director supposed he was now holding against him, but that was life – unfair, mercurial, brutal, and harsh, and too damned short, with the wolf always at the door.

When he was finished eating, he lit another cigarette and waited for the check. Did the prime minister really believe he would go quietly and putter around his garden or some such nonsense after being responsible for the nation's security since the pompous little ass had been in diapers? It was so insulting as to cause the director's breath to catch in his throat, and he had to exert every bit of mental discipline he possessed to calm himself to where he appeared outwardly unfazed.

When the waitress arrived with the bill, he tossed a small pile of shekels onto the tray and pushed himself to his feet. He glanced around at the swarm of youthful humanity going about its mating business without a care, and glared at the ashtray before sighing and beginning the slow march back to his hotel two blocks down the main boulevard.

He had nearly made it to the intersection when a blinding fireball exploded from a storefront just ahead, blowing out the windows of the shops for ten meters in both directions. The blast caught him with its full force and hurled him against a parked car like a rag doll in a tornado. Alarms shrieked and blended with horrified screams as the world spun giddily around him, and the last thing he registered before the night went black was a rivulet of blood streaming along the sidewalk from his head, staining the broken safety glass around him crimson, the shards gleaming with the orange reflection of dancing flames.

CHAPTER 2

Moscow, Russian Federation

The hall in the long-term critical care wing of Moscow City Hospital was empty at the late hour save for a hulking figure slumped in a chair, the man's enormous frame barely supported by the rickety seat. The sonorous drone of snoring rose to the stained acoustic ceiling tiles, and the harsh white of fluorescent lights cast otherworldly shadows along the worn linoleum of the long, sparse corridor. Muted beeping sounded from behind the closed metal doors lining the space. A nursing station glowed in the main area in the center of the physician hub, from which patient wings extended like a seaplane's propellers.

A portly nurse waddled from room to room on foam soles, clipboard in hand, her face etched with disapproving frown lines, her brow perennially crinkled as though she'd tasted something foul in the course of her rounds. She brushed past the sleeping man, eased the door beside him open, and stepped into the room, where a figure lay unmoving on a bed. An IV fed a canula in one arm, a pulse oximeter rested on his left index finger, and a blood pressure cuff on his left bicep connected to a display where his vital statistics blinked on multiple screens by the metal headboard.

She dutifully scribbled the numbers on her sheet and was turning away from the patient when a soft moan escaped his open mouth. The nurse stopped and turned back toward him with a puzzled expression and gasped when his lips quivered in an obvious attempt to form words.

She practically ran from the room back to the nurses' station and snatched a handset from a phone. The keys clacked as she selected the extension, and when it answered, she had a hushed conversation before terminating the call and making her way back to the moaning patient's bedside.

Five minutes later a pair of physicians appeared, and the sleeping man started awake in his chair and glared up at them, blinking away grogginess as he lumbered to his feet.

"What is it?" Leonid demanded of the doctors.

"We don't know," the first answered. "That's what we're here to find out."

They entered as a group, and the physicians moved to the bedside. The smaller of the pair, a lanky man in his fifties with thinning gray hair and spectacles perched precariously on the tip of his nose, leaned in and shone a light into the patient's eyes and then proceeded to perform a short examination. When he was finished, he straightened and turned toward Leonid.

"He appears to be conscious. Or at least no longer in a coma. Good news overall, but he's very weak. He needs to continue resting."

"He's been resting for months," Leonid snapped. "What does this mean?"

The doctor pursed his lips. "I wouldn't get my hopes up, but it's possible that he can make some sort of…at least partial…recovery."

Leonid thought for a moment. "When will you know whether or not he can?"

"We'll return tomorrow morning and evaluate him. For now, we'll monitor his stats and let him rest."

"Will you be able to remove the damn feeding tube from his stomach?" Leonid growled.

"We'll know more tomorrow," the doctor said. "Let's see how he's doing then. But this is an extremely positive sign."

The doctors departed, leaving Leonid and the nurse in the room. Leonid leaned toward the patient and whispered to him.

"Sergei, it's Leonid. Your brother. I'm here for you. Can you blink or something to show you understand?"

The nurse put a hand on Leonid's shoulder. "Don't expect too much. When a patient comes out of a coma, that's miraculous enough on its own."

Leonid shrugged off her hand. "Sergei, I won't leave your side. You have my promise."

Sergei's eyelids fluttered almost imperceptibly, and Leonid stiffened.

"You see?" he said. "You see that? He's back!"

The nurse eyed the big man like he was mad, but managed a wan smile that seemed to turn her face into clay, so unaccustomed was the expression.

"Let's hope so," she said. "Now, let's let him recuperate. Doctor's orders."

Leonid reluctantly returned to the chair where he'd spent weeks of vigil since returning to Russia from Cyprus and lowered himself into the seat, his heart rate as elevated as his hopes since seeing his brother, apparently returned from the void, for the first time in forever.

Across Moscow, in a towering glass skyscraper, four men sat in a conference room with a speakerphone in the center of a long rectangular table, their suit jackets and ties discarded, a bottle of vodka on a service tray, half-full glasses in front of them. A short, fat troll of a man with a sweaty, florid face was shouting at the device, lips writhing like two worms.

"Artem, I'm telling you, Yusef isn't a solution to the vacuum Nicolai's passing has created. There's no way he's sophisticated enough to untangle everything. He's a blunt force instrument, not a scalpel," he declared.

"I can't disagree, but something needs to be done, and I don't make these decisions," Artem said. "As you all know, we're getting constant demands from our partners, and failing to have a new head of the organization is causing a loss of confidence. You need to decide on someone."

"You're the attorney. Figure out some way to stall them," the fat man barked.

"That is precisely what I've been doing, Rudolf, but there's a limit to how long they can be put off. We've already seen several of our allies defect to our adversaries, and I don't need to remind everyone that both the Chinese and the Swiss are circling like vultures. They sense weakness, and they're moving in for the kill. We can't put off a decision any longer."

"It's a shame Sergei is off the table. He knew as much about our inner workings as Nicolai," one of the others said.

"Doesn't he have a brother?" the fat man asked.

"If you were afraid Yusef is a hammer in search of a nail, the brother, Leonid, is a wrecking ball. A felon who couldn't even protect Nicolai in the end. He may be fine as muscle in situations that don't require thinking, but little else."

Artem cleared his throat. "Gentlemen, we're out of time. That's my message to you. A successor needs to be approved, or there won't be any empire left to run. We're shedding credit lines and funds at an alarming pace as our banks digest our predicament. I don't need to remind anyone of what happens if we lose our lines. At that point, we're dead in the water."

"I've taken the liberty of inviting Yusef to come to Moscow from Siberia. He'll be flying in late tonight," a third man said. "I understand his shortcomings, but he's the best possible figurehead now, given the circumstances. We can make all the important decisions as his advisory team, and he can serve as a target for any arrows."

"Nobody authorized you to do that," Rudolf snapped.

"I know. But as Artem has underscored, inaction at this point means death, and we cannot allow our golden goose to die. If you can find somebody better suited to take over, I'm all ears, but this bickering has to come to an end."

"I'll catch a flight from London," Artem said. "We'll want to present a united front when we meet with him."

"Then it's decided. Let's plan to reconvene the board tomorrow. Can you be in Moscow by then, Artem?"

"One way or the other, I'll be there."

Rudolf looked around the group and nodded. "Very well. Safe travels, Artem." He terminated the call and sighed. "Sounds like we need to circle the wagons if we're to have anything left by the time this is over."

"I'm against Yusef, for the record. He's simply not a solution," the man to the left of Rudolf declared.

"Let's not allow the perfect to be the enemy of the good," another said as he rose. He tossed back the remainder of his vodka and eyed the others. "We don't have the luxury of many choices here. Perhaps Yusef isn't the best possibility, but if he can serve as our figurehead until we find someone better, then we've lived to fight another day."

Rudolf slammed his hand down on the table. "Damn Nicolai for keeping everything so tightly held. Seems like everything important was in his head."

"It's regrettable, but the past is the past. Right now we need to focus on avoiding any further defections and solidifying our existing relationships. Will it be easy? No. But do we still present a benefit to our allies? A conditional yes. If we get our act together and they believe we have competent guidance moving forward, we should be able to convince them to give us the benefit of the doubt. We've always performed for them to date."

"Not sure Yusef will instill anything other than disgust. He's practically a stereotype of an unrefined peasant who came into some money."

"Our adversaries need to fear us. He accomplishes that. The respect part…well, we can work on that aspect of his presentation. It may not be a perfect plan, but at least it's a plan, which is more than we've come up with since Nicolai's death."

The men gathered their jackets and departed one by one, leaving Rudolf to stare at the phone, his beady eyes black as a shark's, as he reached for the bottle with stubby fingers. A vein at his temple throbbed like a bellows as he poured his glass to the brim. He mopped his brow with an embroidered handkerchief before swallowing the liquor in two gulps. The contentious meeting had been the culmination of weeks of disorder and panic by the board, whose various factions and self-interests made consensus impossible.

"Idiots," he murmured softly before pushing back from the table and standing, the familiar burn of the vodka spreading welcome warmth through his limbs and softening the rage he'd felt at Yusef having been summoned by his rival, the unspoken inference being that his approval was incidental and he'd be expected to toe whatever line the group decided on. As Nicolai's logistics chief, he'd figured that if he'd dragged things out long enough, he would be appointed the new leader, and to have a thug like Yusef brought in against his wishes was a slap in the face by any measure.

"Idiots," he repeated, and then moved to the boardroom door with his jacket in hand, his footsteps reverberating off the imported Italian marble floor.

CHAPTER 3

Tel Aviv, Israel

A surgeon pushed through the double doors from the operating room and removed his mask as he walked towards the waiting man, who rose when he saw him. The doctor's face was drawn after six hours of continuous surgery, and his pallid skin sagged like a Basset hound's, creased from fatigue and stress. Two heavily muscled men, the bulges in their dress jackets identifying them as security, bookended the operating suite doors, their expressions serious.

"Well?" Noah asked the doctor.

The surgeon offered a slight shrug. "He's old and in terrible physical shape. It's literally a miracle he's alive."

"So the prognosis is…?"

"His gall bladder was ruptured, as were both his kidneys, along with almost every bone in his body. I've never seen damage like this outside of a train hitting a truck, and I spent years as a combat surgeon." The doctor paused. "Prognosis? If he makes it through the day, I'll be surprised. I'm sorry, but it's been a long battle, and I've got a short fuse. Your friend is in critical shape, and he likely won't survive, even though we've repaired everything we can. If he has any next of kin, I'd send for them now."

Noah looked away. "I'll pass the information along." He cleared his throat. "Thanks for the update. We appreciate everything you've done."

The director had been airlifted to the best hospital in Israel, and a team of trauma specialists had been ready for his arrival, but the blast had devastated him, and nobody had much hope he would pull through.

Still, the government took care of its own, and no expense had been spared, the attack an assault on the entire apparatus.

Noah strode down the hall to where nobody could overhear and placed a call. He reported the situation and listened without comment for thirty seconds.

"It would be prudent to assume he was the target," he finally replied. "It's a little too coincidental that the explosion went off when he was nearly in front of the store." He thought for a long moment. "Has the forensic team produced any results, or are they still analyzing?"

"Everything is at the lab. It's receiving top priority. Obviously."

"I want to be notified the second they have anything, understand? Whatever the time. If I'm in a meeting, pull me out."

"Yes, sir."

Noah hung up and checked his watch. He had an all-hands meeting for the section chiefs in an hour, after having spent the night at the hospital. His suit was rumpled, his hair tousled, his eyes red and burning.

He retraced his steps to the nurses' desk outside the OR and offered the stern woman behind it a slight smile.

"You have my office's contact information. Please call with any update about his condition."

"Of course. He'll be headed to ICU in a few minutes, if you want to—"

An alarm sounded, and a red light above the door began flashing. The nurse stood as she raised the phone to her ear, and a half dozen staff came at a run, two of them pushing a crash cart. Noah flattened himself against the wall to allow them to pass, and they slammed through the OR doors, leaving him to stare at their backs as they raced deeper into the operating suite.

"What's happening?" Noah demanded.

The nurse's face was impassive. "Nothing good, I'm afraid." She pointed at a bank of chairs. "Please take a seat over there in case more doctors need to get by."

Noah did as instructed, a knot in his throat, and minutes crawled by with no news. The red light extinguished, and the siren quieted, leaving his ears ringing and his stomach tight. Eventually a different doctor emerged from the OR, and Noah stood.

"I'm sorry," the physician said. "There was just too much damage."

"Then he's…"

"I'm afraid so."

Noah swallowed hard and nodded. "Appreciate the update. We'll make arrangements for the body."

He turned and was already dialing a number as he walked to the elevator bank, shoulders back and head erect, his expression grim.

CHAPTER 4

Sifnos, Greece

The sun was a dying ember sinking into the Aegean Sea as Jet stood in the doorway of the stark white villa the patron had arranged for them, perched high on the cliffs overlooking the water. The hills of Serifos shimmered on the distant horizon. The island was well off the beaten path, the landscape craggy and beige, and was accessible only by ferry or private charter yacht. The patron had recovered sufficiently after ten days to be moved to Sifnos, where he could heal in peace without having to worry about being murdered in his sleep by aspiring rivals. He'd extended an invitation to Jet and Matt to join him, where they would be safe, at least for the moment. After his experience in Seychelles, he'd convinced them to act as his security in the interim, given their performance with the Russians there.

"Can't I go with you?" Hannah pleaded from the entry hall.

Jet shook her head. "No. Everything's closing soon, and it will take too long to shop with you. We can go into town tomorrow. I promise."

"But I'm bored!" Hannah protested.

Matt appeared from around a corner and placed a hand on the little girl's shoulder. "You can help me in the kitchen while your mother gets the rest of the ingredients for dinner."

Hannah pouted before brightening. "Can I pick the good vegetables? The ones yesterday were sour."

"Of course you can," Matt said with a smile, and looked to Jet. "Could you try to get some decent produce so your daughter doesn't have to suffer through another awful meal?"

Jet returned the smile. "I'll do my best. Any special requests?"

"More milk!" Hannah cried.

Matt exhaled heavily. "You can also never have too much beer. Or grappa."

Jet's face crinkled in distaste. "I don't see how you can drink that."

He shrugged. "It's an acquired taste. When in Rome…"

"Or Greece, I suppose. Fine. I'll put it on the list. Now I have to run, or I won't make it."

"Drive safe."

She eyed her daughter and Matt. "Always."

Jet made her way to the small Fiat sedan that came with the villa, and shoehorned herself behind the wheel. The tiny engine sputtered to life and shuddered like a hobo with the DTs before settling into a rough idle, and she ground the gears until she found reverse and performed a three-point turn. She bounced down the cobblestone drive to the gate, punched the button on the remote clipped to the sun visor, and the heavy iron gate wheezed open on rusting hinges, barely allowing the little car to pass through.

The villa was six minutes down a winding road from the Artemonas market, and the sky was painted mango and crimson from the setting sun when she stepped from the Fiat and made her way into the market. It took her longer than she'd hoped to find everything on her mental list, and she earned annoyed glares from the cashier and the security guard lounging by the entrance, her shopping preventing them from closing and heading home. Jet paid for her items and waited as the woman bagged them, and could feel their eyes boring into her as she walked with the groceries to the exit.

Jet approached the Fiat, feeling for the key fob as she neared, and then stopped a few yards away, her eyes narrowing in the fading light. The car's tires had left tracks in the light film of sand and dust that covered the asphalt, but she could just make out where the coating had been disturbed below the little vehicle's trunk – where it had been brushed clear by something, including the tire tracks. Which meant that whatever had made the marks had done so after she'd parked.

Like someone lying on the ground beneath the rear of the car.

She pretended to be unable to find her keys and turned to walk back to the store. She made it ten feet when the car exploded, sending her pitching forward from the concussion, cushioned by the bag of groceries. She hit the pavement hard and rolled as the heat from the blast washed over her, and once it had receded, pushed herself to her feet and surveyed the lot, ears ringing as car alarms from parked vehicles clamored stridently in the dusk.

A dun-colored Renault sedan tore from the lot and sped away along the road that led to the coast, and Jet ran to where a young man was standing by his idling motorcycle, helmet in hand, obviously stunned by the detonation and the spectacle of flames and black smoke belching from the twisted wreckage of her car.

"Sorry," she said when she was beside him, and delivered a targeted strike to the side of his neck. He crumpled, and she caught him before he hit the ground and laid him down gently before she straddled the bike, twisted the throttle, stomped the transmission into gear, and roared off after the Renault, the wind tearing at her as she picked up speed.

She shifted through the gears, redlining the motor with each change, and spotted the faint glow of taillights ahead. They blinked out when the Renault rounded a bend, and she leaned forward, reducing the drag from her body, and urged the bike faster. The engine whined like a banshee as she downshifted to slow for a curve, and then she was revving to the breaking point again, cursing the motor for its anemic horsepower.

Jet came around another curve and spotted the car less than a half kilometer ahead. The last of the light had drained from the sky, and stars had begun making a tentative appearance on the horizon, the landscape whizzing by her becoming less visible by the moment. She was reluctant to switch on the headlight for fear of alerting her quarry, but a near miss with an errant goat that nearly ended her pursuit convinced her to opt for safety; it would do no good for her to go over the handlebars due to an unseen pothole.

She found the button and stabbed it on, and the road blinked white in front of her, allowing her to goose her speed to the maximum as she gained on the car. The sudden appearance of a motorcycle behind him apparently spooked the driver, and he accelerated as she drew nearer, tires screaming in protest as another curve materialized in front of them. She cursed as the more powerful car pulled away from her, eyes stinging from the wind, and instinctively braked when the Renault nearly rear-ended an overloaded truck with no lights that was grinding along the grade, the only warning the drone of its ancient engine and the stench of poorly combusted diesel in a black cloud behind it.

The car swerved around the truck and sped up again, and Jet mimicked the maneuver, her headlight bouncing giddily when she hit a patch of rough pavement just past the heavy vehicle. Her breath hissed through her teeth as the Renault's lights appeared ahead of her again, and her jaw clenched as the speedometer climbed past a hundred kilometers, the handlebars jittering like a living thing.

A flash of red lights ahead lit the road and then disappeared, and she barely made out the screech of rubber on pavement that signaled a misjudged curve. She slowed, and the acrid stink of burning brakes greeted her as she approached a hairpin, the Renault's skid marks black as pitch on the sunbaked gray asphalt. She coasted to a stop at the side of the road and peered down at where the car had gone off the edge and plunged twenty yards down the rocky slope before a boulder had arrested its drop.

Jet swung off the motorcycle, pushed it onto the shoulder, and surveyed the wreckage with hands on her hips as steam rose in a cloud from the car's flattened hood. She glanced up the road at where she knew the truck would soon be coming, and moved to the bike. Jet eased it over the edge and down the side until it was out of sight of the road, and then laid it on its side, leaving the engine puttering for a quick getaway.

She peered down at the sedan in the darkness and picked her way down the incline. Rocks skittered beneath her as she probed for footholds. It took her several minutes to reach the wreck, where the stench of raw gasoline filled the air. She approached the driver's side door gingerly, squinting in the faint light, and stopped when the rumble of the truck on the road above neared with a faint screech of brakes and then receded as it made its way toward the port.

The steam from the crushed radiator hissed softly when she was at the broken driver's side window, and she took in the blood-covered figure slumped over the steering wheel. She cocked her head to listen and then pushed the man off the wheel so she could see his face, which was ruined from its impact with the windshield, the nose smashed flat, a ruby river streaming from it as well as two large gashes in his forehead.

A soft gurgling moan escaped the man's mouth, where his front teeth were shattered, and Jet spotted a rent in his shirt caused by the steering column crashing into his rib cage as the car's motor had jammed its way towards the passenger compartment on impact. The sedan was of a vintage where air bags weren't an option, and the seatbelt was only a lap cinch with no shoulder strap, which explained the damage to the man's face as his upper body had flown forward and then been slammed back again by the steering column before coming to rest over the wheel. Blood coursed from the hole in his chest with each breath, and she understood immediately he was dying, with no hope of help arriving before he expired, no matter what she did.

An eye fluttered open, and he strained to look at her before blinking away the blood. Jet leaned into him and spoke softly in his ear.

"How did you find me? Who are you working for?" she asked in passable Greek.

The man's breath was ragged, and his chest gurgled as his brutalized lungs labored for air. He blinked again, but didn't say anything.

"You're bleeding out. You aren't going to make it. But I can end the pain, or leave you to drown in your own blood. Horrible way to go," she said, her voice flat.

Another gasp, and more blood pulsed from the chest wound. The man groaned and then managed a hoarse whisper.

"Pet…Petr…ko…uh…Petrenko…"

"How did you find me?" she demanded. But the man's eyes had closed, and he was lost to her, fighting for each shallow breath, the pain overwhelming his ability to speak.

She'd seen enough death to know he was finished, and reached through the window and felt for his carotid artery. Jet pressed on it until he lost consciousness, and was debating how to end her assassin's suffering when a louder hiss greeted her from beneath what remained of the hood.

Jet stepped back and peered beneath the car and saw steady drops of gasoline, some of which were hitting the scorching hot metal of the engine before the remainder landed glistening on the rocks. Her eyes widened, and she backed away from the car, aware that the fuel could catch at any moment.

The driver would remain unconscious until he expired, sparing him the agony of death by choking on his own fluids, so there was no reason to further risk another near-miss explosion. She scrambled back up to where the motorcycle lay and was wrestling it onto the gravel shoulder when the tank detonated with a deafening whump, blasting flames high into the air behind her.

A minute later, she was speeding back toward the junction near the market, repeating the dead assassin's last word over and over in her head, committing it to memory, the name meaningless to her now – but with any luck, not for much longer.

CHAPTER 5

London, England

Zhang Lun, his face somber, paced in front of a pair of French doors that looked out on the expansive garden of his rented Kensington mansion. He had elected to remain out of the public eye after the assassination on Cyprus, aware that the Russian's entourage would have suspected that he was behind Nicolai's murder and might be planning retribution. It was unlikely they would be looking for him in England, but he still was uneasy after getting off the phone with one of his subordinates in China, who had described their interactions with Nicolai's network as "chaotic" now that the head of the snake had been lopped off.

Instability meant increased risk, and while he'd planned for it, he couldn't predict how the Russians would react moving forward until he understood who had taken over for the oligarch. His contacts in Moscow hadn't come up with a solid lead yet, which left him in limbo with his family in England – albeit in a luxurious gilded cage of his own choosing.

The roar of high-performance engines intruded from the street, and he turned to glare at the foyer's heavy oak front doors. His wife appeared from one of the three sitting areas, a frown souring her expression.

"Honestly, Lun, how much more of this can we take? It's driving me crazy," she said.

"This is the best area of London, my love. I had no idea it was going to turn into a Formula One racetrack," he replied, his voice tight.

"I can't believe they allow it."

He shrugged. "Money buys tolerance, apparently."

"For the record, I wish we were home. I'm done with this place," she fumed. "I can't hear myself think."

"I know. I'll see if anything can be done about it," Lun said, painfully aware that there was nothing to be done. Superrich children of oil trillionaires from the Middle East came to Kensington to flaunt their wealth. They flew their souped-up supercars in with them and paraded around London, revving their engines and generally making life unbearable for the locals for a month every year. Lun had had no idea that he'd leased the mansion during that month, and recalled having been surprised that it was available.

"Mystery solved," he muttered, and watched his wife pad away, her scowl signaling her disproval of Lun's choice of digs.

Lun had selected London for a variety of reasons, most notably that it was completely off the radar in terms of his usual destinations. He owned homes all over the world, but not in the UK, and after considering how tenuous his situation was until he had a better handle on the Russians, he'd opted to remain out of China until the outlook stabilized. The home was huge, but even so, his wife and daughter were growing weary of their voluntary imprisonment within its walls, and he knew that he was running out of time as well as patience. He was managing to run his business remotely, but he would soon need to show his face or risk speculation that he was ill, or worse – something he couldn't afford, considering how overextended his balance sheet was and how much of the largesse he was enjoying from his creditors was due to personal relationships.

He'd been mulling over strategies and had concluded that he would need to strike first or forever be walking around with a target on his back. To that end, he'd put out feelers for a team of hyper-competent assassins who could eliminate whoever wound up taking over Nicolai's role, and had narrowed his search down to a shadowy group of Chechen mercenaries who claimed they could achieve anything if the price was right.

Lun had been careful to run the inquiries through a German he'd used for sensitive missions in the past, and was confident that it couldn't be traced back to him, which was critical. Taking out Nicolai had been a bold move, but the list of possible suspects behind it was short, especially with the level of firepower that had been brought to bear. Upon reflection, revenge had played too large a part in his decision, but Lun couldn't have allowed his son's murder to stand and had allowed his emotions to guide him – completely out of character for him, which was probably why the Russian hadn't seen it coming.

"What's done is done," Lun murmured, and resumed his pacing, serenaded by the roar of Lamborghini and Bugatti engines from the street. The noise was irritating but bearable, in light of the host of more important issues on his mind, but he would have to do something soon or risk the women in his life making him miserable, a fate in his mind almost worse than being stalked by a hit team.

He removed a scrambled cell phone from the breast pocket of his shirt and placed a call. He spoke in rapid-fire Cantonese, and when he was done, he stabbed it off and glared at it like it had bitten him. He'd ordered his subordinates to find more suitable lodging for his family, preferably in the country, away from the endless noise of the city, which had been overrun by oil-rich Arabs with no sense of decorum.

Lun checked the time on his antique Patek moon phase chronograph and nodded to himself. It wouldn't be much longer before he could resolve his Russian problem for good and get back to business in China, where life was civilized and everyone knew their place, fearful of offending anyone in power lest their social credit score be battered and their existence made miserable with the stroke of a key. Lun had been working with his government to introduce the system globally and consolidate China's power, and he could hardly wait for the day when the spectacle of twenty-something Saudi princes over-revving their supercars would be over, the sand peasants put in their proper place, subservient to their Chinese masters.

"Soon," he whispered softly, and eyed a snifter half filled with an amber single malt scotch so rare it was considered priceless after the distillery had burned down, leaving only a few cases in the hands of the discerning – like Lun. It was early, but he had nothing to do now but wait, and it would make the endless noise more bearable, if only briefly. He crossed to the bar and poured himself two fingers in a tumbler and then sat in an overstuffed chair and swirled it languorously, savoring the heady aroma before taking a sip and closing his eyes in appreciation, the flavor like nothing else in the world.

CHAPTER 6

Sofia, Bulgaria

The streets surrounding the train station in Bulgaria's capital city were alive with activity late at night, with streetwalkers hawking their wares to sex tourists, music blaring through the open doorways of seedy bars, and throngs of inebriated university students roaming the area, shouting at one another over the din. A sheen of moisture left over from an evening rain glistened in the dim streetlights, the cobblestones slick and dark, worn smooth from centuries of traffic. Thunder boomed in the distance from a passing storm, and flashes of light pulsed through the low clouds that hung like a shroud over the town.

A flickering neon sign hanging crookedly over a darkened doorway off a side street announced a cybercafé in Bulgarian and English, some of the letters dead or so dim as to be illegible. Inside the seedy shop were cubicles that lined the garish red walls, screens blinking within. Only a few patrons sat at the stations; a bored clerk at the front was watching a streaming movie while sipping coffee from a chipped ceramic mug. At the rear were three enclosed glass booths, one of which was occupied by a woman with dyed black hair, who was speaking into a headset as she cradled a notebook computer in her lap.

"Nobody knows more about the agency's inner workings than I do. That isn't contentious. And I'm giving you a bargain price," Nabila said, her tone tense.

She listened for several seconds and then cut off the other speaker. "You shouldn't take too long to consider. This is a limited-time offer. I can't believe we're even having this discussion. You know what I bring to the table."

The other party terminated the call, leaving Nabila seething as she shut down her notebook. She stood, pushed the glass door open, and moved to the cashier and placed a couple of coins on the counter. The girl looked up and regarded her with eyes heavily traced with black mascara, and then scooped up the money and returned her attention to the film on her monitor.

Nabila walked out onto the sidewalk, a knot in her stomach like a rock, and glanced both directions up the narrow street before setting off at a fast clip, wary of being robbed at the late hour, the notebook an easy prize for any predators in the area. Her heavy-soled shoes clumped against the roadway with the dull regularity of a pile driver, echoing off the stone façades, her expression dour but determined, the slight drizzle that started as she approached her building appropriate to her mood.

She entered the five-story walkup and trudged up the stairs to the fourth floor, where she had rented a bare-bones studio apartment, paying in cash. She twisted a key in the lock, entered the dingy room, and crossed to the small table that served as her dining room and work space. Nabila shrugged off the shoulder strap of her laptop bag and set it on the table and then walked to the bed and sat heavily on the edge. Her eyes roved over the squalid interior – the kitchen with Soviet-era appliances, the bathroom a bad joke.

Nabila had managed to slip out of Israel, even though the border controls had been tightened and her likeness distributed to all the checkpoints, by dying her hair and cutting it short, and using makeup to darken her skin three tones so she would pass as an Arab tourist using a spare passport she had squirreled away for just such an emergency. Once in Egypt, she'd used her contacts to arrange transport out of the Middle East to Bulgaria, where nobody was looking for her and she'd be safe, at least for a time.

Her problem was that she'd been forced to leave much of her wealth in Israel; she'd only been able to abscond with what cash she'd had on hand, the passport, a fake driver's license, and one credit card. There was also a USB drive with a small fortune in cryptocurrencies – whose value had crashed while she'd been on a freighter in the Black Sea on the way to Varna, wiping out much of her wealth by the time she'd made it to shore.

The objective now was to find a buyer for her knowledge of the Mossad and its operations. But she'd quickly found that the target groups she had approached either lacked the resources to make cooperation worth her while or were reluctant to trust her due to their adversarial stance with her homeland. That left her a product without a customer, and she'd burned too much of her nest egg already to feel secure about her future without a sponsor of some sort.

That, and she was undoubtedly on Interpol's most wanted roster, along with Mossad's termination list, which meant she needed to maintain a low profile for the foreseeable future. While the agency had larger problems than an errant agent, she knew she would be a priority, given the depth of her knowledge. But that cut both ways, as she was sure that Mossad had already begun to take steps to nullify anything she knew, changing out assets, moving safe houses, altering front companies used to fund missions. That meant that her value to anyone was time-sensitive, and dropping every hour as she waited for one of the fish she'd attempted to lure to her baited hook to bite.

Her eyes moistened, and she blinked away tears of self-pity – a luxury she reminded herself that she couldn't afford in her current predicament. She'd rolled the dice, bet it all on red, and lost, and now it was up to her to extricate herself from her situation with her skin intact.

Which didn't make staying in a hovel like this any easier. Nabila had dreamed of villas and private jets and lounging on the Riviera as reward for her years of playing both sides against the middle, and had come so close…

It wasn't fair.

She exhaled forcefully and glared at the notebook. She needed to lock in a client sooner than later, or she would become a liability to anyone she spoke to, subjecting them to risk by association, even though she was communicating via VPNs and proxy masks. It was just a matter of days before someone talked, at which point her old employer's worst fears would be realized – a top-level operative offering to sell their expertise to the highest bidder.

Nabila rose and moved to the window. She pushed the heavy velour curtain aside and looked out at the street, automatically checking for any signs of surveillance. There was nothing suspicious that attracted her attention, but still she scanned every vehicle and doorway, looking for a tell. After several minutes of this, she relaxed and dropped the curtain back into place, and then switched on the lights, confident that for the moment she was safe.

But she was too experienced to believe that would last long.

If her overtures didn't meet with success soon, she'd be radioactive to anyone who might have been interested in buying her knowledge, and would be powerless against the efforts of the agency to silence her at any cost.

Which meant certain death. Or worse, imprisonment in an off-the-books black site back in Israel, tortured and abused until her tormenters were sure they'd learned everything from her, the ordeal finally ended with a bullet to the back of the head and her body dumped in an unmarked grave.

An outcome she would do anything to avoid.

CHAPTER 7

Tel Aviv, Israel

The Mossad headquarter halls were silent; the day shift had long since departed, leaving only the operational teams in the downstairs secure rooms, along with a round-the-clock security detail, and Noah, who had returned to the office after departing the hospital, the weight of his new responsibilities heavy on his shoulders. His support staff had rallied and followed him into the office and were gathered in what had until recently been the director's suite, now Noah's. The old man's few personal possessions had been unceremoniously boxed up and piled in a corner, but the taint of stale tobacco still emanated from the walls and furniture like a curse.

Noah sat at an oval table with three of his immediate subordinates, all of whom had been his peers until his appointment as interim director. Now they looked to him expectantly, their expressions grim.

"I don't need to tell you all how serious this is. We've suffered a grave loss, and finding out who's behind this, and whether the director was the target, is our top priority," Noah said, and frowned at his use of his predecessor's title. In Noah's mind there was only one director, and the idea that he was now gone forever, with Noah replacing him, was only slowly sinking in.

One of the men, Leon, ran his fingers through his short-cut graying hair and nodded. "We've pulled all the traffic camera footage and are analyzing it. And a forensics team is going over every square inch of the blast zone," he reported.

"What about chatter? Even a hint this was coming down?" Noah asked.

Leon shook his head. "Negative."

"What do we know so far?"

"We believe the bomb was left in a backpack by the storefront window. Likely inside. But we need to analyze the feeds to verify that's the case."

"If so, this was likely random?"

"We can't assume anything. Apparently the director…the victim…had dined at the same restaurant twice before, so if someone was watching him…"

"Why blow up half a block if he was the target? Why not a gunman, or a grenade tossed from a moving car?"

"We don't have enough data to say."

Noah shook his head. "Has anyone claimed responsibility?"

The man to Leon's right tapped his pen against the tabletop. "No. Which is why we are thinking the director might have been the objective. As we all know, typically when terrorists detonate a bomb, they're quick to proclaim their brave blow against Israel. But as of now, radio silence from all the usual suspects." He paused. "That, and Eilat isn't on the map for this sort of thing."

Noah cleared his throat. "I think we need to proceed with the assumption that this was an assassination. If so, it's a threat to all of us – it strikes at the very heart of our organization. I want to know who did this and why, and I want to know before the sun comes up." He surveyed the gathering, allowing his stare to linger on each of them before lowering his eyes to the tablet on the tabletop. "One of our own has been taken from us in the most public and dramatic way possible. We'll run interference with the press, but that isn't the point. If this was a targeted attack on the director, word will get out, and if we don't neutralize the responsible parties with extreme prejudice, our standing will be severely compromised. I don't need to tell everyone what's at stake."

Leon nodded. "We'll be here all night working on it."

Noah sighed. "As will we all. I want hourly updates. Call in whatever resources you require. This is an all-hands-on-deck crisis, understood?"

The men stood and filed out of the room, leaving Noah to stare at the one-way bulletproof glass of the window that faced part of the construction that disguised Mossad's current headquarters. He had a sinking feeling in his stomach that matched the sour bile taste in his mouth. The chances that the director had been unlucky were zero. Someone had dared to take him out, and on home turf.

That he had been relieved of his duties, after a long and distinguished career, made it nothing but worse. His death had been pointless and had accomplished nothing from an intel perspective.

Which stopped Noah in his tracks.

What if this had been…the director's retirement package? His severance?

Would the government stoop to eliminating their own loyal servant once he'd outlived his usefulness?

The thought was too ugly to contemplate.

Except that Noah was trained to consider everything. And the more he did, the more he understood it was possible. The director had known every secret worth hiding. He undoubtedly had sensitive information about everyone in the government, at all levels. Would the powerful not be sleeping easier tonight knowing he was dead?

Noah took a deep breath. He would need to tread carefully, even if the chances that this had been an inside job were remote. He'd spent his career planning ops that ran counter to the government's public proclamations and, in many cases, international law. Much as he hated the idea that someone in power might have viewed the director as a liability…it was a distinct possibility. His death had certainly tied up a host of loose ends. And while Noah preferred to think that his government was above cold-blooded murder for convenience's sake, over the years he'd seen too much to dismiss the notion out of hand.

Which meant that nobody, and nothing, could be trusted. Not even his staff. Certainly not his superiors – not even the prime minister, who had ramrodded Noah's appointment through. Until he was confident he knew who was behind the killing, the safest course was to assume the worst, which meant that he might also be in danger if he made conspicuous progress on identifying the guilty party and it turned out to be someone in the administration.

That presented a considerable problem, as he would need to tightly compartmentalize any information that ensued from the investigation, or risk exposure. And while he had worked with his colleagues for many years, the recent betrayal by Nabila, who had been in the director's inner circle, had reminded him that he couldn't assume anyone's loyalty, no matter their station. The woman had disappeared without a trace, leaving nothing for the agency to go on, and one of his first duties had been to closely examine every operation she'd been involved in over the last decade, even if only peripherally. As he'd done so, he'd detected a pattern that now seemed obvious but had apparently gone unnoticed when she'd been in the building.

So any optimistic beliefs about his staff's honesty had to take a back seat to the emerging reality that anyone could be a mole, including government officials and the career bureaucrats who commanded tremendous power behind the scenes. And if one of them had engineered the director's untimely demise, Noah would be next if he got too close.

Which put him at an obvious extreme disadvantage; but nobody had said the new job would be easy.

He moved to the executive chair behind the desk, and his nose wrinkled in distaste. He ran a finger along the desktop edge and made a mental note to have the office deep-cleaned immediately. While the old man had no doubt been brilliant, his nicotine addiction had permeated every crevice of the office, and the odor wasn't helping with Noah's dry mouth and sour stomach.

A condition he suspected would become a permanent aspect of his career from this point forward.

CHAPTER 8

Sifnos, Greece

Jet crept through the brush that encircled the villa, checking for security breaches, before she threw open the front door and rushed to the living room, where Matt and Hannah were seated in front of a television, a Disney animated film playing at low volume on the screen. Both looked up at her in surprise, and Matt rose when he saw her face, which was glistening with a sheen of perspiration in the soft glow of the overhead lamps.

"What happened?" he blurted, eyeing her singed, torn clothes.

"Car bomb," she said. "We need to get out of here. We're blown."

Matt's eyes widened. "How?"

She shrugged. "Doesn't matter. We need to get off the island."

"That won't be easy at this hour." Matt looked to the little girl. "Hannah? Why don't you go to your room and play? Mommy and I need to talk about grownup stuff."

Hannah nodded and stood as she fixed Jet with an intense stare. "Are you okay, Mama?"

Jet nodded and managed a wan smile. "Just a little upset, sweetheart. Do as Matt asks. We'll be up in a few minutes."

Hannah sighed and looked around. "I like it here."

"It's nice that you do," Jet said. "But there are a lot of places in the world this good, or even better."

"Okay," the little girl said softly, and then moved to the stairway that led to the upper floor.

When Hannah had disappeared up the steps, Matt took Jet's hand

and led her to the sofa. They sat, and he inspected her soot-smeared face.

"Start at the top," he said.

"Someone rigged the car. While I was at the market. Almost got me. Closer than I like."

Matt blinked and nodded for her to continue.

"I stole a motorcycle and chased the triggerman. He went over a cliff, but I got a name out of him before he vaporized." She paused. "Petrenko. Which doesn't ring any bells, so I'm guessing he's either a cutout or a contractor."

Matt shook his head. "Could be. Maybe our friend upstairs might know him?" He studied her singed hair and eyebrows. "You positive you were the target? Not Andrew?"

"They had to have watched me enter the store. So it was me they were after."

Matt looked away. "Crap."

"Which brings us to we need to get out of here, stat."

"I get it. Let's talk to Andrew and see what he thinks."

"Doesn't really matter, does it? We're compromised. Best case, the driver was working alone. Worst case, he's part of a team, and they're gearing up for another try right now. You know how these things work."

He nodded slowly. "Did you see any signs of surveillance coming or going?"

"No. Which means they picked me up somewhere along the road to the market. But it doesn't matter. We have to assume they know where we're staying." She released his hand and rose. "Let's tell Andrew what happened."

They hurried up the stairs to the suite that the patron was occupying, and knocked gently on the door. His muffled voice barked from the bedroom.

"Enter."

Matt and Jet strode into the sitting area, and Andrew lowered the submachine gun he was pointing at them from his seat on one of the divans. He looked Jet over and gave a low whistle.

"I'm afraid to ask what happened," he said.

"We need to move," Jet said, and gave him an abridged report of the attack. When she was done, he nodded.

"Agreed. I'll make some calls. Thank God I've mended enough to do so without an ambulance."

"We're obviously in jeopardy the longer we stay here," Matt said.

"It will take time to line up a boat or helo, but anything's possible with the right connections." Andrew frowned in thought. "Speaking of which, the name Petrenko doesn't register, but it wouldn't if he's new or is low on the totem pole. I'll start nosing around once we've got transport arranged. In the meantime, might I suggest you keep a sharp eye out for any hostiles on our perimeter?"

"Of course," Jet said, and looked to Matt. "Will you monitor the security cams while I pack and get cleaned up?"

"I'm on it."

"Give me an hour and check back," Andrew said, and pushed himself to his feet with a wince. He shambled over to where a cell phone sat on an end table and switched it on, and Jet and Matt left him to make his calls.

When they were down the hall, Matt eyed Jet. "What do you think?"

"Logical next steps? I hate to say it, but I've got to check in with the director."

Matt's sour expression spoke volumes. "Wish you didn't have to."

"We're going to need all the resources we can get. Maybe this Petrenko is in the database. Can't hurt to ask."

"Assuming he'll even take your call."

"He loves it when I owe him one. He'll pick up." Jet poked her head into Hannah's room and told her to gather her things, and then turned to Matt.

"I'll see you in a few. Let me make the call and shower," she said, and he nodded.

"Will do."

Matt left for the room where the security feeds were displayed on an array, and Jet entered their bedroom and selected one of the unused burner phones they'd bought when they'd landed in Greece. She logged onto a VPN so the number couldn't be triangulated, and dialed the director's private number. The line hummed quietly between rings, and she cursed under her breath when an automated voice instructed her to leave a message.

"It's the prodigal," she said. "There was an attempt on me. Not sure by whom, but I could use a hand in tracking down a lead. I'll be at the following number for an hour or two." Jet left a number that linked to a blind voicemail box halfway across the planet, and disconnected. She checked the time and looked around the room. They had few possessions, limited to clothes, some hygiene products, cash and diamonds, and weapons Andrew had sourced once they'd arrived in Greece. It would take almost no time to pack, the instinct to be ready to run reflexive after years of living out of suitcases. She padded to the bathroom and stripped off her clothes and was clean within minutes and donning a new outfit when the burner cell pinged from the vanity, indicating a message.

She finished her grooming and dialed the message box and listened as an unfamiliar voice instructed her to call the director's phone again. Jet dialed quickly, and her jaw tightened when the same voice answered.

"Who is this?" it asked.

"I have the same question," Jet snapped. "I need to speak to the director, not an assistant."

A pause, and then the man who had answered spoke in measured tones. "He's unavailable."

"Then I'll call when he is," she snapped.

Another pause. "That will be a long wait."

Jet considered his words. "What's going on? Who is this?" she repeated.

"His replacement. Now you get one chance to explain who you are."

She swallowed hard. "You retrieved my message, obviously."

"Yes. And we ran it through voice analysis, but came up with nothing."

"I know enough to use a filter. I used to be one of you."

An even longer pause. "Code name?"

"Jet."

She heard a heavy sigh. When the man spoke, his voice was tight. "What do you want?"

"Information. Someone tried to blow me to bits. I want to know who."

"And you expect us to help?"

"What happened to the director?" she snapped. "He could have explained our relationship to you."

"He…he's dead. A terrorist attack of some sort. It just happened."

It was her turn to pause and absorb information. "What kind of attack?"

"That's classified."

"You do realize I'll be able to Google attacks and find out within seconds, right?"

A long pause. "It was a bomb."

Jet frowned. "Explain."

"No," Noah said. "That's not how this works. I don't know how you and the director interacted or what your deal was, and I haven't got time to find out right now. So we're not going to be able to help." He hesitated. "You weren't on some sort of off-the-books mission, were you?"

"Negative."

"Then our business is done."

"I need a name run through our system," she said.

Noah's tone turned harder. "There is no 'our system.' From what I know of your exploits, you're radioactive, and we would be better off with zero contact. I'm afraid I can't help you."

"The name's Petrenko. You say the director was killed by a bomb. Was it in a car?"

"I told you, we can't help you. Goodbye. Don't call again," Noah said, and hung up.

She stared at the phone in disbelief and then tossed it onto the bed, her head spinning at the news of the director's death. He had always seemed…perennial. Eternal. An institution who'd been at the top of the Mossad as long as she'd been with it. And now he was gone, and with him, her connection.

The new man, whoever it was, clearly didn't play by the same rulebook as the director had. He'd shown no interest in the amazing coincidence of an attempt on her life in close proximity to the director's death, which told her that he was unsuitable for the job. Even if they were unconnected, a botched assassination on a longtime asset should have set off alarms.

If that was the best the agency could do, its days were numbered. Between Nabila and now this idiot, there was no hope. Not Jet's problem, but still, depressing for her homeland, which needed all the competence it could muster, given the number of enemies it had.

She shook off the shock and drew a deep breath, clearing her head. Jet needed to focus on packing and keeping her family safe. The agency's mismanagement wasn't her concern, although to have her access to its resources cut off so abruptly posed a hardship in the short term.

Jet walked to the closet and removed the two black duffels that she and Matt had used to escape Seychelles, and began removing clothes from hangers, her expression vacant, lost in thought. When she was done, she would make good on her threat to search for terrorist attacks in Israel and get as much information as was online. Perhaps there was something she could use. Perhaps not. But she felt like there was more to the story than the director's replacement understood, and if there was a connection she could glean, that would be more than she had now.

When she'd finished with the clothes, Jet knelt down and reached for the safe, where their passports, valuables, and weapons were stored. Their sojourn in the Greek Isles had lasted barely more than a blink, and once again her family was in mortal danger, hunted by an adversary with no name who was clearly willing to go to any lengths to terminate her.

The notion that she'd ever be safe from the ghosts of the past had turned out to be a hollow conceit, but she had no choice other than to keep pushing forward. There was no refuge in panicking or attempting to hide. She needed to figure out how they'd located her and why they wanted her dead, or it was just a matter of time until they tried again – this time successfully.

"Mama? I'm done," Hannah's tiny voice called from outside the bedroom door. Jet placed two pistols and four spare magazines in the duffel and smiled in spite of herself. Hannah deserved to grow up safe, with a mother, so whoever had decided to come after her had just made the worst mistake of their soon-to-be-short life.

"Okay, baby. Give me a few seconds. I'll be right out," Jet said, and continued stowing their things in the bags, her expression one of grim determination.

CHAPTER 9

Moscow, Russian Federation

Leonid waited on the tarmac of the private aviation terminal at Vnukovo International Airport, his slick black trench coat lending him the appearance of a leather sofa stood on its end, his massive shoulders and arms barely contained by the straining garment. A commercial jet dropped from the night sky and touched down on the runway, and the scream of its engines reversing thrust echoed deafeningly off the buildings behind him as it sent a rooster tail of water into the air. It had rained an hour earlier, which was typical for the time of year, but the storm had drifted west except for a layer of low clouds hanging over the city, leaving Leonid to pick his way through standing puddles near the waiting gray Mercedes limousine that was the arriving Siberian's to use while he was in Moscow.

Leonid had been tapped to act as security for Yusef's visit, even though that was his brother Sergei's strength, not his. Leonid was more of a proactive, bash-heads type than his sibling, but apparently the board hadn't made that distinction, and Leonid wasn't about to tell them, not with his continued need for a paycheck. All Leonid had to do was babysit Yusef and he was home free. The assignment had seemed almost laughably easy, unlike the quagmire he'd been sent into in Seychelles.

Yusef was Nicolai's head of operations in Siberia, where he ruled with an iron fist. His specialty was brute force against those who dared to defy his will, which had worked well in the undeveloped east, where seventy-five percent of the population lacked indoor plumbing and conditions were as brutal as they had been during Lenin's rule. Yusef was an old-school, no-nonsense thug much like many in the Russian mafia, but also highly intelligent, who could operate autonomously with success. This had made him perfect for the role Nicolai had chosen him for, and he'd excelled in running Siberia for the organization for the last fifteen years.

Of course, all those qualities were negatives in civilized interactions, which was why some of Nicolai's board opposed him. Leonid knew all about the Siberian from his brother, before he'd been injured. Yusef had been a thorn in Sergei's side for some time due to his refusal to follow reasonable security protocols, and Leonid had spent long hours listening to him complain about Yusef's stubbornness before Leonid had been imprisoned.

The thought of his brother increased Leonid's pulse rate, and he felt his chest tighten. Sergei's miraculous emergence from the coma was a step in the right direction, but he was still obviously impaired and wasn't registering much. The good news, other than his return to consciousness, was that his vital signs were in the normal range, and he was relatively young and quite healthy despite all he'd been through. Whether he would ever regain his faculties was an open question, but not being a potted plant any longer was certainly hopeful.

The radio clipped to Leonid's belt crackled softly, and he freed it and raised it to his mouth.

"*Da?*" he asked.

"Next one to land is ours."

"Copy that."

Leonid squinted in the darkness at the bright landing lights dropping toward the tarmac from a prop plane, and then a twin-engine King Air touched down softly and immediately began to slow, the runway easily triple the length it required to land. Once at the turnoff that led to the private terminal, it veered left towards the buildings and taxied unhurriedly to within thirty meters of the big Mercedes.

The turboprop motors wound down and fell silent, and the fuselage door opened, and the stairway dropped to the ground. Moments passed, and then Yusef stepped out of the plane and descended to the pavement, a garment bag over his shoulder and a carry-on bag in his left hand. He stopped and looked around and spotted Leonid by the limo.

Leonid waved, and Yusef set off towards him. He was halfway to the vehicle when a high whine stopped him in his tracks. Leonid gazed skyward, and Yusef did the same, and Leonid's eyes narrowed when he caught sight of a pair of black drones dropping from the night sky. Leonid was drawing his pistol as he called to Yusef at the top of his lungs.

"Get down! Drone," he warned, and drew a bead on the closest one, but it was moving too fast to hit.

Yusef ducked into a crouch and was feeling for his weapon in a shoulder holster when the first drone exploded three meters above him in a fireball. The second flew directly at Leonid, who emptied his gun at it. One of the shots hit it and sent it whirring giddily away before it crashed by the plane and detonated in a similar shower of flames as its twin. Leonid winced at the flare and then bolted to where Yusef lay motionless in a steadily spreading lake of blood.

When he reached him, Leonid grimaced at the sight of his shredded back, knowing from the extent of the wounds that he was dying, even if he was still managing to breathe. He reached down and flipped the Siberian over and stood, the stench of Yusef's bodily fluids rank even in the frigid air.

The damage to Yusef told Leonid that the drones had been equipped with some sort of grenades. Leonid had seen enough casualties during his service to know the signs – the man's body turned to hamburger by a hundred small fragments of razor-sharp shrapnel from mere feet away, and his head barely recognizable, the skull liquified by the explosion, leaving little but a jellied blob between his shoulders.

Leonid straightened, ejected his spent pistol magazine, and turned to the car, scanning the surroundings for any sign of the drone operator. Seeing nothing suspicious, he slapped a new magazine into place and raised the radio to his lips.

"Passenger's dead. Plane's history. No sign of the attackers," he growled.

The radio was silent as another commercial flight dropped to the runway and slowed as it rolled toward the brightly lit terminal, and then a brash voice emanated from the two-way.

"What do you mean? Attacked how? Explain."

"Drones with explosives," Leonid said. "We never stood a chance. They were obviously waiting and knew the schedule. Whoever was piloting them is long gone. Which is what we should be, too, unless we want to be held for questioning by the security forces."

"This is a disaster."

"No question. How do you want me to proceed?"

A brief pause. "Abort. Return to base. Tell the driver."

A siren howled from the far end of the field, followed by another, and emergency lights blinked blue and red in the darkness.

"Will do."

Leonid ran to the limo and glared at the driver, who was staring open-mouthed at the burning plane through his open window.

"Change of plans. Get me out of here," Leonid barked, and threw open the door and climbed in. "Step on it," he yelled as he slammed it shut, but he didn't have to, the driver more than motivated to leave the scene before it was cordoned off. Leonid sat back in the rear seat and frowned. Whoever had been behind the hit had been professional, skilled enough to plan the attack on short notice, and sufficiently daring to pull it off.

Perhaps most importantly, they'd been after Yusef. Which meant someone with knowledge of the pickup plan had talked.

The board's inability to keep a secret wasn't his problem, but after the disaster in Seychelles, Leonid's name was already synonymous with failure. Now two for two, any career he'd hoped for with Nicolai's group was over. Even though there could be no reasonable expectation that a single man armed with only a pistol would be adequate defense against a pair of kamikaze drones, the board would be wanting a scapegoat, he was sure.

His only hope lay with going on the offensive and trying to create value in the board's eyes by committing to finding who was behind the assault and terminating them with extreme prejudice.

Which would be a tough sell, he was sure.

But then again, he could be pretty persuasive when his life depended on it.

Which he had no doubt it now did.

CHAPTER 10

Tunis, Tunisia

A pair of dark SUVs rolled down a dimly lit street in one of the port city's primary industrial zones, the warehouses that lined the way looming out of the darkness like steel mountains. Few of the streetlamps were in operation, which was typical of the country in spite of its European pretensions. Although prosperous by North African standards, it still suffered from the corruption and lackadaisical approach to maintenance that was in evidence in the numerous potholes and graffiti on every available surface of the warehouse district, as well as considerable pollution from the number of vehicles crowded into the capital city's confines.

The SUVs slowed at an intersection, where a pack of wild street dogs were chasing an unfortunate cat into the gloom, and then accelerated again towards the seediest area of the district. The condition of the buildings degraded with each block, and as the big vehicles rumbled along, the lead driver cut his headlights, with its twin quickly following suit. They were the only vehicles on the road, the district's heavy cargo semi-rig traffic having stopped as the sun had sunk in the western sky.

The lead SUV coasted to a stop beside a deteriorating sheet metal fence, and the second driver pulled in behind. Four men dressed in black spilled from each of the trucks and hurriedly checked their bullpup submachine guns and then pulled balaclavas down over their faces. One of them pointed at a warehouse a hundred and fifty meters ahead, and they took off at a trot, their boots making muffled thumps on the asphalt.

When they reached the chain-link fence that ringed the warehouse grounds, two of the men ran to the locked gate while the rest hung back. One of them extracted a pair of bolt cutters from the other's backpack and moved to the chain that held the padlock in place. A determined snap, and the lock fell to the ground. The cutter replaced the tool into his partner's bag and motioned to the rest of the men.

They were through the gate in a flash and then moving stealthily in single file, weapons at the ready, aimed ahead, left hands on the shoulder of the man immediately in front of each of them, creeping along like an awkward human centipede. The gunman at the head of the procession wore a night vision monocle, but once they reached the warehouse, he flipped it out of his field of vision, the faint glow of a lamp ahead of them at one of the rusting access doors sufficient illumination.

They crept to the door, and the leader tried the handle, but it was locked. At his signal, one of the men behind him broke from the line and approached with a small wallet in his free hand. He gave the leader his weapon, unzipped the case, and extracted a pair of lockpicking tools before going to work on the tumblers. Forty-five seconds later, he stepped back from the door and retrieved his gun and returned to his position while the leader readied his submachine gun and reached for the handle.

The door swung open, and the men filed through the door into the cavernous warehouse, where pallets of cargo sat in bunches, ready for loading the following day. The leader held up four fingers and pointed at the sheetrock walls of an office at the far end, where a dim light flickered through the blinds of one of the windows.

Half the gunmen approached the office while the rest followed the leader through the pallets until they disappeared from view in one of the sequestered areas. The first group stopped outside the office, and one of them tried the door, happily surprised to find it unlocked. He nodded to his companions and then pulled the door open and swept the interior of the room with his gun as another gunman did the same at knee level.

The space was empty. The light they'd seen was emanating from a computer monitor, where a screen saver bounced a logo back and forth against a black backdrop. The gunmen entered the office and moved carefully around the six desks, refraining from touching anything, weapons in hand. Finding nothing, they returned to the warehouse floor and waited for their leader to return with the rest of the men.

They reunited two minutes later, and the leader spoke in a whisper. "Nothing on the main floor."

"Nor in the office," another said.

"That's impossible," the leader countered.

"Unless our intel was bad," the other gunman observed.

The leader extracted a small cell phone from his pocket, thumbed it to life, and dialed a number, the device's beeping nearly inaudible even in the still of the warehouse. The call connected, and the leader spoke in low tones.

"We're in, but there's nothing here but cargo."

A pause. "There has to be. Our source is sure."

The leader shook his head. "If there's anything, it isn't obvious."

"Go over every inch of the place. It's got to be there."

"Roger that." The leader hung up and turned to the men. "We must have missed something. Split up in pairs and do a thorough search of the area. Look for anything that's out of place."

"No additional info on what specifically we're after?"

"Nope. You know as much as I do."

The leader assigned each pair to one of the four corners of the floor, and they spent a half hour doing a thorough inspection of the main area. When they were finished, the leader led his partner into the office and stopped at the first desk, cocking his head to listen. He stood still as a statue for a full minute while his companion waited, and then turned to him and leaned in close.

"You hear that? Like a soft whistle. Every so often. Faint."

The other man shook his head. "Sorry. I'm not hearing it."

The leader flipped his monocle back into place and slowly scanned the surroundings. He moved cautiously between the desks and froze at the third one.

"Get the men," he whispered, still staring at a row of file cabinets.

His subordinate hurried back to the warehouse, and his men gathered behind him. He turned and pointed at the cabinets.

"There's light coming from between those two. Looks like it's coming from the floor. Could be a trapdoor." He paused. "Move that black one out of the way, but careful. No noise."

Three of the men neared the cabinet and tried to hoist it from the floor, but it didn't budge. The leader walked to them and whispered again, "Too heavy?"

"No. It's bolted down."

The leader thought for a moment and then knelt to open the lowest file drawer. Inside were stacks of manila folders. He felt around and then removed the drawer and ran his fingers along the floor beneath it until he felt an irregularity – some sort of metal cover, like for a weatherproof electrical outlet. He flipped the cover up and felt a button, which he pushed.

The file cabinet creaked and swung forward on its base, revealing a ladder that descended into the darkness.

The leader indicated the hole in the floor and whispered to the nearest man, "Three of you stay up here and keep a sharp lookout. The rest, follow me."

The leader slung his weapon's strap over his shoulder and lowered himself down the ladder. Once at the base, he freed the gun and took several steps into a tunnel that stretched to a bend twenty meters away, then waited for his men to join him. When they were ready, he led the way, slowing to eye the wood timbers that supported the ceiling beams. The passage was tall enough for a man to walk through without crouching, the floor hard-packed dirt with black pools of standing water.

When they reached the bend, he held up a hand, signaling caution. A soft amber glow emanated from around the curve, and he peered down the passage to locate the source. The tunnel terminated at a small vault, the source of the light.

He signaled to his men, and they formed a single-file procession again as they had above, the leader on point. He led them slowly around the bend towards the chamber, and they'd nearly reached the threshold when gunshots exploded from the vault. Slugs thwacked into the beam by the leader's head, and he returned fire, grateful for the darkness in the tunnel that had saved his life and made him a shadowy target. His suppressed bullpup spat ten rounds in a short burst, and then he was running towards the chamber, firing as he moved.

When he reached the room, he saw a single man wearing a blood-soaked shirt sprawled on the ground by a desk, the pistol a meter away from his clenched hand no threat as his life seeped from two chest wounds, forming a ruby pool. The rest of the men joined him, and he cursed softly.

"They're not going to be happy about this," he said to the gunman behind him, and shifted his attention to a knapsack by the desk. He moved to the bag and looked inside and then shouldered it and turned to the others. "Photograph him for an ID, and then let's get out of here," he said, and pushed past his men and retraced his steps to the ladder, his ears ringing from the dying Arab's shots. He was up the rungs in moments and calling on his cell seconds after.

"Target's dead after a firefight. But he had a laptop. I retrieved it, and we're heading back to base unless you have some other destination in mind," he said.

He listened as he received instructions and then hung up. His men emerged from the subterranean passage, and he faced them.

"Back to the trucks. We're done here." He eyed the nearest man. "I'm going to drop a grenade down the hole for good measure. That'll make it harder for anyone to get to the room and figure out what happened. Gather the men by the warehouse door and wait for me," he ordered, and turned to the file cabinet. When the men had left, he removed two grenades from his backpack, pulled the pins, tossed them down the shaft, and depressed the file cabinet button. The cabinet swung back into place, and he took off at a run for the office exit. He was nearly there when the detonations shook the concrete slab floor beneath his feet and blew the cabinet to the ceiling, rending part of it and causing a collapse of debris. He continued to where the men were waiting, and then the group vanished into the night, leaving no evidence of their passage other than the devastation of the secret vault below.

CHAPTER 11

Sifnos, Greece

Jet stared through the second-story window at the haze of fog that had rolled in, and shook her head in frustration. Ordinarily she'd have been asleep in the wee hours of the morning, not awaiting the arrival of a helicopter that Andrew had managed to secure for their transport, so the possibility that the entire island would be fogged in to the point it was difficult to see the trees fifteen yards away hadn't occurred to her. But that was reality, and barring a miracle, there was no way any sane pilot was going to try to land in those conditions.

Which meant they would need a plan B if they were going to make it off the island safely. With aircraft off the table, that left only departure by sea, which had its own set of issues, not the least of which was that the waters could be treacherous even for those who navigated them regularly – but in pea-soup fog, trying to do so would be somewhere between recklessly dangerous and impossible.

That left the traditional route: the ferry off the island that departed just after dawn; the obvious risk being that whoever had found Jet and targeted her for execution would expect her to be on the boat, unless the assassin had been working on his own. Which meant they had a fifty-fifty chance of making it out alive.

She wasn't liking the odds, but the other option – to wait until the fog cleared sufficiently for the helo to come – was even less appealing. In daylight, a helicopter could easily be taken out with a shoulder-fired missile – and those were easy to obtain given Greece's proximity to the Middle East, a literal bazaar for black market weapons due to the ongoing war in Syria and the glut of munitions in Afghanistan and Iraq. Even Turkey had a thriving secondary arms market, as weapons were transported north from Syria by Kurds and then resold to the highest bidder.

So staying put was off the table. They were sitting ducks if they remained on the island, and both Matt and Andrew had agreed it wasn't an option.

Jet sighed and checked her watch again. It would be light out in three more hours, tops. They needed to make a decision, and if it was to be the ferry, they would have to prepare for the worst.

Jet went downstairs to where Matt was still sitting before the bank of monitors in the security room and put her hands on his shoulders.

"Anything?" she asked softly.

"Nope. Quiet as a cemetery," he said. "What's the verdict on the helicopter?"

"Looking like it's a no-go. That leaves the ferry. But I was thinking – it might be best for me to go alone rather than all of us as a group."

He gave her a fatigued smile. "Because anyone who could have found you here wouldn't know your family was with you?"

She frowned. "I know it doesn't make sense. But if anything were to happen…"

Matt shook his head. "You're right. It doesn't make sense. Haven't you ever heard the saying about safety in numbers?"

"I keep confusing it with the one about all of your eggs in one basket."

"Hmm. Do I get a vote?"

That brought a smile to her lips. "Of course. This is a benign dictatorship, remember?"

"Ah. Right. Well, we're all at risk either way, but we stand a better chance of not being picked off if we stay on the move. I've gotten really used to breathing, so I would opt for the boat, even if it's risky, which it is – because staying is riskier. And the longer we sit here, the more time anyone hunting us has to take a second whack at it."

"Me," she corrected. "Hunting *me*."

"Nobody likes a pedant. Look, if they're after you, they're after all of us because we can be used to draw you out. We both know that."

She looked away. "Doesn't mean I need to like it."

"Nope. So…ferry?"

"I'll go tell Andrew to call the helicopter people a final time, but yeah, if nothing changes in the next hour or so, it's the boat."

When Jet made it to his room, Andrew was sitting up in bed, tapping on his tablet, his rifle leaning against the nightstand. He looked up when she entered, and offered a rigid smile.

"Doesn't look like we'll be flying to freedom," she said.

"No, unfortunately it doesn't. What's the smart play?" he asked.

She explained her reasoning, and he nodded slowly. "Makes sense. Oh, and before I forget, one of my contacts said there's an Igor Petrenko who operates out of Belgrade. Ukrainian, but relocated after the dustup with Russia. Specializes in low-end murder for hire, kidnapping, the usual. All the jobs the A-tier players won't touch. I can get more details tomorrow."

"I'd be grateful for anything you can find."

"I'm on it."

Later, as the sun rose over the Aegean Sea, Jet and Matt waited to board the ferry with Hannah beside them, Andrew having decided at the last minute to remain at the villa until he could be evacuated by helicopter so he wouldn't present a burden should they need to move fast, his recovery not sufficient to keep him from being a liability. The fog was still dense, but nowhere near as bad as it had been a few hours earlier, and the big ship had steamed into port and reversed into the commercial jetty without any drama, the trip one it made with ease from Athens, where it would soon return. Passengers trooped off the boat along with a procession of vehicles, and after a seemingly endless wait, departing travelers were allowed on.

Jet had surveyed those in the waiting area and seen nothing that set off any of her well-tuned alarms, the hundred or so early morning backpackers and tourists bleary-eyed and sleepy looking. They filed past the ticket taker and walked up the gangplank and into the vehicle accessway, and then through the parking area to the cabin level, where another attendant checked their tickets and directed them to the passenger lounge.

Matt selected a seat near the bow, and Jet and Hannah sat beside him as the engines rumbled far below in preparation for departure. She glanced around and leaned into him.

"I'm going to take a lap and make sure we're clean," she said, and patted her purse, where her Sig Sauer 9mm pistol was stashed, along with a folding survival knife.

"Didn't see anyone suspicious, did you?" Matt asked.

"No, but better safe than sorry."

Jet stood and casually scanned the lounge. Nobody stood out as a threat, so she moved through the double doors to the rear seating area, where she bought a cup of coffee at the snack bar, eyes roaming the seats as she made change for the clerk. Satisfied the main level was clear, she approached the stairs to the upper-level lounges and stopped when the boat began moving. She waited until it hit cruising speed, and ascended to the higher deck, where she ambled through the forward passenger sections, taking her time, beverage in hand.

At the rear upper lounge, the hair on her arms pricked up, and she sensed someone scrutinizing her. Outwardly unfazed, she made her way to the stern doors that led onto the exterior deck, which was empty given the gloom and cold temperature on the open water. She pushed through the doors and stood to one side, hand in her purse, and was unsurprised when a pair of olive-skinned men followed her out, their frames lean and fit, both with hands in their windbreaker pockets, the bulges of pistols unmistakable. Jet hadn't seen them departing Sifnos, so they must have come from Athens and stayed on board with round-trip tickets, which meant she'd been correct in anticipating that there would be a welcoming committee for her on the ferry.

Jet threw the steaming coffee in the face of the nearest man. He screamed in pain as she pivoted and kicked the other in the solar plexus while he was freeing his gun. He dropped it and gasped for breath, and she had hers clear in an instant and squeezed off two shots, the suppressed subsonic rounds loud pops in the open air. The bullets caught him in the chest, and he tumbled backwards with a strangled scream. She shifted to the other assailant, whose face was bright red and swelling from the scalding coffee, his eyes slits.

"Who hired you?" she demanded in English and then in Arabic.

He screamed a curse and lunged at her. She easily dodged his attempt and shot him as he fumbled with his gun.

She swore silently as she eyed the dead men on the deck. The entire altercation had played out in twenty seconds, and nobody else had emerged from the lounge, which meant that with any luck she might have a chance to cover her tracks. She replaced the pistol in her bag, dragged the first assassin to the rail, heaved him onto it, and pushed his body over. Jet watched as the corpse pinwheeled down to the white froth of the wake and splashed inaudibly, and then repeated the maneuver with the second. She moved to where the first killer's gun still lay, scooped it up, and pocketed the small Walther PPK – an ideal choice for close-in work, she noted, although it hadn't done him much good.

The blood on the deck was a problem, but one that a nearby emergency fire hose easily solved, and barely a minute later she was retracing her steps to the lower deck. She stopped at the bathroom and checked her appearance in the mirror, and after wetting her hands and patting her hair into place, wiped down the Walther and stashed it behind one of the toilet tanks, and then continued to the seating area where Matt and her daughter were waiting.

Matt looked her up and down when she approached, and cocked an eyebrow. "Anything?" he asked in a low voice.

"Nothing I wasn't expecting," she replied. "Want some coffee or a roll? Hannah? Are you hungry or thirsty?"

Matt's jaw clenched. "Not for me. What do you mean, expecting?"

She sighed and looked at him. "It's handled. But we should probably split up. They're throwing resources at this, and they have my description."

"And what? You go to Belgrade in search of this Petrenko?" he asked.

"Basically. And you join Andrew in Slovenia, where he's got that cabin. That's safest. We disembark separately, so if there's anyone waiting in Athens, you and Hannah aren't in the mix."

Before they'd left, Andrew had arranged for a hunting lodge in a remote area of Slovenia, where he was sure they'd be undisturbed, and had promised to call her voicemail with more information about Igor Petrenko whenever he was able to track something down. She wasn't expecting much, in light of the current circumstances, but she had time – it would take some doing to get to Belgrade, as it would for her family and Andrew to make it to Slovenia.

"I hate this," Matt said under his breath.

"Can I have some juice?" Hannah asked, interrupting their tense discussion.

"Of course, sweetheart," Jet said. "Apple if they have it, right?"

"And a muffin, please."

Jet smiled and regarded Matt. "Sure you don't want some coffee? It smelled great."

He shrugged. "That sounds good. You want me to get it?"

"Would you? I want to talk to Hannah." She paused and gave him a sardonic smile. "But be careful. It's super hot."

His stare was puzzled. "Noted. Anything else?"

"Maybe a roll for me. They looked good."

He stood and glanced at her pant legs, which were wet from the knee down. "Dare I ask?"

She shook her head. "I'll tell you when you get back. Better hurry before all the good stuff's gone."

CHAPTER 12

Moscow, Russian Federation

The main conference room was thick with cigarette smoke as the members of Nicolai's board waited for Artem's arrival. Coffee and cognac sat atop the long table, and the members were having multiple conversations in hushed tones, the mood dour after the assassination of their chosen leader before he'd even made it into the office.

Rudolf was huddled at one end with his two closest allies, while the other five board members were split at the other, cognac snifters half full. The custom of alcoholic eye-openers was accepted in the morning, the expectation that it had been a rough night that required early fortification a given.

"Leonid should have seen this coming. He's not up to the job," Rudolf said. "And now we have Siberia in play. This is disastrous. We'll lose all our partners."

"I disagree," the man to his right said. "There was no way to anticipate a drone attack at the airport. Come on, Rudy. I'm no fan of Sergei or his brother, but you can't expect them to be psychic."

Rudolf took a pull on his cognac and frowned. "That's your problem, Lev. You make excuses for failure. There's been too much of that lately."

"Just saying be reasonable. If we get rid of the brother, what are we left with? Hire out? Who's going to vet them? And once they're inside our circle, how can we be sure they won't betray us? We could all be targets now. There's no way of knowing."

"I never thought Yusef would be a good fit anyway. But this has to be addressed, and quickly."

"What do you propose?"

They were interrupted by the conference room door swinging open. Artem strode in, his bespoke Saville Row suit gleaming in the morning light.

"Gentlemen," he said, making the round of the table and shaking hands.

"A terrible day," Rudolf said.

"For all of us," Artem agreed, and took a seat at one of the free spaces. "What precisely happened?"

Rudolf gave him a dry report, and Artem shook his head.

"There has to be a leak," Artem observed. "Who else besides the people in this room knew Yusef's schedule?"

Rudolf thought for a minute. "Leonid and the driver. And of course, the pilots."

"I think we can take the pilots out of the equation," one of the others said.

"Not necessarily," Artem said. "We can't be sure that they knew the plane would be blown up. It could have been a way to end any trail. Although I doubt it. You'd think whoever was behind the attack would have wanted to continue getting intelligence from whoever tipped them off." Artem thought for a moment. "Who is this Leonid?"

"If you recall, he's Sergei's brother," Rudolf reminded him. "The convict."

Artem frowned. "I'd definitely suspect him, then. He's a criminal, and criminals will do anything for money. Likewise, the driver is a low-end flunky. Wave a nice offer in front of him and he'd probably take it."

"Sure," Rudolf agreed. "Any of this is possible. But what do we do about it?"

Artem looked around the table. "First off, we need to choose someone to operate as the head of the organization. As legal counsel, I've been putting out fires with all our partners, and as I said on our call, this is now a critical problem. Of course, that person will be subject to considerable physical risk, as the attack on Yusef proves. Once we have someone selected, then we can move in a productive direction – namely to figure out who was behind Yusef's assassination, who was behind Nicolai's, and who leaked the info. Our business issues are obvious: repairing our relationships and strengthening our position." He paused. "Both of these are pressing enough that I propose that I take on the risk temporarily and become the putative head of the organization for six months. That will buy us the time to organize and implement a strategy, and then I'll gladly step down in favor of whoever you decide will be the best candidate."

If it had been possible for Rudolf's jaw to hit the table, it would have. He looked like he'd swallowed a frog, and Artem pretended not to notice.

"I'll do this with some conditions," Artem continued. "The first is that I appoint my own security. The second is that any investigations I conduct to identify the traitor or traitors are without any restrictions, as are my actions in dealing with them once revealed. The third is that I am fairly compensated for my time and trouble. And the fourth is that I will create an agreement guaranteeing that my acceptance of the position is only for six months, after which it is upon you to fill the slot. Becoming acting CEO makes sense because I know all of our contra-parties, so I'm a familiar face, which will reassure them – and I have a reputation for being even-handed. So that will provide the stability they seek. It will be our little secret that the arrangement is temporary. Once reassured, I would think most of the problems will evaporate. At which point I can return to normal life, and you can decide who'll wear the bull's-eye from there on out."

Rudolf's Adam's apple bobbed like a frenzied animal, and he leaned forward against his forearms. "It's a generous offer, Artem, but I'm not sure we can accept. It places you at considerable risk, as you said."

Artem smiled and nodded. "I had to offer. Can't say I wouldn't be a little relieved for my personal safety if you decline."

The man to his left cleared his throat. "Not so fast. Artem's proposal, as usual, makes a lot of sense. We get what we need now and buy ourselves time to find the right fit."

Rudolf glared at him – one of Yusef's supporters, of course. "You're ignoring that we have qualified candidates sitting at this table," he snapped.

"Do we? Someone who's known to all the players we'll be dealing with? Someone who is…expendable…if the impossible happens again?" He looked at Artem. "No offense, you're highly valued, but you aren't on the board…"

"Yes, I quite understand," Artem said. "Easier to find a new attorney than a new qualified board member."

"That isn't what I meant," the man fired back.

"Look, it was just a suggestion," Artem said. "As you point out, there's a high degree of certainty I won't make it through the month if I become the public face. If one of you feels they want to take that on, more power to you, and I'll write a stirring eulogy. But we need a statement for the public and for our partners, and it can't wait any longer. We need decisive action, not bickering. We're out of runway." He stood. "I'll give you some time to discuss it. I was up with the chickens to get here in time for this meeting, so I'd like to freshen up."

Artem departed, and Rudolf went on the attack immediately. "He's not qualified to be CEO."

"Qualified? Like Yusef was? He'd be a figurehead, nothing more. And a temporary one at that."

"His conditions are absurd."

The man across from Rudolf scowled and studied his fingernails. "I find your objection to a no-lose offer rather puzzling, Rudi. Whoever takes the position could well get killed, as Yusef discovered the hard way. Exactly who are you thinking would be foolhardy enough to take the job knowing that?"

It was Rudolf's turn to frown. "A bit dramatic, don't you think?"

"They're still scraping what's left of Yusef and one of our planes off the runway. Perhaps you should go out to the airport and tell his remains yourself? But wear a flak jacket, and make sure your will's up to date."

One of the others laughed out loud. "It will be fascinating to see which of your mistresses gets the biggest cut."

"We know it will be bigger than any of your wives'!" another cackled.

"I'm serious. We shouldn't make any rash decisions," Rudolf tried.

"I agree. We should put it to a vote. All in favor of accepting Artem's offer?" The man raised his hand. All but Rudolf and one other did as well. The other holdout eyed Rudolf and then slowly raised his.

Seeing his certain defeat, Rudolf did as well. "Might as well make our suicide unanimous."

"That's the spirit!"

When Artem returned, the men toasted his appointment, and Rudolf stared him down. "So what now, Artem?"

"We need decisive action to avenge both Nicolai and Yusef. Anything less would make us look weak, which we already do. We're all aware of the chatter about the Chinese being responsible for Nicolai. So that should be priority one, right after we firewall all further discussions so we can't have a repeat of the Yusef tragedy. And I'll have to move back to Moscow for the duration – which my wife is going to hate, but that's the breaks. While I'd like to think I can run things from London, it's not practical and would send the wrong message. So I'll need to attend to securing competent security, and then relocate, at least for six months." He scanned the men's faces. "Let's hope the next meeting isn't to bury me. I'll inform you all of any decisions that require board-level approval, and submit an offer letter for your signature this afternoon. Thank you for your faith in me. I won't let you down."

"I think we need to monitor your actions more closely than that," Rudolf said.

"I appreciate the input, but if I'm to lead, I'll be moving very fast, and I can't do this via committee. You'll have to trust that the same judgment I've brought to bear for the last decade with our dealings will be in action now. But I can't have back-seat drivers if I'm to be effective. The operating agreement is quite clear about what I require board-level approval for. I'll abide by that. I'm not proposing anything novel."

Rudolf could see he wasn't going to win the battle, so he settled for a smile and another slug of cognac. "Which is fine. What I'm saying is that if you require any feedback from those who have been here longer than you, my door is always open."

Artem's smile was as wintery as Rudolf's. "I'll keep that in mind, and appreciate it. Now, gentlemen, to the minutiae of what must be done over the next few days. Starting with responding to Nicolai's murder."

Rudolf cleared his throat. "We all know it was the Chinese. Why pretend otherwise?"

Artem sat back. "How do we know that, exactly?"

"Zhang is the obvious perpetrator. He had the motive and the connections."

"I don't disagree, but I think we need some sort of confirmation before we take drastic steps, don't you? Zhang is extremely powerful, and it will take some doing to neutralize him permanently. I'd say if we're going to expend the resources to do so, we need to be absolutely sure he was responsible and not base our actions on what 'we all know.'"

"And how would you propose we do that?" one of the others asked.

"Pinpoint his whereabouts at the time of the attack, for starters, and identify a motive. Right now, I'm unaware of one."

"Nicolai hated him, and the feeling was mutual," Rudolf reminded the table.

"Nicolai had made plenty of enemies, as we all know. Give me a few days to research all of this, and I'll let you know what I find out. If it's certain that he was responsible, he will be dealt with, swiftly and permanently – if for no other reason than as a warning to anyone else that we're not to be trifled with. Same will go for Yusef, or we're all targets for our enemies and it's just a matter of time until bullets with our names on them hit home."

The meeting continued for another half hour, and when it ended, Artem again shook hands with the board and allowed himself to be shown to Nicolai's office, where he did a quick inventory and made notes on his phone. He exhaled slowly as he looked around the sumptuous room and suppressed a smile. He had managed to become the head of one of the most powerful enterprises in the world by using basic psychology.

Now the question was how to keep his position and avoid Yusef's fate from any of a dozen unscrupulous adversaries.

A challenge at which he had to succeed, or pay the ultimate price trying.

CHAPTER 13

Belgrade, Serbia

The late afternoon sun was blindingly bright as Jet sat in a taxi. Her flight from Athens had been uneventful if tedious due to weather delays, and as the car crossed the Sava River on the way into downtown Belgrade, she gazed absently at the greenish water as it rushed to empty into the nearby Danube. A bright red vessel, easily ten times longer than it was wide, churned its way toward the junction of the two rivers. The towering buildings on the Belgrade Waterfront side, all modern steel and glass, stood in sharp contrast to the old-world architecture that had whizzed by as they'd motored from the airport.

She'd spoken with Andrew while waiting for her flight; he'd given her the name of a local contact for her to look up and promised to call him to let him know that a friend would be coming to see him and to cooperate however he could. Jet was naturally reluctant to meet anyone she didn't know, but she had no other option and had to be grateful that Andrew was still helping them even after the disaster on Sifnos.

Thankfully, there had been nobody waiting for them to disembark from the ferry when they arrived in Athens, and Jet waited until Matt had led Hannah off the boat before leaving its confines, surrounded by a press of humanity eager to be on dry land after five and a half hours on the water. She had to remind herself that her features were no longer those of the woman she'd been before the surgery in Abu Dhabi, and as such she wasn't at risk of being flagged by the facial-recognition software employed at the port. Still, old habits died hard, and she'd obviously looked similar enough for the assassin to recognize her, so she'd donned a head kerchief and sunglasses and kept her face averted from the cameras she'd spotted on an array over the passenger throughfare.

Once she was confident that she wasn't being tracked, she'd taken a bus to the Athens airport and paid cash for a one-way ticket to Belgrade. She broke her pistol down into components and jettisoned them in three separate airport trash bins, and then settled in to await her flight on one of Europe's countless economy airlines, which cost barely more than taking a train. She would have ordinarily taken a land route, but time was of the essence, and she didn't want to be away from her family any longer than necessary.

Immigration and customs in Serbia had been lax, and she'd been waved through by a bored official who'd barely glanced at her passport. Now, in a cab whose shocks had seen better days, she was untraceable and, for the moment, safe. She just hoped that Andrew's representations about the lodging he'd arranged for Matt and Hannah were true, and that they could relax their guard enough to not be constantly stressed. Her daughter had been through so many changes in her brief life that Jet's heart ached at the thought, and it caused her physical pain to imagine her existence continuing like it had, constantly on the run, the prospect of having to drop everything and flee a country an almost everyday occurrence. Jet had chosen the life she'd led, but her daughter had had no say in hers, and Jet could only hope that the emotional scars circumstances had caused would heal with time.

The taxi reached the Belgrade side of the bridge and headed toward a hotel that Jet had found on her phone – a lackluster two-and-a-half-star affair that would inevitably be staffed by resentful, underpaid personnel who would have no interest in her. There was a certain anonymity to be had by staying at the less popular places, where workers were just trying to get through their shifts with as little thinking as possible, which was perfect for her purposes.

The hotel was everything she'd wanted, from the run-down façade to the surly reception clerk, and when she'd let herself into the postage stamp-sized room, she actually smiled. Stinking of cheap disinfectant and just large enough for a ten-year-old to feel comfortable, it was exactly what she'd been after, and would serve her well for her hopefully short stay.

She unpacked her few items, removed a burner cell she'd bought at an airport convenience store, and powered it on. Jet dialed the number of Andrew's contact, and a deep male voice answered on the third ring.

"We have a mutual friend," Jet said in English. "When can we meet?"

"I have time today. Do you need anything?"

"Some personal protection would be nice."

"Not a problem. Nine mil work?"

"Nine's my favorite number."

"Give me an hour. Write this address down. It's a restaurant. We won't be bothered there." He mentioned a street and a number. "I'll be wearing a brown leather jacket and sunglasses. Sitting in the back."

"See you then."

She hung up and considered her next step. She'd changed money at the airport, so she had some walking-around cash, which she would take with her, along with her passports and diamonds. The hotel, for all its understated charm, didn't inspire confidence, and the room had no safe; and there was no way she was leaving everything she owned in the world with the front desk.

Jet resisted the urge to call Matt. He was probably still traveling, and would leave a voicemail when he'd touched down.

She entered the restaurant address into the phone, and it indicated that it was two kilometers away – an easy walk for her in under a half hour, which would give her a chance to case the place and confirm nobody was lying in wait. She slipped her passports into her back pocket and patted the satchel of diamonds that hung from around her neck. Then she counted the cash she had left after paying for the room and the taxi: fifty-five thousand dinar, the equivalent of about five hundred euro, which from the prices she'd seen posted in shop windows on the drive in would last her a good while.

Jet set off down the street with her map software guiding her way, and marveled at how crowded the sidewalks were. The population was attractive, seemingly fit, and certainly thin, for the most part, their clothes the usual international brands that had erased most national differences in favor of ubiquitous athletic shoes and shirts and jeans that would have been equally at home in San Diego or Buenos Aires or Paris. Jet fit right in with her usual black ensemble, and she strode determinedly through throngs of university students and shoppers, her dark brown dyed hair tucked beneath a knit sailor's cap.

She reached the restaurant with plenty of time to spare and ducked into an optician's shop to consider his display of sunglasses while watching the restaurant and studying the vehicles parked nearby. With the amount of pedestrian traffic, it was difficult, though not impossible, to spot a watcher. She took her time as she tried on half the inventory after waving away a shopkeeper who insisted on hovering right behind her as though she were going to make a break for it with a pair of knockoff Ray-Bans.

Jet didn't see anything amiss and departed the shop with an annoyed glare from the clerk. She strolled slowly along the sidewalk on the opposite side of the street from the restaurant. None of the cars had anyone in them, nor did the windows on the buildings seem unduly suspicious. She rounded the corner at the intersection and then peered around it to watch the restaurant entrance as she pretended to be talking on her phone.

Five minutes before her meeting, a red Citroën pulled to a stop in front. A man in a brown leather jacket got out of the passenger side, carrying a backpack. He had longish black hair, gaunt features, and the customary three days of stubble dusting his face that seemed the norm for any male over the age of thirteen. The car rolled away, and he entered the restaurant, leaving Jet to monitor foot traffic to confirm they were alone.

Ten minutes later, she crossed the street and ducked through the glass door. The restaurant was empty, and she immediately spied her man at the rear of the dining area. She walked to him and offered a professional smile, which he returned with equal sincerity.

"Gustav," she said as she sat across from him.

He nodded. "And what shall I call you?"

"Sylvie works," Jet said.

"Well, Sylvie Works, nice to meet you. How is our mutual friend?"

She shrugged. "Fine."

"He told me he'd suffered some setbacks."

"I try not to poke my nose in other people's business."

His tight smile signaled approval. "Are you hungry?"

She shook her head. "Big lunch. But I could drink something. Mineral water?"

He signaled for a waiter who was standing by the entry, looking out at the street. He hurried over, and Gustav ordered in Serbian, pointing to her and then himself. The server scurried off, and he sat back and studied her.

"Your man is a lowlife," Gustav started. "Involved in drugs, murder, organ trafficking – anything he can get paid to do. Runs a crew of about fifteen thugs. Business must be tight, because for the last few months he's been mostly doing loan sharking and protection, which is usually just disguised extortion. A real charmer."

"Your English is quite good," Jet said.

"Thanks. I went to uni in London for a couple of years." He regarded her. "You're not American or British."

"A citizen of the world," she said. The waiter reappeared with a bottle of Perrier for her and a local microbrew beer for him. The thin man set both on the table and made himself scarce, and Jet sat forward.

"Where can I find him?" she asked.

He patted the backpack. "I've written a list of his protection racket customers. Might take some time, but it's the end of the week, and it's likely he'll be picking up his payments."

"In person?"

His eyebrows rose. "Maybe. Maybe not. At his level, he may not have anyone he trusts with the money. He does own an auto body shop as his front. It's a laundering operation. I took the liberty of including the address. Word is he isn't there regularly, but you never know." He paused, and she opened the bottle and took a long sip. "I included a couple of photos from his arrest record, but they're rather outdated. Still, he's not hard to miss. Looks like a Neanderthal. You'll just have to hope he shows himself."

"That's doing it the hard way," she said.

"No question. Oh, and I put your gift in the bag, along with a couple of spare mags. Beretta nine with the numbers removed. Untraceable. Homemade suppressor, never used. Carton of fifty rounds."

"What do I owe you?"

He smiled again. "Dinner next time."

"Seriously."

"I am serious. Don't worry about it. I've been our friend's associate for a long time. We do each other favors whenever we can. I'll bank this one."

"At least let me pay for your meal."

He laughed. "I own the place. Save it for taxi fare." He handed her the backpack. "I do hope you'll take me up on dinner, though. It's been some time since I had such charming company."

She gave him a genuine smile this time. It never hurt to have someone interested who could help her if she needed it. "I'll think it over. Thank you, Gustav."

"My pleasure…Sylvie Works. Good luck."

She stood and hefted the backpack. "If I need to hire someone discreet to watch some of the shops, I presume you could arrange that?"

"With ease. Going rate's a couple of hundred euro a day. Want me to set it up?"

"Please. Short notice. As you say, it's the end of the week, so if he's going to do collections, it'll probably be within the next few hours."

"Let me make a call. How many do you need?"

She thought about it. "Two. I'll ring you in half an hour. Is that enough time?"

"Sure."

She set half her wad of dinar on the table. "I'll only need them until the shops close. Will this do the trick for the help?"

He eyed it. "Should be. Where do you want to meet my people?"

"I'll give you an address," she said. "First I want to go look the shops over."

"I'll leave my phone on."

Jet left the restaurant and hurried through the pedestrians to a side street, where she paused in a doorway to look over the backpack contents. Two minutes later she had the photos in her pocket, with the addresses, the pistol, in serviceable if well-used shape, left in the bag for now. She entered the first shop into her navigation program and then set off at a brisk walk; the district where her target operated was only ten minutes away, which she could cut down to six if she pushed it.

And given the circumstances and the stakes, she'd push it.

CHAPTER 14

Bohinjska Bistrica, Slovenia

Matt and Hannah stood in front of the bus stop in the quaint alpine town, the air so crisp it felt like a different planet after the warmth of Sifnos and the pollution of Athens. Colorful wooden houses lined the streets, making the area an idyllic mountain enclave for skiers in the winter and tourists in the summer. Andrew was scheduled to arrive any moment, and then he would escort them to the cabin he'd secured in a location so remote that nobody would ever find them, much less think to look.

Hannah took his hand and squeezed it tightly. "I miss Mama already," she said, her voice plaintive.

Matt returned the gentle pressure. "Me too, Hannah. But she won't be gone long."

Hannah frowned. "You always say that, and she always is."

"I know," Matt admitted. "But I'm betting this time is different."

Hannah considered his words. "I hate it when she leaves."

"I'm not a big fan of it, either. But sometimes she has to."

"I wish she didn't."

"That makes two of us." He released her hand. "But look at this place. Isn't it beautiful? Everything's so green!"

The little girl looked around and nodded wordlessly. Matt decided to switch tactics.

"We've got a super fun cabin in the woods. And I hear there are rivers here full of fish."

"I don't like to fish."

Matt checked the time on his phone and was about to respond when a van pulled to the curb, and the passenger window lowered. Andrew waved to them.

"You made it! Come on, then. Climb aboard," he said.

Matt helped Hannah into the vehicle, opened the cargo doors and tossed their bags in the back, and then climbed in and sat beside her. When they were underway, Andrew tilted his head to speak to them.

"Nothing to report in Greece, so that all went smoothly. Don't worry about the driver. Doesn't speak a word," he said. "Glad to see you got here in one piece."

Matt nodded. "I could say the same for you."

"I'm improving every day, but I'd be lying if I said that I'm not feeling every bump in the road."

"That which does not kill you…"

"I'm strong as Hercules at this point."

The van rolled out of the small town and began climbing up a windy secondary road. Ten minutes later it turned onto a private gravel drive and stopped in front of a two-story hunting lodge that could have housed a football team.

Matt eyed Andrew and grinned. "A humble little place," he observed.

Andrew shrugged. "No point to having some mad money if you aren't going to spend it." He opened the passenger door, and Matt did the same.

"Let me give you a hand," Matt offered.

"Appreciate it. My mountain climbing days are a thing of the past, unfortunately."

The interior of the lodge was less impressive than the exterior, and once Matt and the driver had carried their luggage inside, Andrew gave Matt and Hannah a tour.

"I've stayed here before. It's really way too big for the three of us, but I didn't want any more surprises, and it's a known entity," he said.

Matt considered the rough-hewn wood floors and the soft sough of wind through gaps in the window frames and nodded. "We appreciate you getting it for us."

"Not a problem. Besides, I need someplace quiet where I can recover, and this perfectly fits the bill. There's a market in town that has most everything we'll need, and the lodge comes with pots and pans and dishes, so we're set. Propane tank and septic and a backup generator, so we're self-contained for the duration. Comes with a Jeep, too. Keys are in the pantry off the kitchen. If memory serves, it doesn't run great, but it runs." He indicated one of the bedrooms. "I'll take this one. There are four others. You're welcome to whatever suits your fancy."

Matt escorted Hannah to one of the smaller bedrooms at the rear of the cabin and set her bag on the floor inside. "I'll be right next door, sweetheart."

"I'm hungry," she said.

He smiled. "So am I. Maybe I'll take the Jeep and see if I can find that market before it gets too late? Either that or we'll have to try to trap a raccoon or something for dinner."

She grimaced. "I don't want to eat a raccoon."

Matt's countenance was serious. "Pretty certain that no raccoon wants to be dinner, so it's mutual. Come on, let's go see if there's anything you can eat there, okay?" Matt called out down the hall. "I'm going into town, Andrew. Want anything special tonight?"

"No, thanks," he replied. "I haven't had much of an appetite since I got shot to pieces. And I ate on the plane."

Matt smiled again. Andrew had chartered a jet in Athens rather than flying commercial, as he and Hannah had. So of course Andrew had enjoyed a catered meal of his choosing. Matt reminded himself that money wasn't an issue for them either, and to stop being parsimonious, but rationalized that his funds weren't exactly liquid, and blowing ten grand on an hour and a half flight wouldn't have been practical, not with the amount of cash he was carrying.

He extended his hand to Hannah and looked at the front door. "Come on, young lady. Let's find out just how badly that Jeep runs, shall we?"

CHAPTER 15

Belgrade, Serbia

Jet met Gustav's watchers and briefed the two women on the task they were to perform, and took them to the two shops she'd selected from the list. She showed them the photos and noted their reactions – one took a snap with her cell; the other merely nodded as though she'd committed the images to memory. She supposed they seemed as professional as she could expect, considering the short notice and the price, and they agreed to phone her if Petrenko showed. They took up position across the street, and she left them for the auto body shop, which was five minutes away.

The neighborhood was seedy, which she expected, and the shop packed with vehicles. Jet sat at a collapsible table outside a market fifty meters away and ordered a mineral water from the girl who came to attend to her. When it arrived, she sipped it judiciously, making it last as dusk approached. The body shop workers called it a day after a half hour, and a pair of them walked to the market and emerged a few minutes later with a case of beer and a bottle of rakija – a particularly potent local liquor that could blow up to fifty percent alcohol, a favorite of the working class in how quickly it could get the job done.

The laborers leered at her, which she ignored, and toted their purchases back to the shop, where the crew had dragged crates to the curb and were lounging, clouds of acrid tobacco smoke rising from them like a forest fire. They cheered the arrival of the alcohol, and Jet ordered another water when the shop girl came to check on her.

Time crept by, and the workers grew louder in inverse proportion to the level of their bottle. The light had completely bled out of the sky when Jet was getting ready to call it an evening. She finished her third mineral water and was preparing to leave when a black BMW 7 Series sedan braked to a stop in front of the laborers, its bulk ostentatiously out of place in the district. Two men got out of the car, and Jet's eyes narrowed when she spied Petrenko, hair trimmed a quarter inch off his skull, wearing a knockoff Versace windbreaker, a heavy gold chain draped across his chest. He was carrying a black leather satchel that was practically bursting at the seams, and she could make out the bulge of a pistol jammed into his waistband at the small of his back.

The pair greeted the workers, and Petrenko entered the shop while the second man stationed himself at the door. The workers offered him a pull of their bottle, but he declined with a laugh, patting his stomach.

Jet weighed her options and, in the interest of time, decided on a direct approach. She paid the clerk and crossed to the body shop, keenly aware of the full attention of the half dozen men, who watched her near with undisguised interest. When she reached them, she offered a shy smile and batted her eyes for good measure.

"I'm sorry," she tried in English. "The bathroom at the market is broken. Do you have one I could use?"

The men exchanged confused glances, and then the guard grunted and looked her up and down.

"Very dirty," he said in heavily accented English. "No good."

She shifted from foot to foot. "I don't care. Emergency."

He gave her an annoyed glare and gestured at the men. "Pigs. Very bad."

"Please," Jet begged. "I'll buy more beer."

One of the workers stood unsteadily and leered at her, then grinned at the guard. "Come on, Marko," he said in decent English.

Her face registered surprise, and he laughed. "Three years in Chicago. Cousin there."

The worker and Marko had a heated exchange in Serbian, and then Marko exhaled loudly and stepped aside.

"Thank you. Thank you so much," Jet said to the worker. "I meant it about the beer."

He grinned crookedly in what she imagined was his most charming playboy manner, his blue eyes twinkling with alcohol. "It very dirty. Marko no lie."

"I'll just be a minute. It really is an emergency," she said, and Marko heaved the steel door open for her and pointed to another at the rear of the shop. She nodded and pretended not to notice how he forced her to squeeze past him, brushing him with her breasts as she did.

She crossed the shop and swung the toilet door open. It was everything the men had promised, and worse: no seat, rank from lack of ventilation, and looked like it hadn't been cleaned since the war. Jet gagged and held her breath, and her eyes flitted to the front of the shop to confirm the front door was closed before she slammed the toilet door hard enough for the men in front to hear it, and then sidled towards the open doorway of the office, where a single overhead lightbulb lit the small space.

Jet had the pistol out by the time she reached the office. When she stepped through the doorway, Petrenko looked up in surprise from where he was counting money, and his face twisted in anger.

He snarled something in Serbian, and Jet took a step closer and motioned with the pistol.

"You speak Russian," she said in Russian. "Raise your hands and keep them where I can see them."

"You picked the wrong person to rob," he spat in kind, and slowly set the money aside and put both hands palms down on the desktop.

She cocked the hammer on the pistol. "I'm not after your money. I'm here for answers."

He glared at her. "I don't understand."

"You sent the wrong guy to try to kill me in Greece," she said. "He gave me your name before he died. I want to know who hired you – who you're working for."

He blinked, but other than that his poker face was good. "I don't know what you're talking about."

She smiled as though amused and lowered the aim of the pistol. "I'll start with your knees. After that, I'll move higher. Strike three will take you out of the gene pool for good. Probably not smart to test me unless you want to be walking on sticks the rest of your life." Jet paused. "If they told you anything about me, you know I won't hesitate."

"I… I don't know who the client is. It was all handled on the dark web."

She shrugged. "Looks like you want to lose a kneecap. I've heard that walking is agony after that, no matter how good your surgeon is. And I'm guessing Serbia doesn't have top specialists."

"No. Wait. I can give you the contact info. A phone number."

She nodded. "That's a start."

The creak of rusty hinges startled her, and she spun to see Marko, gun drawn, bearing down on her from the front of the shop. He began firing at Jet, the slugs blowing divots from the brick office wall on either side of her. She ducked low and squeezed off three shots, one of which punched into his stomach and another which shattered his left hip. He dropped like a sack of rocks. She twisted to deal with Petrenko, and grimaced at the sight of him splayed back in the chair, wide lifeless eyes staring at the ceiling, one of Marko's rounds having taken half the top of his skull off and painted the wall behind him with a good portion of his brains.

She swore and rushed to scoop up three cell phones on the desk in front of the dead man and then cautiously moved from the office into the shop, where Marko was moaning in agony. Jet looked around the vehicles in various stages of repair and spotted a steel door at the rear. She ran to it and slid the heavy bolt aside and was swinging it open when alarmed voices yelled from the front, signaling that the laborers had worked up the courage to see what the shooting was all about.

Jet was through the gap and outside in a flash. She sprinted flat out down the alley that stretched behind the buildings. When she reached the corner, she rounded it and kept running for two full minutes, putting three blocks between her and the scene of the crime.

When she reached her hotel, she avoided the desk clerk and crept to her room. Once safely inside, she debated her next move. It was unlikely the workers would say much to the authorities, given that the shop owner was a criminal. More likely was that they would grab all the extortion money and vanish before the police arrived, leaving them to conclude that a rival gang had taken Petrenko out – something that happened regularly to murderers and mobsters everywhere in the world. If she was lucky, Marko would keep his mouth shut or bleed out by the time the cops arrived, but she knew far too well not to rely on luck. If she were smart, she'd get out of town immediately and vanish without a trace.

Something she was exceedingly good at.

Although doing so left her empty-handed, with no more information than she'd had before she arrived.

Which left her to make a difficult choice. Ultimately, though, her immediate priority was to learn what, if anything, the phones could provide in terms of intel, because without Petrenko alive to question, she was at a dead end.

Jet took a deep breath and thought hard. Technically, she wasn't a murderer if Marko didn't die. Ballistics would show that it had been one of his rounds that had killed Petrenko, so of all her sins, killing the mobster wasn't one of them. But that would complicate the job for the police; if the bodyguard was actually the shooter, whatever story he told would be assumed to be false, especially given Petrenko's line of work. Vetting his explanation would eat up hours or days, granting her a slim window of opportunity. Of course, if Marko had died, then she was in the same boat, only with an even more convoluted scenario for the police to piece together, which again might translate into delays and a lack of enthusiasm in light of the remoteness of an easy solve.

She packed her things and called Gustav.

"Things got messy," she announced. "I need a favor."

A pause. "Name it."

"I have some phones I need hacked. You know anyone?"

"I can find someone." Gustav hesitated. "How messy?"

"Bad enough. What do you want me to do with your gun?" she asked.

"Throw it in a river." He paused again. "Are you going to stick around?"

"I'd rather not. But I need the phone information." She thought for a second. "I could use someplace to wait it out."

"I can put you up in a safe house for the night. After that, you'll need to get out of town. The authorities here are lazy and crooked, but if you make it too easy for them…"

"I'll take you up on that. Can you get a tech for the cells?"

"I'm going to give you an address, and I'll have someone meet you there in an hour. Let me make some calls. I probably won't be able to find someone to help you with your phones until tomorrow, though. Those types don't work nights."

"Fire away."

He named a street and a number, which she committed to memory.

"If there's any blowback, you never met me," she said. "Tell your people if they breathe a word about the job I paid them to do, I'll find them."

"You don't have to worry. Goes with the territory." He gave a low chuckle. "I guess this means our dinner will have to wait."

"Maybe next time," she said.

Gustav sighed dramatically. "Always the bridesmaid…"

Jet hung up and considered the risk involved in waiting for Gustav's contact. It was a calculated one, and she'd need to plan accordingly. If the police moved faster than he thought, they might think to seal the borders, although that wasn't necessarily impossible to overcome. She'd slipped in and out of enough countries to know it not only could be done but was relatively easy in places like Serbia.

Although Jet didn't like staying in place, she had no choice, because it would be just a matter of time until whoever had hired Petrenko would hear about his untimely demise, and any information she could glean from the phones would be useless.

She shouldered her bag and caught a glimpse of herself in the bathroom mirror. Outwardly, she looked calm and collected.

Which couldn't have been further from the truth, given the uncertainty of her future and the safety of her family.

But for now, she'd take it as a win.

CHAPTER 16

Tangier, Morocco

A white Gulfstream G-250 with maroon stripes running nose to tail touched down at the Tangier Ibn Battuta Airport and taxied past the commercial terminal to one of the darkened hangars near the end of the runway, where a dozen military jets were parked and several transport aircraft sat partially disassembled. It stopped near the long metal building, and the pilot killed the motors. The jets whined to a halt, and the plane door popped open as a black Mercedes van appeared from the gloom and approached the sleek jet.

Seven men emptied from the plane, jogged to the van, and piled in; the Mercedes rolled away as the last was pulling the door closed behind him. The vehicle exited the airport grounds and sped away. The arrivals from the plane were seated in the back, their attention fixed on an older man at the front, who sat on a bench seat facing them.

"All right," he said in Hebrew. "The goal is to capture the target alive. We're authorized to use force and to take out anyone who gets in our way, but we are not to terminate the subject." He paused. "You've all been briefed on what we're walking into. Bin Amir has been known to us for years, but we've never been able to get a fix on him. This time we have. The laptop we salvaged clearly implicates him in the attack on the director, and he's believed to be behind at least eight other terrorist attacks. But we don't think he's acting on his own, and to understand who is ultimately responsible, we need him alive." He studied the men's faces, all between twenty and thirty years old, hard, chiseled, lean and serious, their eyes intelligent but flat, death a familiar companion to them. "Any questions?"

One of the fighters cleared his throat. "If we need to, we can wound him?"

The older man shook his head. "I'd rather you didn't. That can go wrong too easily. That said, if he's shooting at you, you can shoot back; but use your best judgment to avoid killing him. That order comes from the very top. You don't want to have to explain why you didn't follow it."

Like most demands from politicians and desk jockeys, the edict ignored the realities of a firefight, where split-second decisions might be called for, and trying to incapacitate rather than kill wasn't usually possible in any but the most ideal of circumstances. But these commandoes were used to impossible orders and would do their best, even if it meant sacrificing their own lives to carry out the mission.

"OK. Check the weapons. We're about twenty minutes out," he instructed, and the group unloaded two rucksacks loaded with submachine guns, magazines, and night vision headsets that had been waiting for them in the van. They went about their work with quiet efficiency, nobody speaking, the only sound in the cabin the rumble of tires on pavement and the snicking of magazines being slid into place and firing mechanisms being checked and rechecked. One of the fighters opened a hard aluminum case and passed around stun grenades and then carefully removed a pair of explosive charges suitable for taking down any barrier they might encounter in a single blast. When they were satisfied with their weaponry, they donned the night vision gear and adjusted it. Then they sat back, waiting to arrive at their destination and earn their pay the hard way.

A cell phone trilled from a desktop near where a trio of men sat with cigarettes smoldering, the room filled with smoke and the sour tang of an onion-rich meal long abandoned on a table by the door. One of the figures eyed the man closest to the phone and growled to him in Arabic.

"See who that is."

The slim young man adjusted the soiled fez atop his head and moved to the phone. He raised it to his ear, murmured a greeting, and after fifteen seconds, crossed the room and handed it to his companion.

"What?" the seated man barked into the cell.

After a half minute of listening, he switched off the phone and looked at the others. "We have ten minutes," he said, and pushed himself to his feet, cigarette abandoned in the overflowing ashtray, his dark features tense.

The van stopped at a run-down manufacturing district comprised of crumbling, faded buildings, and the men spilled from the vehicle and followed the mission leader to a single-story structure with a water tower beside it. A half dozen derelict vehicles sat in its yard, some on blocks, a couple almost completely stripped, their chassis rusting from the salt air of the Atlantic only a few kilometers to the west. An ancient crane jutted into the night sky, its hook and steel cable dangling near one of the cars, swinging ever so slightly from the stiff ocean breeze that cooled the desert sands.

The team spread out, and three of the gunmen moved to the iron door at the side of the building, their night vision goggles lending them the look of alien insects in the darkness. They studied the heavy barrier, and the mission leader indicated the steel rungs of a ladder that ran up the wall to the roof.

He tapped his earbud and spoke softly. "Eli, get up to the roof and see if there's a way in there. We're at the door, and it looks like it could take a hit from a locomotive without budging. The rest of you, keep a lookout."

"10-4," Eli said, and slung his gun across his chest and heaved himself up the ladder to the flat roof above. He surveyed the surface and spied a raised section in the center and crept toward it. He scrutinized it for several moments and tapped his earbud.

"There's a skylight. Big enough for us to rappel through three at a time. But we'll be exposed, and it looks like heavy tempered glass, so cutting it isn't an option."

"We can blow it," the leader said, "and then toss in the flash bangs. Seems better than tackling the main entry. Everyone, up to the roof."

The men did as ordered, and when they reached the skylight, the mission leader flipped his night vision goggles out of his field of view and peered into the space below. His expression changed from determined to shocked, and he was screaming a warning when the skylight erupted in a gigantic blast of fire and debris, vaporizing the nearest men instantly and sending two flying. They slammed against the roof, bones snapping like twigs, and lay helpless as three grenades clanked onto the surface around them and then detonated, ending their suffering and collapsing half the roof into the space below.

The van tore away as AK-47 rounds stitched its rear doors, tires screeching in protest as it careened around the first corner, its big motor revving it to speed while it distanced itself from the inferno behind. Black smoke belched in inky clouds as fire engulfed the plant, and several more big explosions lit the night sky when solvent barrels inside the building ignited, obliterating any evidence of the dead team's remains and collapsing the remainder of the roof into a pile of blazing rubble.

CHAPTER 17

London, England

Kenneth Simms stood outside a stately home at the corner of a tree-lined drive in West Brompton, one of London's more affluent districts. Arms folded and brow furrowed, he supervised the crew that was loading Artem's family's essentials into a moving truck, his eyes never stopping scanning the length of the street in both directions.

Simms was an ex-British Special Air Service major who'd retired and started one of the most highly regarded private security firms in the United Kingdom. Artem had hired him to handle his relocation to Moscow and ensure there were no incidents like the drone attack. Simms had arrived the prior day to reconnoiter the neighborhood before posting guards in strategic locations, including two on the roof of the stone edifice equipped with a portable radar array that would detect any incoming threats before they were in range, so the client would be warned and could seek shelter while his men dealt with whatever was thrown at them using shotguns loaded with double-aught buckshot, Skywall 100 anti-drone projectile launchers, and more mundane H&K UMP submachine guns for land-based adversaries.

The truck had parked in front of the house at seven a.m., arriving with the morning sun, and Simms's team had been in place a half hour before, ensuring that all approaches were covered before the movers arrived. He'd sat down with the family and told them what to expect, and had suggested that they depart before the truck arrived and allow him to handle things for safety's sake; Artem's wife, however, had flatly refused, indicating that she wanted to confirm that their prized possessions made it onto the truck unharmed. Simms had tried reasoning with her, but Artem had cut him off and later pulled him aside to explain.

"Her family fled the USSR with nothing but the clothes on their backs," Artem said. "There's no way she's going to allow anyone to oversee her things being moved. Sorry. It isn't rational, but that isn't the hill I'm going to die on, if you understand what I mean."

Simms had nodded. "Yes, sir. Of course. I simply wanted to point out that it would be foolproof if you weren't here when all the activity took place."

"Perhaps, but you don't have to live with her for the rest of your life. I do. She'll never forgive me if I force the issue."

So Simms was now stuck with a less-than-desirable security scenario, where Artem and his wife were exposed as she micromanaged their things being packed onto the truck, and Artem stood on the steps with their ten-year-old son, watching the laborers carry boxes to the street.

Simms raised a handheld to his mouth and depressed the transmit key. "Stations One and Two, report," he said softly.

A moment later, the small device crackled, and a voice emanated from the speaker.

"Station One. All clear. Nothing to report but ordinary traffic. Over."

"Station Two. Same. Only a few vehicles. Locals heading to work."

Simms nodded once to himself. "Stay alert. We're about halfway through. Over."

He lowered the radio and climbed the steps to where Artem was standing. "All due respect, might it not be more secure to watch from inside, sir?"

The lawyer's wife pushed past them and threw Simms a dark look before descending to the truck with her cell phone to photograph how her treasures were being stowed. Artem sighed and tousled his son's hair.

"Solidarity, my good man," Artem said with a frosty smile. "All in this together, and such. Just do your job, and we'll be fine."

"Of course, sir. I'm just concerned. We can detect and neutralize most threats, but no system is a hundred percent. A determined sniper…there are too many possibilities to rule all of them out."

"I'm more worried about my wife killing me right now than anything. This looks to be over within another fifteen minutes or so, and then we can get out of here."

"Just give me a few moments' notice so I can have the car pull around," Simms said, his tone neutral, only his gray eyes demonstrating the disapproval he felt. Clients came in all shapes and sizes, from the hyper-paranoid who welcomed his conservative approach to those who treated it all as a game or an annoyance – which unfortunately best described these Russians. But the money involved in taking the contract was epic, and Simms was in the business to glad-hand his charges and make them feel safe, not alarm them unduly. Frankly, he was far more concerned about the situation when Artem touched down in Moscow, but he would worry about that when they landed. The lawyer had chartered a Challenger 300 private jet to carry his family and Simms, along with three of his most seasoned operatives, to Russia. Together they would be working with their counterparts in Moscow, with Simms overseeing security while the Russians handled logistics based on his input. A less than ideal situation, but at a hundred grand per week, one that Simms would grin and bear.

He descended the steps to the street and was walking towards the front of the truck when his radio crackled again, and a strained voice called out.

"Base, this is station two. We have a pair of incoming motorcycles on the A intersection headed your way at high speed. Probably eight to ten seconds out."

Simms frowned and spoke into the handheld, his voice tight. "Could be nothing, could be legit. All stations, prepare to engage."

He spun and took the steps two at a time as he called out a warning to the lawyer. "Get inside the–"

Simms was cut off by the muted rattle of a suppressed weapon on full automatic, whose rounds peppered the stairs and caught him in the small of the back. The last thing he saw as he dropped face forward against the stone steps was the attorney dragging his son into the house and slamming the heavy wood door shut as answering fire from the roof sprayed the street where the motorcycles were now tearing away, their engines howling as they redlined.

Several rounds hit the second bike, and the rider lost control and skidded on its side before it crashed into a parked car. The lead bike tore away down a side street and disappeared from view, leaving only the whine of its engine accelerating away to accompany the hysterical screams of Artem's wife from beside the truck.

Simms's men spilled from the house and ran down the block, weapons in full view. One of them knelt by him and checked for a pulse before shaking his head to the others. A pair of his men trotted to where the motorcyclist lay unmoving, his weapon dropped ten meters behind his resting place, body twisted at an impossible angle, the bike's motor still sputtering in a rough idle. They moved to the crash site with their guns pointed at the rider, and the nearest nodded to his companion.

"Cover me," he said, and crept closer. When he reached the vehicle, he eyed the body's three wounds and crouched beside it. He felt for a pulse and then twisted to his companion. "Dead."

The other gunman lowered his weapon and approached, and the first set his gun on the pavement and pulled the rider's helmet off. They both stared with stony expressions at the face of an Asian youth no older than his late teens. The one holding the helmet frowned at the dead youth and looked to his partner.

"What the hell is this, then?" he said.

"And who do we even tell? Boss is history."

The first man shrugged. "File a report and hope we get paid. Russians are usually good for it."

The other man shook his head. "All those years. Iraq, Afghanistan, Syria…and he gets his card punched by this clown? I've got bloody boots older than this lot."

"Crying shame, that's for sure." He turned to look at where the client was coming down the steps with his arms outstretched to comfort his wife. "Bloody cock-up, the lot of it. He's right out in the open if they want another try at him."

"Come on, then. Job's gotta get done, one way or the other. Cops will be here shortly. We need to get them out of here."

"Right then. Double time." He tapped his earbud. "All stations, Alpha is down. Repeat, Alpha is down. We're evacuating the client stat. Bring the car around, and let's get ready for the bobbies. Time's a-wasting."

CHAPTER 18

Belgrade, Serbia

After an uneasy night at the modest flat that Gustav had provided in a working-class area of the city, Jet hurried along the sidewalk towards the address he had texted her. The streets were mostly empty at the early hour, a few office workers making their way to work and a garbage truck the only traffic to speak of as she neared her destination. She'd slept poorly, snatching only a few hours of rest between monitoring the apartment block approach through moldy curtains in case she'd been double-crossed and working through possible next moves in her mind, and she decided she could afford five minutes to buy a cup of coffee at a stall a hundred yards from the address.

She gulped the steaming liquid without waiting for it to cool, the sensation and taste reviving her and stimulating her synapses. By the time she tossed the cardboard cup into the nearby bin, she felt human, if not as alert as she'd have preferred. She eyed a television behind the server, which was broadcasting a news channel, but it was all soccer scores and highlights, with no mention of any gunfights or murders. Which didn't mean she was out of the woods, but it did ease her concern slightly.

Jet circled the block where the phone tech's small shop was located to ensure she wasn't heading into a trap. When she was comfortable that she wasn't being observed, she walked to the glass door and depressed the bell to the side of it. The shop's hours were posted on the window, and it didn't open for another two hours, but Gustav had told her he'd arrange for the technician to be available early to attempt to solve her problem. She waited for one minute and then another, watching the reflection of the street in the glass, and then a short man with a thick graying beard and a glistening shaved head materialized inside and twisted the dead bolt open.

"You must be Sylvie," he said in rusty English. "I'm Vaz. Come in."

Jet nodded and pushed past him. He locked the door behind her, and she waited as he skirted her and indicated a doorway at the back of the shop. She followed him past a chaotic sprawl of computer hardware on stainless steel racks affixed to every wall, a pile of older monitors in the center of the floor leaving little room to maneuver, and into his workshop, which was similarly disorganized.

"You have the phones?" he asked, and took a seat on a barstool at the workbench.

"I do." Jet retrieved the devices and handed them to him. He studied them with an expression of distaste and then shifted his gaze to her.

"These are burners. Cheap, but solid security," he said.

She nodded. "I checked. They're password protected."

"That's not unusual," he said, pursing his lips.

"Can you crack them?"

"Oh, sure. Not difficult, but it will take a little while. You want something to drink? Tea? Coffee?" He paused. "Something…stronger?"

"No, thanks, Vaz."

He nodded. "There's the question of price and payment."

"Your time's valuable, I'm sure," she acknowledged.

He named a sum, which was a little over what Gustav had guessed it would be. She didn't blink.

"Done," Jet said.

"Cash, obviously."

"It's the only way to fly," she said, and the corner of her mouth twitched with a faint smile.

"My kind of customer, Sylvie."

"Glad to hear it, Vaz. How long?"

"You can come back in an hour."

She shook her head. "I'd rather not. I've grown attached to those phones."

He glanced around the workshop. "You can clear those hard disks off that chair, then," he said, and after perching a pair of reading glasses on the bridge of his nose, scrutinized the charging outlet of the first phone before reaching for a tool with which to pop off the back.

Jet did as he'd suggested, and after shifting a half dozen boxes onto the floor beside the chair, lowered herself onto the seat, eyes glued to the phone. Vaz switched on a stereo mounted above the work area, and eighties synth pop warbled from hidden speakers. He hummed along with the tune and worked methodically and, once the back was off the device and the circuit board exposed, began probing it with a voltmeter and another implement she didn't recognize.

Several minutes later he looked up at her with a triumphant expression. "We're in," he declared, and then popped the board cover back into place and thumbed through the menu, peering at the screen with laser intensity. He held the phone up for her to see, and shook his head.

"Never been used. Nothing to see."

Vaz repeated the process with the other two phones, and the final one yielded a couple of outbound calls, but no numbers, the identities blocked.

"Can you pull up the numbers?" she asked.

"Negative. They've been wiped. Whoever was using these was ultra-paranoid or had some sort of obsessive-compulsive disorder."

"Then it's a dead end?"

"Maybe. Maybe not. Some SIM cards will show an empty register when you erase them, but don't actually wipe the phone book clean. With the right hardware, we might be able to pull something up."

"I trust you have the right hardware?"

He smirked. "Child's play for someone who knows what they're doing. You came to the right place."

"Buy cheap, buy twice," she agreed, and Vaz unsnapped the case again and went to work on the phone.

"There's only one number," he announced after a few minutes. "El Burro. Does that mean anything to you?"

Jet shook her head. "No."

He squinted at the screen and then grabbed a pen from a wire desk organizer and scribbled the number on a scrap of paper. Vaz presented it to Jet like it was treasure, with a small bow of his head, and she eyed the number with curiosity.

"Do you recognize that area code?" she asked.

"It's a country code. Poland, if I'm not mistaken. I could try to narrow it down further, but if it's another burner, it won't necessarily correlate to a city prefix."

"Is there anything else on the phone?"

"No. That's it."

She reached into her bag, withdrew a wad of cash, and counted out the agreed upon number of euros. When she handed it to Vaz, he grinned like a kid on the playground.

"Pleasure doing business with you, Sylvie. Anytime you need anything, come by."

"I'll do that. Thank you, Vaz."

"No problem."

He showed her out and bolted the door behind her, and she took off at an unhurried pace, not wanting to draw any attention to herself now that the sidewalks were filling up with more pedestrians. That she'd been able to recover anything from the phones had been a longshot, but one that had paid off. Now she just needed to figure out whose number it was, and what its link was, if any, to whoever wanted her dead.

"Child's play," she muttered in an exaggerated impression of Vaz, and resisted the urge to smile at her own inside joke as she retraced her steps to the apartment so she could get clear of Serbia before her luck ran out for good.

CHAPTER 19

Tel Aviv, Israel

After only a few days at the helm of the Israeli intelligence agency, Noah was already beginning to show signs of stress. The dark circles around his eyes had deepened, and his face was haggard from lack of sleep. He could only wonder at the stamina of the old man who'd run the Mossad for decades, because the pressure involved was weighing on him and he'd only just started. He was used to operational deadlines from his time working the Eastern European desk, but as the new director, it felt like everyone was coming at him from all directions at once, and it was unnerving in the extreme.

The speaker on his desk buzzed, and he glared at it like it had tried to bite him.

"Sir? They're ready for you," a tinny woman's voice announced from the box.

He punched a red button as he stood. "Thanks, Sarah."

Noah donned his suit jacket and inspected his reflection in the window and then walked forcefully to where his subordinates were waiting around the conference table in headquarters' soundproof meeting room. He pulled the door shut and moved to the head of the table and then sat and stared at his staff for a long beat before checking the time on his watch with a sour look.

"I've got to leave for a meeting with the PM in ten minutes. What have you got for me?" he asked.

One of the men cleared his throat and checked his notes. "The entire team was eighty-sixed. There were no survivors. We've been debriefing the driver, but he hasn't been much help. He didn't see anything of note."

"None of this is news. Tell me we've made any sort of progress."

"We have all hands on this, but it's slow going. That said, we were able to get a fix on the explosive used in the blast. C-4. Forensics isolated the signature." He paused. "It's the same that was used on the director's assassination. And in a nightclub bombing in Dresden last year."

"Well, well. Our man has certainly been busy," Noah said. "What else?"

"That's all we have for now."

"Who took credit for the Dresden attack?" Noah asked.

"Nobody. There were rumors and buzz, but it was like the American 9/11 attack: all supposition, and no actual organization laying claim to it."

"How many dead?"

"Dresden saw twenty-seven casualties and almost that many wounded."

"Connection to Israel?"

"None anyone could ascertain. There were two Israeli citizens among the dead, but they were students. No political activism, no suspect relationships. We concluded they were just in the wrong place at the wrong time."

"That's it? That's everything?"

"Yes. We're trying to get security feeds from any traffic cameras, but this is Tangier we're talking, not New York, so it's a long shot. And the locals aren't particularly receptive to us sticking our noses in. They want to know how we're involved, obviously, and we can't come out and say we had a commando team operating on their soil without authorization."

Noah frowned. "That wouldn't go over well. All right. Keep at it. I'll go talk to the politicos and fill them in."

Everyone rose, and Noah hurried out, anxious about his coming meeting – the first with the PM since he'd earmarked Noah for the position. He had precious little to offer in terms of actionable intelligence; but then again, things didn't happen overnight, even if politicians wanted them to.

An SUV was waiting at the subterranean garage level and whisked Noah away as soon as he was strapped in. It took an hour to get to the PM's residence, where Noah's arrival wouldn't be noted by the press.

The PM's expression was grim when an assistant showed Noah into his home office.

"Please. Sit," the PM said, indicating a chair facing a sofa, a coffee table in the middle.

"Thank you, sir," Noah said, and did as asked.

"What news do you have for me?" the prime minister began. "I don't need to tell you how much of a stir this nightmare has caused. We've kept a lid on the loss of the men, of course, but internally it's a body blow. I want to understand how this could have happened."

"Well, sir, it's still unclear how the bomber knew about the team. But we're working every lead. We've identified the explosive that was used, and it's the same as the one that killed the director," Noah said.

"Bastards," the PM blurted, and slapped his hand on the table as he sat across from Noah. "We have to go scorched earth on this, do you understand? This can't stand. Examples need to be made." He fumed in silence for a long beat. "It's obviously the damned Palestinians. I want to lock down the West Bank immediately. Turn over every rock until you find these terrorists and drag them to justice."

Noah swallowed hard. "There's no evidence of Palestinian involvement, sir."

The PM glowered at him. "Of course it's them. It's always them, with help from Hezbollah and Iran. Who else would it be? They're like cockroaches. We need to move swiftly and decisively. They can't be allowed to get away with this."

"Perhaps we should base our actions on data rather than impressions, sir? If we start rounding up the usual suspects, it could tip the hand of the culprit, and if it's not the Palestinians, that will hamper our efforts to identify them."

The PM sat back and considered Noah as though he were a lab

specimen on a slide. He steepled his fingers and locked eyes with the younger man.

"Noah, you know I like you. I lobbied to have you replace the director, which, trust me, wasn't a popular decision. But it was time. I felt we needed new blood, which is what you are. But please don't think for a minute that I won't replace you if you decide to oppose my wishes. I run the country. You run the Mossad. We can either scratch each other's backs, or we can be at each other's throats. And trust me when I say that you do not want me as an enemy." The PM slowed his cadence so each word was emphasized. "I made you. I can unmake you just as quickly. So if I say it's the Palestinians and we need to make a show of force and demonstrate there will be repercussions, it isn't a suggestion or a request. Do I make myself clear?"

Noah swallowed a knot the size of a baseball and matched the PM's stare without blinking.

"I completely understand what you're saying, sir," Noah said. "But as a longtime friend and associate of the director, and as the leader of Israel, I have to believe that finding and punishing the actual guilty party is your ultimate objective. And we don't have any evidence that the Palestinians are behind this." He also paused. "We lost a lot of good men yesterday, sir. Loyal men with families and dreams. I think we owe it to them to put in a full effort to bring their murderer to justice."

The PM nodded as though in agreement. "Are you done?"

"Sir?"

The PM slow clapped for effect. "If you were running for office, that would have been a brilliant speech. But you already got the job. If you're still here arguing with me in thirty seconds, you'll lose the job. I don't know how else to say it. Of course I want justice for the director and the team. And I'm confident that my gut instinct is correct." He glared at Noah. "We're finished here. You have your marching orders. Or do I need to pick up the phone, relieve you of your duties, and promote any of a dozen station heads who would sell their souls for your slot?"

Noah rose and shook his head. "No, sir. I understand. No offense intended. I just want to ensure we get the right guy."

"As do I. If you learn anything that conflicts with my Palestinian theory, by all means tell me, and we'll reconsider. But in the meantime, I need to understand you're on the same page as I am, and your loyalty isn't in question."

"You can depend on me, sir."

Noah departed the PM's office and walked somewhat shell-shocked to the waiting vehicle. He slid into the back seat and settled into the soft leather, his head spinning at the overt power play he'd just been subjected to, and realized that he was in deep water without a floaty.

The PM had made it plain that Noah was an errand boy who would do as he was told – or else.

Which left him in an ugly position. Because while the older man's instinct was to blame his usual adversary, Noah saw none of their typical chaotic incompetence with either of the bombings. And the prime minister's attitude further cemented Noah's feeling that he would have to tread extremely lightly in case the director's assassination had been an inside job.

He watched the landscape blur by as the SUV took him back to headquarters, his face a blank, lost in thought, mulling over his next step. It would be easy to give the PM what he wanted, and Noah would have to take the appropriate steps, at least on the surface. But he would have to somehow continue a real investigation in parallel, yet in complete secrecy.

An almost impossible challenge he had to succeed at or he'd be hung out to dry and replaced within a fortnight.

Of that he was more than sure.

CHAPTER 20

Bohinjska Bistrica, Slovenia

The woods around the lodge were eerily quiet in the early morning, the only sound the plaintive mating cries of birds. The mist that drifted through the trees slowly evaporated as the sun rose into the azure sky. A plume of cooking smoke rose from the lodge's stone chimney, where Matt had started a fire at dawn after discovering that the cabin's propane generator wasn't operative. Unsure of how full the tank might be, he had opted to chop wood rather than use the gas stove until they could locate a repairman to isolate the problem. Barring that, he would have to troubleshoot the system, but between attending to Hannah and helping Andrew, his hands were full.

The market had been closed when he'd gotten there, so the prior night they'd been forced to consume the lodge's provisions, which consisted of freeze-dried food that was barely more appetizing than the MRE meals he'd been issued when in the service. Needless to say, dinner had been a lackluster dining experience, and faced with a breakfast using powdered milk and whatever was in the cupboard, Hannah was sure to rebel.

When she emerged from her bedroom and padded into the kitchen to keep Matt company, he smiled at her and checked the time.

"Not sure there's anything you're going to be thrilled about eating in here, sweetheart," he said. "I'm thinking we can do another run into town and see what time the market opens. You want to come?"

"No raccoon," she said firmly.

"No. We'll try to get something more appetizing. Besides, I didn't see any this morning, so you're out of luck."

Hannah looked relieved, and he offered another smile.

"Put your shoes on, and let's hit the road," he said, and she ran off to her room.

Matt looked in on Andrew while the little girl was dressing, and explained he was taking the Jeep to make another store run.

"Oh, and the generator isn't firing up," Matt said. "Do you have a contact for maintenance here?"

"Somewhere. Probably one of the chaps in the village. But we have electricity from the street…"

"I know. But the generator's here for a reason, and it would be nice if it worked. The gas tank's meter is on the blink, so I can't tell how much propane is left. That might be part of the problem, but I don't have the tools to field strip the system and isolate what's wrong."

"I'll see if I can find the number. After last night's feast, I don't need to tell you to stock the Jeep up with supplies, do I?"

"Negative. I'm way ahead of you. I'll buy a solid week's worth of food so we don't have to sweat it."

Matt returned to the kitchen and found Hannah waiting patiently with a forlorn expression. He held up the keys and shook them.

"All right! Let's make tracks!"

The road into town was in the same dismal repair as the lodge's drive, and Matt had to go slowly in order to avoid blowing a tire on one of the deep ruts that dotted the pavement. By the time they rolled into town, there were people on the streets, and the market's parking lot was a third full with early morning provisioners.

He parked and helped Hannah from the Jeep, and they walked hand in hand to the double glass doors. Two lanky men stood to one side, giving Matt their best thousand-yard prison stares, their facial tattoos and close-shaved heads indicating that they'd spent sufficient time behind bars to perfect them. Matt wasn't interested in conflict and wanted to avoid any undue attention, so he lowered his gaze and focused on Hannah, ignoring their aggressive glares. They lost interest as he entered the store with her, and ambled away from the entrance after one of them spit by his boots and the other barked a harsh laugh.

Once inside, Matt freed a wheeled cart from a column and pushed it along the aisles, selecting products he could identify easily by their packaging, surprised by how many were in English as well as Slovenian. He'd done a cursory investigation of the country when Andrew had told him about it, but hadn't realized that apparently English was a mainstay language that was widely understood, judging by the product selection.

He wheeled the overflowing cart to one of the pair of checkout stations and waited as a stout woman with a downtrodden expression scanned the contents, her periodic frowns when the scanner didn't recognizing a bar code and forced her to enter it by hand indicating that her job was an endless hell of broken dreams and constant disappointment.

When she eventually finished, Matt paid in cash and then bagged his own groceries while she eyed him imperiously, that service apparently under no circumstances provided by the staff. Hannah stood by, watching with a bemused look, Matt's systematic packing apparently fascinating to her child's brain, and when he was done placing the sacks into the basket, beamed at him.

"You're good at that," she observed.

"Years of practice when I was in high school," Matt said, and glanced around to confirm he hadn't missed anything. "All set. Let's get going," he said, and led her back to the entrance, keeping an eye through the glass for the pair of thugs.

When they got outside, the lowlifes were nowhere to be found, and he uttered a silent mental sigh of relief. Often in smaller towns the local hoods had nothing to do but pick fights, and while Matt could have easily taken them, that wasn't in keeping with the low profile he was determined to keep. Better that they'd wandered off in search of other stimulation and left him to his shopping, he thought, and paused to kneel to tie his shoe, the lace having worked its way loose in the store.

Hannah continued walking. The growl of a nearby engine roared from the row of cars, and then a lifted Nissan Pathfinder careened backwards from a space, burning rubber, on a collision course with the little girl. Matt leapt for her and snatched Hannah out of its path a split second before it would have crushed her, and sat with her hugged tight to his chest on the asphalt as the driver shifted gears and sped away, the pair of skinheads plainly visible in the cab.

"Are you okay, honey?" he asked, his voice tight.

"I'm sorry. I didn't see…"

"It isn't your fault, Hannah. Don't worry. It's over now. Some people are crazy drivers."

"I guess."

Matt pushed himself to his feet and watched the Nissan disappear down the town's main street, and was glad he didn't have his pistol with him or he'd have put a half dozen rounds through their rear windshield to give them something to think about. Instead, he leaned down and finished tying his shoe, and then made his cautious way back to the Jeep, where someone had been kind enough to put their cigarette out on the hood – leaving Matt two guesses as to who.

He packed the groceries into the cargo bed and helped Hannah up into the passenger seat, and then rounded the back and slid behind the wheel, his heart still hammering in his chest at how close he'd come to seeing his adopted daughter killed within arm's length, promising himself that if he saw the two miscreants again, he'd make an exception to his low-profile stance and beat them to bloody pulps just for practice.

Matt's face betrayed none of his thoughts, and he twisted the key in the ignition and gassed the Jeep to life and then threw Hannah a grin, lightening the tension they both felt.

"Seatbelt, Hannah," he said, and she dutifully fiddled with the buckle before snapping it into place, and then they were off, heading along the same street the Nissan had torn down, keeping to a sane speed, now the only vehicle on the road.

CHAPTER 21

Tel Aviv, Israel

Noah sat at his desk, swiveled half away from his monitor, staring glumly out the window as he replayed the disastrous meeting with the PM in his head. It seemed like only hours ago that he'd been giddy with excitement at the unexpected promotion to director of the Mossad, his career aspirations wildly exceeded by any measure. Now, as the reality of the position hit home, he felt nothing but depression as he realized that he was only a political pawn to be discarded whenever the game required, any autonomy the job appeared to have a hollow mirage.

He fidgeted with a pen his wife had given him, a Montblanc, black with a white cap tip, a congratulations gift intended to commemorate his newfound good fortune. It now seemed silly, like awarding a gold star to a toddler for guessing the correct shape or color, and he narrowly resisted the urge to hurl it across the room in frustrated anger.

The speaker on the desktop buzzed, and his secretary's voice rang out from the box.

"Sir? Your meeting is here."

He sighed and turned toward the desk and depressed the red button. "Send him in."

"Yes, sir."

His office door opened, and a tall man in his early thirties entered, his midnight black hair swept straight back off his forehead, a light dusting of beard lending him the image of an Italian B movie star; not exactly handsome, but what women might describe as interesting or brooding.

Noah indicated a seat in front of his desk, and the man sat down, his expression serious.

"Congratulations, Noah," he said.

"Thanks, Ian. I appreciate it. I wish I'd invited you here for a celebratory drink, but I'm afraid that isn't the case," Noah replied.

"What's up?" Ian asked.

"We have a situation. We're at a kind of dead end on the investigation into the explosion that killed the director. The government wants us to take action against the Palestinians. They figure that it was likely them, and that's that. But I'm not so sure. Which puts me at odds with the administration."

"Sounds like politics," Ian observed. "Typical, right?"

"Yes, but it does put me in a difficult spot. Which is why I need you. I want to launch a parallel investigation, but one that's absolutely secret. There can't be any discussion about it with anyone." Noah regarded Ian. "We go back a long time, so I can trust you."

"I thought it might be more than my good looks you were after."

"Good guess. This has to remain completely off the books. Officially it isn't taking place."

"Fair enough, but what do I tell my control?"

"I'll take care of that. If asked, tell him that it's above his pay grade. You're now my special assistant."

Ian nodded. "And what, pray tell, does that include other than getting you coffee and maybe a back rub now and then? Laundry? Book dinner reservations?"

Noah's face cracked with a smile. "Wouldn't that be nice? No, you'll need to prep your go bag."

"Where to, and to do what, exactly?"

"We're about to find out."

Noah held up an encrypted cell phone and pressed the redial key. The phone rang four times, and then a female voice answered.

"Yes?"

"You know who this is," Noah said.

"I thought I was dead to you," Jet replied.

"I might have been hasty. We're getting more intel on the director's murder, and I thought it might be a good idea to put our heads together on it."

A long pause. "Why?"

Noah let out an exasperated sigh. "I took the liberty of looking into your relationship with him. It's quite a read. And…it…occurred to me that it would be stupid to shut you out…if you were willing to help."

"Yes, that's exactly how it would be. Which is what you did," Jet snapped.

"I know. I'm sorry. I have a lot of balls in the air, and I made a…premature call."

"A stupid one. Your own words."

"Can we agree that it was misguided and move on? It would be in our best interests."

Jet paused for a long moment. "I'm unclear on how this helps me. What am I missing?"

"You'll have access to our database. You said yourself that we might have a mutual enemy in whoever did this," Noah said.

Jet paused again. "Fine. What do you have?"

"Well, we located a suspect and sent in a hot team, but…it appears the target tripped to our plan and neutralized them."

A sharp intake of breath. "The whole team?"

It was Noah's turn to hesitate. "Yes. I'm afraid so. They were good men. We're still unclear on what happened, but it's possible that we have a leak."

Jet snorted. "So that's it. You played fast and loose, and you lost. So now you need my help because I'm deniable. Nobody but the director knew of our operations, and if there's a leak, I'm outside your loop."

"I can see why the old man worked with you," Noah acknowledged.

"But you have no idea why I was willing to work with him, do you?"

"I assume mutual self-interest."

"Correct. I would help him out of a jam when it got bad enough. In return, I received his support. Which you should know since you read my file."

"I get the feeling there was a lot left out of the official accounts. Like what sort of support. I see that you have a full pardon."

"And an agreement signed by the PM that releases me from any obligations to the agency," she pointed out. "Look, tell me what you have, and I'll tell you what I've dug up. Fair's fair. I won't play any other way. No holding out."

"Very well. We identified the bomber."

"This was before he took out your team?"

"Correct. He was in Morocco. He got wind of the raid and blew half the block up once we were on-site." Noah and Ian exchanged a look. "We don't know his real identity. The only thing we've nailed down is that he's got some sort of fixation with Mexican culture. We have no idea why. Possibly he's Mexican. Maybe one parent. Maybe he went to school there. But he's used code names like 'Taco' and 'Jalapeño.'"

"Well, we're on the same trail, then. I located a phone number for someone who uses the alias 'El Burro.' A Polish number." She hesitated. "If I give you the number to run a trace and locate on, you can't go in half-cocked like you did in Morocco, understand? It's information I'm giving you for my use, not the collective's. This bastard tried to kill me. So it's personal."

"I promise I'll share any info we get as a result of the number as soon as we have something. You have my word as director."

Jet chuckled. "For the record, I'm recording this call, so I'm going to hold you to that."

"No need, but I understand."

She gave Noah the number. He repeated it back and then sat forward in his chair. "I'll put this through signals and call you as soon as we have something. Leave this phone on," Noah instructed.

He hung up and looked at Ian. "She's the real thing. I can't share all the details, but she's an ex-operative with more successful wet missions than anyone in our history, by far."

"You obviously feel she can be trusted," Ian said.

"I know that anyone besides you in the agency can't be at this point, so she's the best option I have."

"Where do I come in?"

"Once we have something for her, it will be clear. Just get prepped for travel. Possibly extended."

"Any guidance on weather?"

Noah studied the number. "I'd bet on cold, but stay tuned."

Three hours later, Noah called Jet again, and this time she picked up after the first ring.

"I have good news," he said. "We isolated the number to an area in north Warsaw. According to the cell company, it was last used fourteen hours ago."

"Can they get us a real-time position once I'm there?"

"I can try, but our contact in Poland isn't at that level. No promises."

"Fine. Give me the details."

"I will. But I'm also going to send you one of our top agents to work with. He's as seasoned as they get."

"No deal. I work alone. You obviously didn't read my file that closely," she snapped.

Noah's voice developed an edge. "It isn't negotiable. This prick killed the director, so regardless of his attempt on you, he answers to us for that. If we're going to share as we agreed, we share everything. So you'll be working with our agent, or we'll be mounting an entirely fruitless campaign in the West Bank while you're spinning your wheels in Warsaw. Those are my terms."

She didn't speak for ten seconds. "I don't take orders from him, or you. Is that understood? And if he gets in my way or slows me down, and I have to junk him or worse, it's on you. Those are my terms. That, and tell him to arrange for weapons and money in Poland. Nine millimeter, suppressed, subsonic ammo. You know the drill. Standard package."

"His handle is Ian," Noah said. "Does your phone get data?"

"Of course."

"I'll send a photo shortly. He'll meet you in Warsaw. How long will it take you to get there?" Noah asked.

"No more than five or six hours, tops. Depends on flights or train times."

"Ian will be there in about the same amount of time. I'll forward a meet location with the photo."

"Make sure he understands our deal," Jet said, and terminated the call.

Noah set the phone on his desk and considered the bargain he'd made, and then reached for another phone with which to call Ian and get him on a charter flight to Warsaw within the hour. However this turned out, they were already farther along than they'd been before he'd contacted Jet, and she had the beauty of being completely off the radar if things got ugly. Ian was another matter, but Noah needed eyes and ears on the ground, and Ian was his best bet for an operative who could keep up with Jet's skills and think on his feet.

Which didn't eliminate Noah's feeling that he had just thrown his friend to the wolves.

But as with all things, time would tell.

CHAPTER 22

Moscow, Russian Federation

Artem arrived at Nicolai's corporate headquarters in an armored Mercedes G550 SUV, where he was met by four armed bodyguards, the largest of whom he recognized from photographs as Leonid, Sergei's brother. He brushed past the entourage and strode through the doors and then moved straight to the elevator bank, leaving the guards to catch up. One of the steel slabs slid to the side, and he stepped into the elevator, speaking softly to the men as they approached.

"You can wait here in the lobby. I trust I'll be safe in our own boardroom."

"Yes, sir," Leonid said, and turned to the men to ensure they'd heard their orders.

The doors closed, and the carriage soared upward in whisper quiet. Artem admired the German engineering that had made the conveyance possible. Much as he disliked the Germans, he had to admit that their cars and their machinery were the finest in the world, their precision unmatched, even by the Japanese. He supposed a great part of his animosity stemmed from his grandfather's experience in the Second World War, when he'd been one of the surviving troops at Stalingrad. His ancestor's experience with the Teutonic war machine had been passed down through his father to Artem, who ever since he was a small child had been told the stories of the tens of millions of Russians who'd died in that war stopping Hitler.

But could they ever build an elevator.

He arrived at the penthouse level, and the door opened, and he emerged to find himself facing the entire board, along with several younger senior members of the management team, all of whom gave him an ovation. When the applause died, he smiled and raised a hand in greeting.

"Thank you. Seriously. Thank you all."

Rudolf gave Artem a cold smile and motioned to the conference room door, and Artem allowed the crowd to file in before entering and taking the seat at the head of the long table. He waited until everyone was settled, and when he began speaking, his voice was strong and confident.

"I'm sure everyone here has heard about the attempt on my life this morning," he said. "Thankfully it was unsuccessful. But it was close. For that reason, I'll be maintaining the highest level of security while we're dealing with the perpetrator."

"As we would expect," Rudolf said. "And may I say how relieved we all are that you're fine."

"As am I. But my wife is quite shaken, as is my son, so I'll be assigning appropriate resources to their security as well."

"Of course," Rudolf agreed, nodding overly enthusiastically.

"Now to the subject of the perpetrator's identity. The assassin was Asian – probably from one of the triads that import drugs into England. I would say that's a safe bet. Which obviously points to the Chinese."

"Not unexpectedly," Rudolf said.

"This is further evidence that our suspicion that it was Zhang was correct. The coincidence is simply too much."

"We have gotten confirmation of his whereabouts," one of the younger men said, and after a theatrical pause, continued, "He's in London."

Rudolf nodded. "Where he could oversee the attack in person. The man's diabolical."

"I think this is adequate confirmation of his involvement," Artem said. "The question is how to proceed. My sense is that we need to neutralize him permanently. That's how Nicolai would have handled it. His actions have crossed important lines that remove any restraint we might have shown, so the gloves can come off."

"How do you envision us doing that?" Rudolf asked.

"I would just as soon keep that operational detail confidential for now, until I've decided the most effective mechanism. I hope you'll understand." Artem checked his phone screen. "Oh, and I hear Sergei has shown some improvement?"

"Yes," Rudolf said. "But it's unclear whether he'll regain his faculties. Although we have been able to clear his brother of suspicion. He had no information about your London move, so he couldn't be the leak. Neither did the driver. So both are clean."

"I thought I saw him downstairs. It's good that he's blameless. We're going to need all the loyal assets we can get while we right the ship, and he seems capable in a security role."

"Nicolai clearly felt so."

"Good. Then I'll want to have a word with him once we're done here. Now let's move on to more pressing matters. Where are we with filling the empty Siberian slot?"

The meeting went on for two hours, and by the time it was over, a number of critical issues had been decided and the underlings given their instructions. Artem thanked the board members for their support and ignored Rudolf's thinly disguised hostility – his resentment was obvious, even though he'd dodged a literal bullet by being passed over for the leadership position.

When the room emptied, Artem withdrew a burner cell from his jacket pocket and placed a call. When the line picked up, he spoke in low tones.

"Good job on London. It went off perfectly," he said. "You should check your wallet. The bitcoin transfer has been made, so you're golden."

He listened for several moments and then continued, "You should consider relocating from Eastern Europe. The infrastructure isn't the best." He paused. "Oh, really? Well, you've got more than ample resources to do so now. Nice choice. Lovely canals."

He disconnected and smiled to himself. The attack had been a masterstroke in sealing his leadership authority by creating a perceived emergency and delivering him as the solution to the problem of his own creation. Classic Hegelian dialectic, which he'd learned from his years with Nicolai, who was a master of the Machiavellian.

So now he had carte blanche to proceed as he liked against Zhang, who was more of a diversion than any real threat to him, but whose execution would seal Artem's grip on power by demonstrating his decisiveness and willingness to be ruthless when required. That in turn would give him the moral authority to continue in the leadership role after his six months had run its course. Rudolf would be furious, of course, but that couldn't be helped, and Artem could arrange for him to meet an untimely end before his enmity became truly problematic. For now, Rudolf was playing ball with Artem in the belief that he would step down, and there was no reason for Artem to tip his hand. Better to allow the fat troll to believe what would keep him useful, and then blindside him at an opportune time, making it seem like an accident.

For now, he needed to work up a plan for the Chinese that would remove him from the board, but do so with deniability, so he wouldn't be battling Zhang's organization in perpetuity. It would be complicated by the mogul's natural caution born from decades of being a target of violent rivals. He was no doubt expecting some sort of reprisal after Nicolai's murder, so it would have to be accomplished with absolute stealth, but also in a manner where whoever replaced him at the top of his group understood without losing face that a grievance had been addressed and balance restored.

Otherwise they wouldn't respect Artem's leadership and would view him as weak. So it would have to be achieved in a way that could be unrelated to the Russians yet was obviously their work, albeit deniable for official purposes.

The truth was that the Chinese and Russian interests were intertwined, and their prosperity depended on a productive working relationship. So Zhang's replacement would be eager to avoid burning bridges over possible Russian involvement when it better suited the Chinese to move past his death and focus on the future.

A future where everyone would understand that Artem had done what needed to be done, and had accomplished it in a manner clever enough that everyone could pretend that it had been random and had nothing to do with him.

It would be a difficult trick to pull off, but one that Artem had been thinking about for days. A plan was formulating, and he'd need to make some calls to verify he could put the necessary pieces into play – but if he was successful, it would be a masterstroke that would establish Artem as a force to be reckoned with, both internally and in the minds of the organization's enemies.

He looked around the conference room and moved to the windows, where he could enjoy the panoramic view of Moscow, the Red Square and the Kremlin seemingly close enough to flick a cigarette at. This was the ultimate position of strength, with billions at his fingertips and the power of life and death his to use as he saw fit. Nicolai had built it all with his help, and Artem would steward the juggernaut to even giddier highs.

And now that he was ensconced at the top of the organization, he would allow nothing to stand in his way.

As his adversaries would learn the hard way.

CHAPTER 23

Bohinjska Bistrica, Slovenia

Matt straightened and stretched his back, which was aching from the hours of work he'd put in on the generator and the propane tank regulator, trying to get it to work. The promised maintenance man from town had never shown up, and Matt had decided to busy himself with the project, using the rudimentary tools he'd found in a cabinet off the kitchen. He'd isolated the problem to the fuel line, since the gas stove was also refusing to work, but he'd confirmed that the tank had propane, because the gas hot water heater was functional, albeit barely.

The front door banged shut, and Hannah skipped along the path to the side of the house where Matt was standing.

"Did you fix it?" she asked.

"No, sweetheart, I think it's the regulator. It's the only thing that makes sense."

Her face scrunched in puzzlement, and Matt pointed at a metal gizmo attached to the copper gas line. "That thing keeps the pressure from getting too high so things won't work."

"Oh," she said.

"The problem is I need a big wrench to remove it, and I don't have one. These pliers aren't going to do the trick."

"Then…what?" Hannah asked.

"Another trip into town, I'm afraid."

Hannah frowned. "I don't like the truck. It's smelly."

"Yes, that Jeep's seen better days. You all right staying here? Shouldn't take me long at all."

She shrugged. "I can draw."

"Smart choice. Let me get cleaned up and grab some money."

They trooped back into the house, and Matt changed out of his sweaty T-shirt. He stuffed a wad of currency into his pocket and went to Andrew's room to check on him. The patron was propped up in bed, reading Tolstoy, his brow furrowed in concentration. When he looked up at Matt, he seemed annoyed at the interruption.

"I'm headed into town," Matt announced. "Could you make sure Hannah doesn't burn the place down?"

"I think I can manage that. You figure out the problem?"

"Hope so. We'll soon know for sure."

Matt made his way to the Jeep, and the engine started on the first try. His opinion of the vehicle had improved the more he'd driven it, even though the interior did smell like exhaust from a pinhole in either the muffler or the tailpipe. But its oversized tires made it surefooted, for all its other flaws.

He backed out of the overhang that protected the vehicle from the elements and headed down the long drive to the road. The trip into town took ten minutes with no traffic on the way, and once at the hardware store, he quickly located a pipe wrench and some other useful odds and ends that would be necessary to restore the regulator to working condition. Matt paid cash, and the owner bagged his purchases, and Matt carried them to the Jeep and made another quick stop at a small market for some water before retracing his route to the lodge.

He was halfway home when he caught a glimpse of the truck that had nearly killed Hannah in his side mirror, gaining on the Jeep. Matt increased his speed, and the truck continued barreling down on him, its engine howling behind him. He floored the gas, and the Jeep surged forward, His speedometer inched past a hundred and thirty kilometers as the old SUV labored for traction on the loose gravel that plagued the rural highway's pavement.

Matt sped past the turnoff for the lodge and continued hurtling down the road, cursing between clenched teeth whatever had possessed the thugs to pursue him. He rounded a bend and lost sight of the truck, and then it reappeared behind him, still moving at reckless speed considering the conditions. He dared a glance at his gas gauge, he had a little over a quarter tank, so he could lead them on a chase for some time without running dry.

But then what? Two against one, and he didn't have his gun. Even with his skills, if they were armed, he'd be in trouble. So that left the unappealing option of outrunning them, which seemed unlikely in light of the Jeep's age and its design limitations.

Another bend, and tree branches brushed the side of the Jeep as he narrowly avoided skidding off the shoulder into the brush, reminding him that he needed to maintain all of his focus on driving, not playing out distracting scenarios in his head. The curves got more treacherous, and he nearly lost it again, and he had to force himself to slow somewhat so he could avoid rolling the vehicle on one of the hairpins. Matt hadn't driven this section, there having been no reason to, but it was rapidly deteriorating with the elevation, and was now little more than a two-lane ribbon pocked with potholes and gaps where the pavement had washed out or been eroded by snow.

He cut a sharp curve too wide and nearly careened off the road where it dropped precipitously down the tree-lined slope to where a stream frothed a quarter mile below. The big knobby tires protested with a scream of tortured rubber but gripped well enough to avoid disaster, and he downshifted for more traction and stomped on the gas, urging the SUV forward.

When the road straightened, he picked up speed again, and his gaze flitted to the rearview mirror as the engine climbed into the redline again. No truck. He slowed and kept an eye on the mirror as he approached the next turn, but there was now nothing following him. So the miscreants had either tired of their chase or had turned off on one of the other drives that fed onto the road, their amusement exhausted for the time being.

Matt pulled to the shoulder and sat for several minutes, waiting, and when nothing appeared on the road behind him, he executed a three-point turn and headed back, his heart pounding from the adrenaline spike the high-speed chase had engendered. The twisting two-lane seemed far less threatening at a third of the speed, and he took his time, half expecting to be ambushed around each turn.

When he reached his drive, he twisted and glanced in both directions to ensure nobody was lying in wait, and then turned off and rolled up the gravel way until the lodge loomed into view. Once parked, he carried his purchases into the house and drained half the water he'd bought in three swallows, the sour tang of acid in his stomach a remnant from the unexpected adventure with the local miscreants.

He had no idea what he'd done to draw their wrath, but from now on he'd be packing whenever he ventured into town. Matt had little doubt that the pair had it out for him, and if it was a fight they were after, he'd bring one – but at a place and time of his choosing. His commitment to keeping a low profile only extended so far, and trying to run him down had crossed an important line and demonstrated they were going to be a continuing menace to both himself and Hannah.

And Matt had ample experience putting down dangerous threats. He suspected the pair of skinheads wouldn't be missed by anyone if they disappeared in the woods, and if they were going to make another try for him, they'd learn that it didn't pay to rile up an old dog who was more than capable of biting.

Hannah came running to him and hugged his legs.

"Did you miss me?" he asked, dropping to one knee.

"I saw a mouse. It was scary."

"A mouse? Inside?"

She shook her head. "No. By the wood you chopped."

He made a face. "Well, then. He's probably just nosing around, having a look. As long as he isn't inside, outside is where he lives, so we'll just leave him be."

"I don't want to get bit."

He smoothed her hair and looked her in the eyes. "Don't worry. I won't let anything happen to you."

"Promise?"

"Cross my heart."

CHAPTER 24

Warsaw, Poland

The Warszawa Centralna train station was humming with activity when Jet walked through the automatic glass doors and made her way past a futuristic shopping arcade on the main floor to the escalators that led to the upstairs level. She did a slow walk around the station, which was as modern as any she'd been in, and then took the escalator to the McDonald's that occupied a prominent position on the upper floor. Inside, she went to the counter and ordered a diet soda and slowly scanned the interior as she waited for the girl at the register to make change.

Her contact was seated at a booth near the back of the dining area, a burger half eaten on a tray in front of him. She pocketed the coins the clerk handed her, carried her drink to the booth, and sat across from him, her expression impassive. He eyed her with a similar lack of emotion and pushed the burger away.

"I don't see how anyone eats this crap," he said in Hebrew.

"Probably best we stick to English, don't you think?" she suggested.

"I already did a scan of the place. We're clean."

"Still. Let's stick to protocols."

He shrugged. "It's your movie."

She nodded. "That's right. And we'll get along better as long as you remember that."

He took a sip of the coffee that he'd ordered with the food. "It was drilled into me. You have any issues getting here?"

She'd flown commercial, and the short flight had been uneventful.

She shook her head. "None. Our…friend…indicated you would have a full briefing for me from the phone data?" she said.

"That was overly optimistic. Our contact here can do so, but he insists on meeting in person. I suspect it has something to do with being paid in cash."

She sighed and shook her head. "Two minutes in and you're already useless."

He tried a smile. "Not my call. It's a local. He isn't a pro. You know how amateurs can be."

"Does he know who you are?"

"No. Just that I'm from the embassy. On terrorist watch. The usual cover."

"There's no way I'm meeting with him. So this one's on you," she said.

"Fine by me." He paused. "We dug up some more on the bomber. He's more of an enigma than anything. Just rumors. Everyone we queried either denied knowing anything or clammed up when we asked – all except one prisoner we've been holding for a couple of years without a trial. He was willing to talk in exchange for some favorable treatment. He didn't know much, but he was able to confirm that our man travels freely throughout the Middle East, Africa, and Europe. Apparently he's a hired gun and, while he's sympathetic to the Palestinian cause, doesn't play favorites – he's a contract hitter who specializes in explosives."

"Did he have a name?"

"He goes by many. He's known in Arab circles as the Mexican."

"Because of his nationality? Race?"

"He didn't know. It was all secondhand information."

"Basically as useless as anything else you've brought me."

"We have confirmation he's real."

She shrugged. "Doesn't get us any closer, and we both know it."

"The phone's our best bet," Ian conceded.

"When do you meet your man?"

He checked his watch. "This evening. He gets off work at eight. He suggested a bar by his apartment at nine."

She thought for a moment. "That gives me time, then. I'll change my appearance so he couldn't pick me out of a lineup."

Ian eyed the food on his tray in disgust. "Where are you staying?"

"Somewhere safe and anonymous."

He patted a satchel on the yellow plastic bench beside him. "I have all your toys and some mad money."

She nodded. "Give me the name of the bar and the address. I'll meet you there."

Ian lifted the satchel and passed it to her. "Don't get caught with that or you're on your own."

"Amazing I've made it this far without your valuable insights."

He frowned. "I'm trying to be as pleasant as possible. I get that you like to work alone. I didn't pick this assignment, so can you ease off the venom a little?" He removed a pen from his jacket pocket and scratched a name and address onto a napkin. "That's the meet. Anything else?"

She slipped the napkin into the bag and stood. "See you in a few hours."

"What am I supposed to introduce you as?"

"Your assistant. Sylvie."

"Fair enough. See you there."

Jet turned and walked away, eyes roving over the other diners as she neared the exit. Once back on the escalator, she descended the steps hastily and made for the exit, uneasy at having been exposed in a public place, even though it was with a trusted party. Nothing had triggered her internal alarms, but that didn't mean much with hundreds of travelers milling around, and she'd need to search the satchel once outside the station to ensure that it was free of tracking devices.

She stopped on her walk at the halfway point to the Airbnb loft she had rented and checked the bag and its contents, meticulously going over every seam and item. When she detected nothing unusual, she made her way to a store near the rental and bought makeup and then continued to the loft and went to work on her appearance. By the time Jet was finished, she looked fifteen years older, with dark circles beneath her eyes and thick eyebrows, her almost imperceptible crow's feet accentuated with detailed application of contrast and concealer. She inspected her work and smiled and topped it off with a surgical mask so her nose and mouth wouldn't be visible – one benefit from the public health guidance of late being she could literally hide her features and not draw attention.

The bar turned out to be a boisterous beer hall with loud music, dim lights, and at least a hundred working-class men in their thirties and forties, most going to fat and showing the types of bloated features that announced their dissolute natures from across the room. Ian was waiting just inside, a baseball cap pulled low over his brow, his jeans and dark jacket deliberately unremarkable.

When Jet nudged him with her elbow, he did a double take and then whistled softly.

"Wow. That's incredible," he said.

She nodded. "The mask helps."

"I wouldn't have recognized you."

"That's the idea, isn't it?" She looked around. "Where's your man?"

"He texted me that he's running late, but he'll be here in ten."

Her eyes narrowed. "Problem?"

"I don't think so."

She exhaled in frustration. "You had one job…"

He chuckled and took a pull on his beer. "Relax. He'll be here. You want one?" he asked, motioning with his glass.

She shook her head. "No, thanks. I try to keep my wits about me during a mission."

He shrugged. "Suit yourself."

Time crawled by, and with each passing minute, Jet's annoyance increased. She was about to tell Ian she was leaving and their deal was off when a man entered the bar, and Ian leaned into her.

"That's him. He described what he was wearing. Let me go introduce myself."

"Make it snappy."

Ian returned with the man a few moments later and indicated Jet. "My assistant. Sylvie."

"Pleasure," the man said in accented English. "Rupert."

"Nice to meet you," Jet said, and Ian motioned to the bartender.

"A drink for my friend," he said. "And another for me."

Jet kept the anger under control, but her green eyes flashed dangerously, which Ian either didn't catch or chose to ignore. The two men toasted when their drinks arrived, and spent five minutes talking soccer while she fumed. When they finished their drinks, Ian checked the time and looked to Rupert.

"You have anything for us?"

Rupert looked around. "Not here."

"Then where?" Ian asked.

"My apartment. I have a rig I use to log into the system, and once in, we can see everything."

Jet and Ian exchanged a glance, and Ian extracted some cash and placed it on the bar. "Lead the way. I trust it's close?"

"A block away."

Rupert headed for the door, and Jet murmured to Ian as they followed, "I don't like this."

"I know. I'm not enjoying it, either. But we'll play along to get whatever he has."

"He makes a move, I'll gut-shoot him."

"I think he's just enjoying the role."

"For his sake, I hope you're right."

Rupert lived on the third floor of an older walk-up that had seen better days. He unlocked his door and ushered them in. The interior proved to be a stark contrast to the outside, all white and maple flooring and ultra-contemporary furnishings. He crossed to an expensive workstation with two large monitors and pointed to a yellow leather sofa nearby.

"Have a seat. This won't take long," he said, and he smiled complicitly as his fingers flew over the keys.

The monitor on the right blinked, and a screen popped up. Rupert typed some commands and then the phone number, and a long list of call data appeared. He squinted at it and looked to them.

"Goes back a few years, so he's been using it regularly." Rupert pointed at a couple of calls near the bottom of the list. "You said you were interested in Germany? These originated from Dresden." He tapped the screen with his index finger. "See the date?"

Ian nodded. "Where is it now?"

Another screen flashed, and he frowned. "It isn't pinging at present, so it's either off or he's junked it."

"Can you pull up where the last few calls were made from?" Jet asked.

Rupert nodded. "I can do better than that. There's the last month. Looks like most of it was from an industrial area in the north end. On the outskirts. Rough neighborhood. No place for a lady."

"Can you narrow it down?"

"I already have. The data's from the cell tower there. According to my triangulation software, it would have to have come from a two-block area to the northwest. That's as close as I can get without pinging the actual device, I'm afraid. If I could, I would get you to within three meters. Or if I was at work – but that would raise way too many questions."

Ian nodded and removed an envelope from his pocket. "Here's what we agreed upon. Thanks for helping."

Rupert took the envelope, eyed the contents, and smiled. "Sorry I couldn't narrow it down more."

"That's a good start. We'll be in touch if we need anything." Ian paused. "Obviously, not a word to anyone about this. Forget you ever saw the number."

"Of course."

Outside, Jet glanced around the dark street. "You think he'll keep quiet?"

"Yes. He's done so in the past for us."

She checked her watch and looked to Ian. "Feel like seeing Warsaw's glamorous industrial sector by night?"

He managed a dry smile. "I thought you'd never ask."

CHAPTER 25

London, England

Lun reclined on the sofa in the villa's home office, his tone agitated as he spoke with one of his assistants on a scrambled cell phone. He listened intently for several moments and then cut the younger man off.

"That doesn't sound believable," he snapped.

"Our sources say that the Russians are in disarray, sir. They apparently have appointed one of Nicolai's attorneys to run the company."

"Why wouldn't one of his directors have taken over?"

"That isn't clear. Perhaps infighting? Although I was told that the post was considered too dangerous now, after Nicolai's passing and the incident at the airport."

Lun eyed the glass of single malt scotch on the coffee table in front of him before responding. "And what do we know of this attorney?"

"He's low profile. Lives in London. A contract law specialist."

"He must be a decoy of some sort. There's no way a man like that could head up the Russians' organization. Think what you will about Nicolai, but he was a force of nature."

"Anything is possible, sir. I'm still trying to get more information. But our sources have reported that the attorney has implemented compartmentalized security protocols that make it extremely difficult. Apparently everyone is on edge, suspicious, lying low."

"Sounds typical of how a paper pusher would operate: establish bureaucratic controls rather than taking decisive action," Lun said, and hung up.

He took a sip of his scotch and thought. Perhaps he was in the clear after the change of leadership. The sort of brutality that had ended his son's and the Russian's lives wasn't a sustainable business model in this day and age, and someone who operated outside of the jungle mentality would recognize that and reject it as counterproductive. That, and if you were going to live by the sword…

The thought of his son brought an ache to Lun's stomach. The boy had been anything but perfect, but he'd still been young, feeling his oats, enjoying his youth when he'd been struck down. True, Lun had been too soft on him and allowed him to be overly reckless, but that couldn't be undone. And the boy hadn't deserved his fate at the hands of a paid assassin. The Russian could have made any number of other moves, and both would have been alive today.

He drained his glass and sighed. Such a waste. Now he had nobody groomed to take over for him. Certainly not his daughter, who was more interested in fashion and makeup than empire building, or his younger brother, who had shown no interest in the business and was involved in too many shady enterprises to risk handing the reins. And Lun's subordinates were all too meek – desirable while Lun was still in what he considered his prime, but not for carrying on his legacy. Sending a sheep to do the work of a lion was a recipe for disaster – which he hoped would be the case with this Russian attorney, whom he recalled from a meeting with Nicolai in London years ago when they'd consummated their relationship. Upon reflection, the man had been just another wonk in a suit, who'd contributed little and had been in no way memorable.

Hardly the stuff of leadership, as far as Lun could tell.

His laptop pinged from the desk, and he rose and walked over to it. He opened his chat application and saw a message from another assistant that brought a smile to his face. Lun reread the text and nodded in satisfaction. Finally some good news, or at least a pleasant diversion.

An Indonesian politician Lun had been courting for months had finally responded and had invited him to Scotland to play golf at St. Andrews, a course Lun had wanted to play for much of his adult life but for which he'd never seemed to have had the time. But now, cooped up in the London house, he had nothing but time to play the oldest course in the world, fondly known as the Grand Old Lady, and could finally fulfill another of his lifetime fantasies.

He peered at the screen and jotted down a number and then placed another call on the scrambled phone. The politician's assistant answered, and after a short delay, the man himself was on the line.

"I hope you can get away from your busy schedule," the politician said, his voice silky.

"How could I possibly say no to the opportunity?" Lun responded.

"Great to hear. Can you get to Scotland by tomorrow afternoon? I have a one o'clock tee time, and the weather is supposed to cooperate. Never a given there."

"I will move heaven and earth to join you."

"It will be an honor."

"No, the honor is mine for the generous invitation."

"I shall see to it that we want for nothing. Small-production single malts, my private sushi chef, delightful company if you wish… We shall make a day of it. I'll take the liberty of booking you a suite at the hotel. It's the only place worth staying. An icon, as is the course."

"That would be wonderful. I'll time my arrival for no later than noon. Can I ask you to arrange for a set of clubs? I don't have mine handy."

"Of course. It will be my pleasure. Just bring yourself; I'll take care of everything else. How many rooms will you need for your entourage?"

"Don't worry about them. I can make arrangements."

"Very well, then. See you tomorrow," the politician said, and disconnected.

Lun grinned and considered pouring himself another finger or two of scotch. General Hatar, now the next in line for the premiership in his country, was known for his appetites, and his promise of the very best wasn't an empty one. He had managed to loot a small fortune from his country over a long career in the military and then in politics, and he wasn't shy about spending it.

Lun had decided that another drink couldn't hurt and was just pouring it when his wife rapped at the door and entered.

"Good evening, my dear! Don't you look lovely!" he said.

Her eyes narrowed, and she looked disapprovingly at the glass and bottle.

"You're in a good mood. Is there something to celebrate?" she asked.

He told her about the invitation, and her lips tightened.

"Are you sure it's safe? I thought the reason we couldn't go home was because it was too dangerous," she said.

"Nobody will know I'm there. I'll book the jet myself. Not even my staff will know."

"What about the bodyguards?"

"If nobody has any idea I've left, I won't need them. Just don't tell anyone where I've gone. It will be a quick in and out. One night."

"If it's safe to do this, why isn't it safe to go home to China? I don't understand."

"They know me too well there. If anyone was going to make an attempt on us, it would be too easy there. In Scotland on a public course? I'll be just another tourist. Nobody will give me a second look." He paused. "You're welcome to come if you like, but this will be mostly business."

She pursed her lips and shook her head. "If you don't need me, I'd prefer not to. There'll be nothing for me to do while you're playing golf and drinking with your clients all night."

"Then it's settled. I'll call around to some charter companies and get a flight in the morning. It's a short hop. Less than an hour, I'm sure."

Her expression was flat when she turned to leave, and then she looked over her shoulder. "What time would you like dinner?"

He checked his watch. "Oh, the usual. This won't take much time."

"I'll tell the staff."

She departed, and he carried his drink to the desk and opened a browser to find charter companies in London. He couldn't have one of his people book the flight or he might compromise himself, but fortunately there were a number of large operators in the city, and in minutes he'd booked a Hawker 900 for takeoff the following morning at ten. Dundee Airport was only a short drive from the hotel, so he would have plenty of breathing room to check in and change into his golf togs before tee time. The charter company had no problem charging the ten-thousand-dollar fee for the overnight to his black card, so he had nothing more to do but enjoy his cocktail and indulge his family their passive-aggressive disapproval that he was getting to spread his wings while they were stuck in this gilded London cage.

A burden he would gladly shoulder in exchange for what was to come.

CHAPTER 26

Warsaw, Poland

Ian crept down the main access road for the industrial district in the car the local Mossad contact at the embassy had provided, Jet in the passenger seat. The streets were deserted at the late hour. The major trucking hubs were in a different area, a more modern section of the city outskirts where the boulevards allowed for less congestion, and this one had been relegated to manufacturing, which was a daytime endeavor.

"What are you looking for?" Ian asked, his voice low.

"I'll know it when I see it."

"Needle in a haystack comes to mind."

"That could be. But it's all we've got. We know he's using a building here. We just need to figure out which one."

"Not necessarily, right? He could have a day job. Wouldn't be the first," Ian observed.

"Doubtful."

"Right. But how do we know?"

Jet turned to look at him. "First off, *we* don't know anything. I do. I looked at the times of the calls. They were all over the map. Some at night, some during the day. So the likelihood he's a worker is slim. Not zero, but slim. And if you look at his MO in Tangier, he had his own building, right?"

Ian was forced to nod. "That's correct."

"Then until we discover otherwise, it's likely that he has one here, given how often calls originated here. So what we're looking for is anything that seems…off."

He chuckled and then caught himself. "That's it? We're looking for *off*? What exactly is that?"

She eyed him. "It's something that doesn't fit the pattern for the area. Or draws my attention for whatever reason. Like I said, I'll know it when I see it. This isn't a science."

"I...see."

The district was in good repair, and the buildings were relatively clean despite their industrial nature, most with well-maintained parking areas, newish paint, and corporate logos emblazoned on their sides. After a drive around the area Rupert had identified, Jet chewed her lower lip and thought for a few beats.

"Pull over and park. I want to walk it on foot."

"Works for me," he said.

"Tell me everything you know about the Morocco operation."

"We had solid intel, but he'd booby-trapped the building, and we believe he was tipped off. It was a carpet warehouse, and the company was a front – we're still trying to verify who actually owned it."

"It'll be a shell, of course. Owned by a trust in the Cook Islands or Nevis," she said.

"Probably. He'd rigged it with explosives. Our men never stood a chance." He continued for three minutes, reporting on what he knew from his briefings with Noah. When he was done, Jet opened the door and stepped out.

"You can stay here if you want. Or come along. Up to you."

"I need to stretch my legs. Doesn't look like anyone's around, so it isn't like we'll be noticed."

"Let's move."

Jet set off along the sidewalk at a rapid pace, and Ian adjusted his stride to match hers. She walked down the primary road and then methodically performed a grid search, moving like a wraith in the night. Eight minutes later, she stopped and turned to Ian.

"That warehouse doesn't fit in," she said, indicating a dark hulk.

"Fit in how?"

"Business must be booming. All the buildings so far have been occupied – you can tell they're seeing daily use by their parking areas and their loading docks. But this one looks abandoned. Which doesn't make sense. If space is in demand, you'd think the owner would have rented it."

He considered her words. "I suppose that's as good as anything, as hunches go."

"I want to take a closer look. Stay here and watch the street."

"We haven't seen a soul since we got here."

"Then it should be easy to spot any threats," she said, and walked to the chain-link fence. She knelt in front of the padlocked chain that secured the two sides of the gate, and glanced at Ian. "It's seen regular maintenance. No rust, no grime. Not really in keeping with an abandoned building."

"Could be a caretaker," he observed.

"That's true," she said, and then tested the chain before squeezing through the narrow gap, barely making it through the tight fit.

"I'll be back," she whispered over her shoulder, and then set off toward the warehouse at a run, her black ensemble rendering her nearly invisible in the darkness, nothing more than a faint shadow crossing the lot.

Jet reached the main doors and again studied the lock. No signs of the expected corrosion. Her gaze drifted upward to a box near the roofline, and she strained to make it out in the darkness. She eyed it for half a minute and then removed her phone from her pocket and called Ian.

"Yes?" he answered in a hushed voice.

"Pretty sophisticated alarm system for an empty warehouse. The casing looks like it's almost new."

"So?"

"I'm going to see if there's a way in through the roof. Because if that thing's activated, the doors are a nonstarter."

"Not great news. Be careful."

She hung up and slipped the phone back into place and then slowly circled the building, noting that the few windows had steel frames and were protected by heavy bars. When she'd come full circle, she moved to a rain gutter that ran along the corner from the flat roof, and pulled on it to check it for stability. It didn't move, so she tested it with her full weight, and when it remained in place, pulled herself up to the roof hand over hand.

There, she saw the outline of several air-conditioning compressors. As she neared them, she saw a long, raised skylight. She approached it cautiously and looked down into the warehouse, which was pitch black. Remembering Ian's description of the disastrous Tangier operation, she palmed her phone, switched on the flashlight, and shined it down into the space, focusing on the interior rim.

As far as Jet could tell, the building was empty, but she caught the glint of a fine wire affixed to the corner of the skylight frame. She studied it for several beats and then returned to the drainpipe and lowered herself back to the ground.

When she'd returned and slipped back through the gate, Ian's expression was expectant.

"Well?" he queried.

"It's our man. Skylight's rigged. If I hadn't been forewarned, I might have missed it."

"So…what do we do now?"

"The alarm's got to be engaged. The simplest way forward is to tell your boss we need a relay transmitter we can wire in that will tell us when it's deactivated." She looked around. "Until then, we keep watch the old-fashioned way. Which means a long night. You want to call Noah, or should I?"

"I can handle it."

She told him what she needed. He listened intently and then walked a few meters away and placed the call. When he finished speaking, he returned to her.

"It'll be in the air within the hour," he said.

Jet checked the time. "Won't be here till nearly dawn. It'll be close."

"You're comfortable wiring it up?" he asked. "Or should I request a tech?"

Her look was withering. "I can manage." She glanced around. "Get the car. We'll want to park it where we can see the gate, but not where it will be noticed."

"Not much chance of that with all the trucks here."

She pointed to a spot by a dumpster halfway down the block on the far side of the street. "That would work."

Ian went in search of the car, and Jet considered the warehouse with a frown. Catching the bomber was still a longshot, but they'd just narrowed the odds considerably. All of which assumed that he would be returning to the building any time soon. She hated the variables in the scenarios, but resolved to make peace with the uncertainty. Either he or one of his accomplices might appear at any moment, whereas only hours before they'd had nothing.

And even a slim possibility was better than nothing.

At least that was what she told herself as she waited for Ian's return.

CHAPTER 27

Bohinjska Bistrica, Slovenia

A sprawling, single-story house sat at the end of a long gravel drive on the outskirts of town, out of sight from the main road, its weathered wooden plank exterior a ramshackle eyesore. Smoke rose from a steel chimney pipe at one end of the structure, and a barn hulked adjacent to the opposite side along with three battered SUVs, all with oversized tires to handle the roads.

Darkness had fallen earlier, and an amber glow seeped from shuttered windows. Inside, six men sat around a table, bowls of stew and bottles of strong beer before them, an ashtray playing the role of centerpiece. Thrash metal pounded from the speaker of an old-school stereo system, and the peeling walls were bare of art or photos, matching the stark furniture and dearth of anything remotely homey.

"They should have been back hours ago," the oldest of the men growled in Romanian, his face heavily lined and sun-burnished, his nose crooked from countless bar fights, his balding hair cut close to his scalp.

"You know them, Nicu," another said. "Probably stopped someplace and got too drunk to drive. Wouldn't be the first time."

"I don't like it," Nicu said. "They aren't answering their phone. They could be in custody. In which case, we're all screwed and should be out of here."

"We would have been tipped off if that had happened. Besides, it isn't like we can move the lab in a hurry," the man responded. "We'll need a box van or a cargo truck. Not to mention how explosive the chemicals are."

Nicu pushed his plate away and fished a pack of cigarettes from the breast pocket of his denim vest. He lit one and blew smoke at the others and pointed a pair of stubby fingers at them.

"Go find them, Cristi. I don't like surprises," he snapped.

"All of us?"

Nicu frowned. "You and your brother. Andrei can stay here and keep me company. The cops are still looking for him, so he shouldn't leave the house."

Cristi nodded and regarded the other men. "Good point. What about Luca and Dorian?"

Luca stared at Cristi without expression. "You need us to hold your hand?"

Nicu laughed. "Just the two of you. Not like it's that big a place. We don't need to attract a bunch of attention."

Cristi stood. "Come on, Stefan."

The brothers left, and Nicu shook his head as he reached for his beer. "Whatever those morons have gotten themselves into, we should never use them again," he said.

"They know how to cook the dope. And they're loyal. Nobody ever said they were responsible," Andrei shot back.

"If they got themselves arrested, it's on you. They're your buddies."

"They may be idiots, but they know better than that. Nobody wants to go back to jail."

"Then what's your excuse?"

Andrei offered a crooked grin and held up two fingers, signaling for a cigarette. "I had no idea she was fifteen. That'll blow over soon enough. They have better things to do."

"I had no idea she was human. I thought you'd found a hog to slaughter," Luca said. Everyone laughed, and Nicu tossed the packet of smokes to Andrei.

"Seriously, though," Nicu said. "Dorian, how long do you think it would take to pack up the lab if we have to?"

Dorian studied his boots. "Maybe half a day. But we've got

shipments to make, remember? We stiff anyone and they won't care why."

"I can handle that, if it comes down to it. But let's hope we don't have to move. This place is perfect." Nicu took a long drag of his cigarette. "I told everyone to lie low. This really pisses me off."

Andrei nodded. Nicu was a meth manufacturer and as ruthless as they came. He was infamous in the business for a zero-tolerance attitude for nonpayment or excuses, and Andrei knew of at least a half dozen he'd killed for treachery since they'd started the business six years earlier. If Lucian and his dimwitted cousin had done anything to jeopardize the enterprise, Nicu wouldn't hesitate to slit their throats.

Cristi and Stefan bounced along the road into town, their ancient Mitsubishi SUV's shocks far past the point of no return, the interior reeking of stale smoke and body odor. Once on the main drag, they cruised past the usual bars Lucian and his cousin frequented, looking for their truck, but saw nothing. They parked at the most popular watering hole and took a lap inside, but didn't see their boys, and after repeating the exercise in three other places, got back into their vehicle and stared at the dashboard.

"What now?" Cristi asked.

"Maybe they got into an accident? Got shitfaced and ran off the road? I've almost done it enough times," Stefan said.

"You think they might have gotten arrested?"

"If so, their truck would be in the lot by the police station. We'll go by on the way out of town."

Stefan started the engine, and they rolled along the street until they reached the police station. It was a small building, and the impound lot consisted of nothing more than a parking area beside it, encircled with a fence. A sorry collection of old economy cars was parked inside collecting dust, but there was no lifted truck.

"Well, that's a relief, I guess," Cristi said.

"Yep. Now we have to look for accidents. Stupid bastards…"

They retraced their route to the house and drove slowly, high beams on, looking for any signs of skid marks. They were at one of the hairpin turns three-quarters of a kilometer past their drive when Cristi grabbed Stefan's arm and pointed. "There, see? Over by the shoulder."

Stefan pulled to the side of the road and squinted into the darkness before swinging his door open. His brother opened the glove compartment and removed a flashlight, and together they made their way to the edge of the drop. Cristi directed the beam down the hill and swept it, but saw nothing but brush and trees.

Stefan turned to him. "The bushes are flattened. They must be down there, but a decent way. I can't make anything out from here." He peered into the gloom and removed his cell phone and switched on the flashlight. "Come on."

They picked their way down the drop and stopped at a rock outcropping, below which was an even steeper slope. At the bottom, they could just make out the truck below them, crumpled against a tree like a flattened tin can, missing two of its wheels.

"Damn," Cristi whispered.

"I'll say. Let's see whether they're in there."

Stefan led the way to the cab and recoiled at the sight of the driver, obviously dead, hanging halfway through the shattered windshield, his skull crushed and half his face torn off. Cristi played the flashlight over Lucian in the passenger seat and then called to his brother, "He's alive!"

Stefan redirected his phone light to where Lucian was wedged between the dashboard and bench seat, covered in blood, his nose ruined and one eye bulging from the socket, struggling for breath. He shuddered at the light and managed a hoarse whisper.

"Help me…"

"It's Stefan and Cristi. What happened?" Stefan said.

Lucian tried to twist to look at Stefan, but gave up, the pain too much.

"We…ran off…the road. Other guy…must be…a cop. Drove…like a…pro…"

"What other guy?" Stefan demanded.

The injured man coughed, and blood trickled from his mouth. "Help me."

"The other guy, Lucian. Who is he? Describe him."

"Old…Jeep. Tall."

"Hair color? How old?"

"Please. I'm…hurt bad."

"We'll do what we can. But what color hair did he have, and how old is he?"

"Cristi, it's…that guy from…the market…yesterday…"

Cristi had been in town with Lucian the prior morning, bored and looking for amusement as they stocked up on supplies, and he remembered the man.

"With the little girl?" Cristi asked.

"Urgh…yes…"

Cristi straightened and looked at his brother. "I know who he's talking about. Looks pretty hard. Could be a cop."

"Get…me…out. Help. Please," Lucian said, and ended with a gurgling moan.

Stefan stepped away from the cab. "It's a miracle he's still alive. It's been hours."

"How are we going to get him up to the car?"

Stefan shook his head. "We'd have to get him to a hospital…and that would open us up to all kinds of questions. Assuming we could even get him out of there. He looks like the dash cut him in two. There's no way."

Cristi's eyes widened. "We can't just leave him. He'll die."

"He's going to die anyway. There's nothing we can do."

"Jesus…"

Stefan rounded the truck, flicked open a butterfly knife, and then drove it through Lucian's bulging eye as Cristi looked on in horror. Lucian stiffened, and a tremor shot through his body, and then he exhaled a long groan and fell still. Stefan withdrew the blade and looked at his brother. "At least he won't suffer."

"You…killed him."

"He was too far gone. You want to go explain to Nicu how we could have saved a guy who was nearly dead anyway? Who picked a fight with a cop, or nearly led him to the lab? You were with him yesterday. What happened?"

"Nothing. I mean, you know Lucian. He can get…but we didn't *do* anything. Except on the way out, he was flooring it. But he didn't hit the kid."

Stefan's tone grew cold. "Did he almost hit her?"

Cristi was silent for a few moments. "I mean, I wasn't driving…"

"Were you high? Sounds like it."

"Maybe a little."

"Crap. And now you have a cop on our tail? Nicu would snap your neck like a twig if he knew."

"What do we tell him?"

Stefan shut off his phone light and wiped the knife blade off on the tall grass before pocketing it.

"Let's get back to the truck. We'll figure out a story that won't get you killed."

"What about the wreck? The bodies?"

"It could be years until someone finds them. If ever. We couldn't see them from the road. Neither can anyone else. By that time, they'll have been picked clean by the buzzards. Now get it into gear. We have bigger problems to worry about. Like what the hell you two got us into, and how to explain enough of it so we can figure out what to do."

CHAPTER 28

St. Andrews, Scotland

Lun watched his final putt of the day sink into the eighteenth hole and smiled for the fiftieth time, his face aching from the unfamiliar expression. The course had been magnificent, just as he'd expected and as challenging as any he'd played on, with the additional gravitas of the area's history making every hole a personal challenge for him. He wiped away a trickle of perspiration from his brow and gazed skyward to where a pair of seagulls were noisily circling the course, and looked to the Malaysian politician.

"Wonderful game. Truly," Lun said. "A delight I shall never forget, Hatar."

"It was indeed, was it not? I'm so glad that you were able to make it. There are some things that transcend description."

Lun nodded. "I completely agree."

Their caddy gathered their clubs and placed them into the back of his cart, and Lun and Hatar followed in their own back to the golf club. Hatar smiled broadly as he pulled to a stop in one of the reserved slots and turned to Lun.

"I don't know about you, but I'm parched after all that exertion," he said. "The beer was half warm."

"And half flat," Lun agreed.

"Best if we stick to scotch from here on out, don't you think?"

"I can't think of a single argument against it," Lun said and accompanied the Malaysian into the club's bar – a storied affair that, like the course, reeked of history and tradition.

Hatar checked the time on his platinum watch. "I told my chef to expect us in an hour or so. Does that work for you?"

"Yes. I'm hungry after eighteen holes."

"And thirsty, I hope," Hatar said, signaling for the barkeep. A server hurried over, and Lun spoke to him in English.

"Do you have a list of your best scotches?"

"Of course, sir," the man said, and went in search of it as Hatar and Lun took in the place. When he returned, he presented a laminated card to Lun, who perused it before setting it on the table.

"Two glasses of the Bowmore 1984. Neat."

Hatar nodded approval as the server departed to get their drinks. "A fine choice."

"Yes, their list is extensive."

"I took the liberty of arranging for a bottle of Dalmore Constellation 1973 Cask Ten for us to try with dinner. Have you had it?"

Lun shook his head. "No, I'm afraid not."

"It's truly remarkable. An experience, not a whiskey. Rare as hen's teeth."

"I look forward to it."

The server returned with a bottle on a tray and two glasses. He set them down on the table and poured an inch into each. He waited until Lun tasted his and nodded acceptance, and then disappeared, leaving them to their drinks. They both took appreciative sips, and Hatar set his glass down as Lun swirled his and sniffed, the better to appreciate the aroma.

"My chef is a master," Hatar said. "I stole him from one of the top restaurants in Okinawa. A magician, truly. The man has a gift. I'm glad you'll have the time to dine with me."

"Today has been one of the best in recent memory," Lun said. "I can only imagine how it could improve."

Hatar leaned into him and whispered conspiratorially, "I have a pair of young lovelies from London who would be charmed to make your acquaintance. One phone call and they can join us for dinner."

Lun's face was impassive. "What is the saying about when in Rome?"

"I suspected you would approve. They are both gorgeous…and discreet."

"A spellbinding combination, I'm sure."

"You have no idea."

They drained their scotch and ordered two more, after which Lun insisted on paying, flipping his black card casually to the server. He left a generous tip, and Hatar escorted his guest to a private suite, where Hatar's chef was waiting in full sushi chef regalia with a trio of helpers by his side, their garb traditional Japanese.

The young women appeared fifteen minutes later and were, as promised, barely out of their teens, gorgeous, and friendly in the manner only professionals could be. The dinner proceeded, and delicacy after delicacy was served until everyone was at the bursting point. The chef's helpers whisked the trays away, and Hatar snapped his fingers for the scotch. One of the helpers hurried to retrieve the bottle, and Hatar did the honors of pouring the nectar into a pair of glasses, not offering any to the girls, who were content with their flutes of Dom.

Lun toasted Hatar and took a preliminary sip and then closed his eyes and savored the smoky elixir, reveling in the complexity of the flavors as they played across his palate. When he opened them, he smiled with genuine warmth, fueled in part by the scotch and two bottles of sake consumed during their meal, and sat back in his chair.

"As you said, it is an experience, not a whisky," he said.

Hatar nodded. "It will change with each mouthful. Remarkable, is it not?"

"Absolutely."

The girls giggled and stood, and one of them beamed at the men. "We're going to the loo to freshen up, okay?" she said.

Hatar waved them away. "Don't stay too long."

"We'll be back."

Lun finished his drink and blinked several times. Hatar refilled his glass and held his aloft again in salutation.

"To a night to end all nights," he proclaimed.

"Indeed!" Lun agreed, and swallowed half his drink in a gulp.

The chef approached, and Hatar spoke in Japanese to him,

congratulating him on an exquisite meal. Lun responded in kind, his Japanese was markedly better, but he pretended to speak at the same level as the Malaysian so the politician wouldn't lose face. The chef bowed and left, and Hatar nodded again.

"The girls will be back shortly. Which do you fancy? Or do you want them both?" he asked.

Lun blinked several times again. "I… I think you'll have to keep them entertained, my friend. The day is catching up with me. I'm going to go to my room." He put a hand over his stomach. "I'm sorry. I seem to have a bit of heartburn from all the celebration."

Hatar rose. "No need to apologize. I'm honored you took the time to join me. I'll try to console the young ladies. Think nothing of it, Lun. I'll have one of my men take you back to the hotel."

"Thank you. For everything."

By the time Lun made it to his room, he was trembling slightly, and his mouth seemed flooded with saliva. He removed his togs and climbed into bed and pulled the covers over his head. His heart was pounding so hard it seemed determined to tear out of his chest, and he concentrated on his breathing, trying to slow it as the room spun.

Eventually it slowed, but Lun was overcome with weakness, and it was all he could do to call the front desk and ask for them to send a doctor. He was at an age where he took things like food poisoning seriously, having traveled all over the world and experienced its ravages firsthand too many times, and he knew that the sooner he got five hundred milligrams of ciprofloxacin into his system, the faster his symptoms would abate.

After a seeming eternity, a soft rap at the door announced the doctor's arrival. Lun groaned and struggled from beneath the blankets, but his legs seemed unwilling to obey his brain's commands, and his knees buckled after three steps toward the door. He moaned at the pain from his hip striking the marble, and after two failed attempts to regain his footing, dragged himself the rest of the way, exhausting himself by the time he made it. Lun mustered all of his resources to reach the knob and unlock it, and then fell backward onto the cool stone as he shuddered and struggled for breath.

"Mr. Zhang?" a male voice asked from outside the door. "This is Dr. Reynolds. May I come in?"

Zhang managed another moan, and the doctor swung the door open, nearly battering Lun's legs. His expression changed from concern to shock at the sight of Lun, convulsing, saliva streaming from both corners of his mouth, eyes clamped shut, face contorted in an agonized grimace.

An hour later, at the hospital, he stood beside a specialist, monitoring Lun's vitals, a grim frown in place.

"He's in full-blown respiratory failure, and his labs show his kidneys are shutting down," the specialist said. "We're going to have to vent him."

"Damn," Reynolds said. "How much longer until the tox screen comes back?"

"Should be any moment."

The specialist left and minutes later returned with a pair of orderlies, who were pushing a ventilator. A nurse accompanied them, and they were intubating Lun when the specialist's cell buzzed. He glanced at the screen and then did a double take before turning to Reynolds, his expression dour.

"It's hemlock. He's been poisoned." He paused. "We're going to have to notify the police."

Reynolds shook his head. "Poor bugger. Am I correct in my recollection of my medical school days that there's no antidote for hemlock poisoning?"

The specialist nodded. "You are. Unfortunately, his respiratory system will fail, and eventually he'll fall into a coma, after which his vitals will stop. I'm afraid it's lights out for your lad."

"How long does he have?"

"Maybe an hour or two. Is there a next of kin?"

"The hotel is researching. I'll alert them. I was waiting until we had a definitive."

"Well, you do now. He's dying, and there isn't a damn thing we can do about it."

Reynolds shook his head again. "Horrible way to go."

The specialist grunted. “Hard to see how this could be accidental, given how rapidly he’s deteriorating.” He hesitated. “Whoever did this wanted him to die in the most awful way imaginable. It had to be deliberate.”

Reynolds stepped back and allowed the team to go to work, well aware that all the effort was for naught – once a patient’s renal system failed and their breathing essentially stopped, it was game over, and there was nothing anybody would be able to do but unzip a body bag and wait.

CHAPTER 29

Warsaw, Poland

Jet stretched and cracked an eye open, instantly awake, and Ian stirred on the twin bed beside hers. The equipment she'd needed had arrived an hour before sunrise, and she'd raced to the warehouse to hook it up to the alarm system before traffic had begun arriving in the industrial district. Their all-night vigil had produced no results, but she hadn't been deterred, and now, as daylight seeped from the sky once again outside their cheap hotel room, her idea to remotely monitor the alarm had just paid off, with the receiver on the nightstand beeping loudly to signal that the system had been deactivated.

Ian sat up and looked around the room, hair matted down on the side upon which he'd been lying. Jet threw the blanket aside, swung her legs off the bed, and slipped on her boots – she'd slept clothed to cut down on time if the device sounded, and Ian had done the same.

They were on the road in three minutes and at the industrial park in ten. The area was quiet again as dusk darkened the surroundings, the workers having left hours before, leaving the district as deserted as it had been the prior night. Ian killed his headlights and parked a hundred meters from the warehouse. He ferreted in his backpack and withdrew a pair of binoculars and, after a brief surveillance of the warehouse, grunted and passed them to Jet.

"I see one guy by the front door. Gate's still locked," he said.

"Looks like a guard, based on his body language and posture. We'll have to take him out quickly to get to whoever's inside."

"How do you know someone's there?"

"No other reason for a guard to be watching the street, much less for the alarm system to be switched off," Jet explained impatiently.

"How do you want to play this?" he asked.

"I'll circle around the back and call you when I'm in position. Then you create a distraction that draws him to the gate, and I'll deal with him."

Ian didn't appear convinced. "That's a lot of risk if anything goes wrong."

"Just do your part and don't worry about me," she said. "Unless I missed where you have a sniper rifle in your bag of tricks."

He shook his head. "Afraid not."

"Then we do this the hard way."

"Any special requests for the distraction?"

Jet smirked. "Impress me," she said, and screwed the suppressor on her pistol and chambered a round with a soft snick.

She slipped from the car and took off at a run, leaving Ian to devise a disruption that would draw the guard's attention long enough for her to dispatch him. Jet covered the ground to the yard next door to the warehouse and slowed as she jogged through tall grass, the brick-and-mortar side walls hiding her approach.

When she reached the far end of the lot, she stopped, cocked her head, and listened for several seconds before slipping the pistol into her waistband and feeling for fingerholds in the wall. She found a gap where shoddy bricklaying or time had degraded the mortar, and felt for a second with her other hand. When she found one, she pulled herself up, using the toes of her boots for additional leverage, and then cursed when she slipped and fell back onto the ground.

Jet picked herself up and studied the wall and backed away a dozen meters. She inhaled deeply and sprinted flat out at the intersection of the side and back wall and was halfway up the back when she pushed off and hurled herself at the side wall. Her hands clamped onto the top, and she hauled herself up and paused to survey the warehouse grounds at the crest before dropping to the pavement, landing in a crouch.

She freed the pistol and moved to the building, eyes locked on the front of the structure where the guard was stationed. When she was halfway there, she removed the cell from her pocket and hit redial. Ian answered, and she whispered to him.

"I'm in. Make it quick."

Jet disconnected and waited. A minute went by, and then another, and then the sound of Ian singing an American pop song at the top of his lungs reached her from the street. She rolled her eyes at the improvisation and crept towards the front of the building, where Ian materialized out of the darkness beyond the gate and grabbed onto it, still howling a garbled rendition of either Maroon Five or Frank Sinatra – such was his ability to carry a tune she couldn't be sure which.

The bodyguard detached himself from the front entrance and stalked towards the gate, and Jet moved quickly, darting to within ten yards of him before squeezing off three shots in quick succession, the subsonic pops muffled by the suppressor. The man stumbled two steps and fell face forward onto the asphalt, and his finger reflexively squeezed the trigger of his gun. The sharp crack echoed off the front of the building, and Jet ran to the guard and put a final round into his skull before looking up at Ian, her jade eyes glittering catlike in the gloom.

"Cut it," she said, and Ian retrieved bolt cutters from his backpack and severed the links while Jet dragged the dead man by the legs toward the building. She was nearly there when gunfire roared from behind her, and she instantly dropped and spun as slugs ricocheted off the pavement around her.

Jet fired at the muzzle flashes coming from the front entrance of the warehouse, and when the steel door slammed shut, yelled to Ian.

"Cover me. I'm going in."

She ran towards the building and flattened herself against the wall adjacent to the entrance as she ejected the magazine from her pistol and slapped another into place. Jet waited to see whether the shooter would open the door again, and when he didn't, crept over and pressed her ear against it.

The sound of running boots on cement greeted her, and she threw the door wide and tumbled through the gap, rolling until she could make out the fleeing figure near the far side of the space. She fired a half dozen times, and the shooter returned fire, but one or more of her rounds found home, and he crumpled to the floor even as he squeezed off another few shots that went badly wild.

Jet darted to the nearest wall and stayed in the shadows as she drew closer to the wounded man. When she was five meters away, she called out in Arabic, her tone flat.

"Throw your gun where I can see it."

Several beats went by, and then a pistol clattered in the gap between them. She stepped into the faint light seeping through the skylight and kicked the gun away, then walked slowly to where the man lay on his back, clutching his abdomen, blood staining both hands, wincing in pain.

"You're the one they call El Burro," Jet said, more statement than question.

"You'll never get…out of here…alive…" he whispered hoarsely.

"Well, then we'll both be going to hell together," she said. "The Eilat bombing. Who ordered it?"

He looked away and moaned.

"Gut shot is the worst way to go, they tell me," Jet said. "Cooperate and we can get you to a hospital."

He glared at her. "Lies."

"My fight isn't with you."

"I have…no idea…"

"Looks like you want to go out hard. Fine by me," Jet said.

"It's…the…truth."

The front door creaked open behind her, and she dropped into a crouch and spun, pistol leveled at it. Ian moved to where she could see him, and she lowered the weapon and returned her attention to the bomber.

"How were you paid?" she asked.

"Crypto."

"How did you connect?"

"Knew…my work…"

"Murder for hire, you mean?"

He coughed and then turned to the side and vomited blood. Jet looked to Ian.

"He won't last long," she said. "We need to get him to an ER. Drag the guard in here and help me carry this one to the gate."

"Okay," Ian said, and disappeared out the door. He returned a few moments later lugging the dead guard. "If anyone heard the shooting, we're out of time."

"I know. Get the car. I'll take care of him. That'll speed things up."

Ian left, and Jet replaced her gun in her waistband and considered the wounded bomber.

"Is there anything in here that will help me get you to the door, or am I going to have to drag you?"

"Fork…lift," he managed, indicating one of the dark areas.

"Don't go anywhere," she said, and moved to where the big conveyance hulked in the gloom. The key was in it, and she figured out the controls and then drove it to where the wounded man was bleeding out, dropped the forks to the ground, and hopped down.

"This is going to hurt," she warned, and then lifted him by the underarms and slid him across the forks. He screamed in agony, but she ignored it. The pain of the director's murderer wasn't her concern. The only reason she cared to keep him alive was to extract more information. After that, he could rot in prison the rest of his miserable life, for all she cared.

She climbed back into the operator's seat and guided the forklift to the door, and was getting off when she heard the car pull up outside. Jet dropped to the floor and moved to the entrance and then ran down the three steps to where Ian had parked.

"He's in a bad way," she warned as she opened the rear door and leaned in. "Put your seat up as far–"

A deafening blast exploded from the building, and the windshield starred white as debris struck it. Ian slammed the transmission into reverse and backed away from the warehouse, half dragging Jet along with the car. She pulled herself up and onto the rear seat, and Ian coasted to a stop at the gate as tongues of flame licked from the loading dock doors and the front entrance.

"What the hell was that?" Ian exclaimed.

"Bombs, obviously," she said. "So much for getting anything else out of him."

"He killed himself?"

She stepped from the car and threw open the front door. Once in the passenger seat, she kicked at the windshield until it collapsed in a heap on the hood, and glanced over at Ian.

"Are you hurt? Can you drive?" she asked.

"I'm fine. Just…shaken."

"Get us out of here. If the shooting didn't draw every cop in Warsaw, this sure as hell will."

CHAPTER 30

Bohinjska Bistrica, Slovenia

Nicu glared at Stefan and Cristi, his displeasure evident. They'd been gone hours the night before, and he'd been asleep by the time they'd made it back. The next morning, they'd told him a long story that he'd doubted on its face, even though when he tried to poke holes in it, they'd both been consistent in their responses. But his gut told him at least some of it was invention – the question being how much, and whether it changed the fundamentals of the account.

The day had passed quickly as he'd considered his options. If, as they'd indicated, the mysterious stranger was a cop, the smart move would be to pack up the lab and hit the road. But they were nearly done with a two-hundred-kilo production run that had taken weeks to make, and breaking down the lab would eat into time, as well as mean they'd be short for their customer – a gang that didn't react to surprises well and would smell a rat, even if none existed.

Which could be deadly in this business.

At the very least, they'd question his reliability as a supplier, in which case he would get lower prices for his product and might even be cut out entirely if they found someone else. There was no shortage of meth labs in the region, the drug being one of the most popular in the former Eastern Bloc countries, and he couldn't afford to be displaced and have to find another buyer.

He'd sent his men out to see if they could spot the stranger, but they'd come up dry. Now they'd lost too much time, and he needed to make some tough decisions.

"If he's a cop, why haven't we heard anything from our contacts in town?" Nicu snarled at Andrei.

"Could be national. They don't share with the locals."

"They'd at least let them know, wouldn't they?" Nicu demanded.

"Depends on whether they think the locals are bent, I'd guess. Could be he's undercover. That's what makes the most sense." Andrei paused. "Or maybe he's Romanian. That would explain it."

The gang they sold to was in Romania, even though they picked up their loads in Slovenia. If they had a leak in their organization, the Romanians would be involved, in which case the natural move would be to send agents to locate the source in Slovenia without raising eyebrows with the local force.

Nicu shook his head in irritation. "A lot of guesswork. We pay too much to the cops to get blindsided by a wild card."

"So what do we do? We asked around, we've been searching every inch of the town, and nothing," Cristi said.

"We need to find him," Nicu said. "Now that it's dark enough, we can use the drones to see if we can get a hit on the car. What did Lucian say it was?"

"Older Jeep. Silver."

"There aren't a million of those around here. It's worth a shot."

"And if we don't get lucky?" Andrei asked.

Nicu thought for a long time. "Then we close up shop and burn it all down."

The brothers exchanged a worried look, which Nicu ignored. "Get the drones ready. We can do a search of every house we know of." He tapped his laptop. "Thank you, Google Earth."

"What if we get a hit?"

"Obviously we have to learn what he knows, or we assume the worst."

"Crap."

"Exactly."

Matt stirred and rolled over, the bed hard but tolerable after years in the jungle sleeping on dirt. He exhaled and adjusted his pillow, and then his eyes snapped open.

Something had woken him up.

A sound. Out of place in the silence of the deep woods.

He sat up and listened for a half minute and then slipped on a pair of shoes and walked to the window, staying out of the frame in case anyone was watching. His ears strained for a hint of what had roused him, and he heard it again: a faint buzzing, like a hive of bees, only higher pitched.

Matt instantly recognized the sound and moved to the bedroom door. Whoever was operating the drone was looking for something, and in the middle of the night, it wasn't likely to be innocent.

The pair of miscreants jumped into his thoughts, and he swore softly. They could have decided they wanted to escalate, and finding the Jeep would tell them where he was. At that point it wouldn't be safe to stay, and Matt didn't have anyplace else to go that was secure. Which meant that he needed to get the Jeep hidden or risk having to deal with the local thugs, which wasn't really consistent with staying off the radar.

He had no idea why they'd targeted him, but it barely mattered. He knew the type, and once they got the scent, they would figure he'd be easy pickings since he hadn't engaged – and his losing them on the road could have been construed as weakness. Bullies and thugs sought out soft targets, and even though it couldn't have been further from the truth, Matt had acted as one in order to avoid unnecessary conflict.

A move that was coming back to bite him in the ass.

He rushed through the lodge and bolted out the front door to the storage shed, where he'd stowed the tarp that had covered the Jeep when they'd arrived. He quickly found it, ran to the old SUV, and draped it over the vehicle in under a minute. There was no wind, so no need to fasten the straps beneath the undercarriage while drones were overhead. The quicker he was out of sight, the more likely he was to go undetected.

He retraced his steps to the lodge and watched the grounds through the partially open door. Several minutes later a drone appeared out of the night sky and hovered over the front of the house before continuing past it to the tree line, where it vanished from sight.

Matt continued to monitor the area for another half hour and only paused to retrieve his pistol. He spent the rest of the night in a chair at the door, watching and waiting, unsure of what was to come but ready for whatever it was, any willingness to back down now gone. He was almost a hundred percent convinced he'd covered up the ancient Jeep in time, but *almost* wasn't completely sure. Although as dawn painted the black sky with vivid orange and red, his certitude increased, and he yawned, his back killing him, the chance that anything was going to happen decreasing with each passing minute. If scumbags were going to make a move, it was going to be in the dark, not when he could see them coming. Lowlifes operated under cover of night, which meant he'd successfully evaded them. If they'd found him, they'd had hours to come for him, and they hadn't.

He yawned again and shifted the chair to the side and then bolted the door. He didn't want Hannah to wake up and see him with a gun and get worried; there was no point in that nor in alarming Andrew, who for all his bravado wasn't completely out of the woods yet.

Matt returned to his room and stashed the weapon and then padded to the kitchen to make some coffee, any chance of sleep eradicated by the drone and the implications of its nocturnal visit. Whatever happened next, it was becoming obvious that if he didn't want to go to war with the local toughs, he'd need to prepare for a move to greener pastures.

The only question being where those might be.

CHAPTER 31

Warsaw, Poland

A pair of tall men stood watching the warehouse burn, the contents aflame even though the roof was concrete and rebar and the walls brick. Firehoses shot geysers of white water at the conflagration to little effect, and clouds of black smoke billowed toward the sky like a volcanic eruption of aerosolized ink. A building at the rear of the lot was also ablaze, probably from sparks blown by the light wind, and the firefighters appeared to be successful in containing it, the problem being its distance from the hydrants and trucks.

One of the men shook his head as he observed the flames.

"What do you think?" he asked the other.

"Too soon to tell. But I'd guess either a chemical or gas explosion, or arson."

"It's always one or the other in commercial buildings, isn't it? That or electrical fire."

"This has been burning hot for too long. No telling what they had stored inside, but whatever it was, it's not going out on its own."

An hour and a half later, the flames had been replaced by steam rising from the skeleton of the building, and the firemen were standing by their trucks, exhausted after the prolonged fight to extinguish the blaze. A white panel van coasted to a stop in front of the site, and a powerfully built man in his forties stepped from the passenger side and made his way to the rear. The driver joined him as he opened the cargo doors and rummaged around inside, and then the pair made their way towards the uniformed men, rucksacks slung from shoulder straps, high-power handheld spotlights in their free hands.

"Hanz," one of the officers greeted them. "Levik."

"Gentlemen," Hanz said, a trace of German lightly accenting his Polish. "I presume it's safe to go inside?"

"Yes. There's damage to the roof, but it's holding."

"That's positive, I suppose," Levik said. "Boss?"

"Might as well get started," Hanz replied. "Anything we should know going in?"

"Negative. The men were able to drown the hot spots from out here. Nobody's been in but a recon team, and they called for you."

Levik exchange a look with Hanz. "Lucky us."

"Come on, then," Hanz said, and led Levik to the front entrance, the red brick framing it now charred black.

When they emerged after an hour inside, both technicians bore serious expressions.

"Looks like there were a couple of people in there. No way to know cause of death right now – they're both cooked well done. We'll need the coroner," Hanz reported.

"That's strange. The building was supposed to be unoccupied. A storage facility per the business license."

"Well, there's two bodies inside. Charred crispy," Levik said.

"Right. Any idea what caused it?"

"That's going to be tough. But first glance, looks like a series of explosions blew the hole in the roof, as well as the loading dock doors. Whatever they were storing was volatile. It'll take a day to comb through it all to confirm what the primary cause was."

"Then nothing obvious?"

"No, although the blasts by the roof are curious. I would swear they look like explosive charges were used. Whole chunks of the concrete were pulverized."

"Explosives?"

Hanz nodded. "Bigger than grenades, that's for sure."

The uniformed officers scowled at the news. "Why would they have explosive charges rigged on their roof?" the senior of the two asked.

Levik frowned. "If you were going to rig the skylight to blow if anyone attempted an entry, that would account for it."

"Why would anyone…"

"Do you have any information on the owner? That's where I would start. Not to tell you your job," Hanz said.

"It's being pulled. But you know how things work. The offices don't open for another hour or so." A pause. "Is there any way to tell whether the bodies were dead or alive when the place went up?"

Hanz shook his head. "Not my field of expertise. Coroner would be able to tell you. Maybe. Not a lot left of them other than bones and grilled flesh."

"Although…neither was twisted up like they were trying to shield themselves from the fire. You normally see defensive body language. Arms up or something," Levik observed.

Hanz shot him a dark look. "We aren't going to speculate. We'll need to get the big bus down here and set up a mobile lab to establish a definitive cause."

The tall officer offered a wan smile. "Always lovely to see you two."

Hanz's lips twitched. "Likewise."

The techs returned to the van and stowed their gear and then hopped in and drove off, leaving the officers to scratch their heads at their preliminary take. The senior of the pair turned to his partner and spoke in a low tone.

"What the hell have we walked into here? Drugs? Arms trafficking?"

The partner shrugged and wiped a thin layer of soot from his face. "I honestly have no idea, but it sounds like things are going to get interesting."

"Understatement of the year."

"Let's hope I'm wrong."

"I doubt it."

CHAPTER 32

Bohinjska Bistrica, Slovenia

The sun beamed through thin gauze curtains, dust motes dancing in the morning light, the lodge redolent of coffee Matt had made earlier. Hannah came running down the hall to where Matt was dozing on the sofa in the great room, her bare feet slapping against the varnished hardwood floor. Matt started to full consciousness and looked at her with concern.

"What is it, sweetheart?" he asked.

"It's your friend. He…go see him."

"Andrew? Is something wrong?" Matt asked, pushing to his feet.

"I think he's sick. He asked me to get you."

"All right. Stay here."

Matt made his way to the patron's room and rapped on the door. "Andrew?"

"Come in," Andrew answered.

Matt pushed the door open and entered. Andrew was sitting up in bed, his face covered in a sheen of sweat.

"I'm afraid I've taken a turn," Andrew said, his usual strong voice tremulous and weak.

"Damn. Let's get you to a doctor."

He shook his head. "No. It's a fever. Could be worse. But if it doesn't improve, yes, I'll probably need someone to come." Andrew coughed. "Can I ask you to go into town and see about a doctor? Just in case?"

Matt's expression soured. "There's been a complication." He told

Andrew about the truck and the drone. When he finished, Andrew closed his eyes.

"That's unfortunate. Who are they? Is it possible we've been compromised? Nobody knows we're here."

"I don't think this is related to your or Jet's business. These are lowlifes. Locals with too much time on their hands."

"The drone implies sophistication, however. And persistence. That's out of character for small-town riffraff."

"Agreed. Not sure what to make of it. I didn't do anything to draw their attention."

"All well and good, but if I require a doctor, not positive. And I could really use some aspirin to cut the fever."

"Can you call the handyman and get someone's number?"

"He still hasn't responded to my call the other day about the generator."

Matt thought for a moment. "I have an idea how I can make it to town. They're looking for the Jeep. But what if it was a different color?"

"How are you going to manage that?"

"There's some spray paint in the equipment room. Black primer. A case of it. Seems that's their idea of maintenance – spray some on whatever's rusting and hope for the best."

Andrew nodded weakly. "That could work."

"I'll give it a try and then head into town."

"I hate to ask you, but…"

"No. You're right to."

Matt walked back to where Hannah was waiting for him.

"Sweetheart, I'm going to work on the truck for a little while and then give it a test drive. Can you hang out here while I'm doing that?"

The little girl nodded. "I wish there was TV."

"Yes, that would be good. But don't you have your books? Maybe *The Little Prince*?"

"I've read it a lot."

"Well, try it again. They say it gets better every time."

Matt exited the lodge with a glance skyward and, seeing no drones, proceeded to the maintenance shed, where seven cans of paint sat in a rotting cardboard box. He removed three of them and a roll of masking tape and then walked to where the Jeep was still covered by the tarp.

An hour later, he stepped back and inspected his handiwork. The rusting silver heap was now flat black and looking like a teenager's dark fantasy. It was unmistakably a Jeep, but nothing about it would arouse suspicion unless they examined it closely. From a distance it was a different car. He'd taken care to remove the Jeep logo from the front and back, further obscuring the make to any but SUV enthusiasts.

Matt returned the empty cans and the tape to the shed and then started the engine and put it into gear. He eased down the drive and onto the road, the area as still as a mountain lake at dawn, the only sound the motor and the mating calls of birds.

Matt pointed the truck toward town. He was halfway to the outskirts, rounding a curve, when he braked hard. He squinted at the road ahead where it straightened after another bend, and frowned as he pulled the truck off the pavement and into the trees. He drove thirty meters until he hit a game trail and then parked where the Jeep wouldn't be seen and killed the engine.

Matt lowered himself from the driver's seat and closed the door after himself, taking care to do so softly lest the sound travel. He picked his way to the game trail and followed it as it paralleled the road. Ten minutes later, he paused at a thicket and peered through the trees at where a police car blocked the two-lane. He could see a cop standing nearby, smoking and talking in a low voice to a skinhead who could have been a twin of the thugs who'd nearly run Hannah down at the market.

Matt cursed at the sight and considered the implications. Whatever he'd stumbled into, it wasn't good if the bad guys had enough clout with law enforcement to mount a roadblock. He tried to tell himself that they weren't looking for him, since he hadn't done anything wrong; but after the drone, he feared the worst. For whatever reason, this group or gang was after him, and the cops were on their side. There was no other reasonable conclusion to draw.

Matt watched them for several minutes and then made his way back up the trail to his vehicle. There was no way he was going into town now. Never mind the Jeep – he was a stranger in a small berg, and he'd stick out wherever he went.

He twisted the ignition key and backed down to the road and then retraced his route to the lodge, his mind racing over the implications of the situation. With Andrew worsening and Hannah to worry about, he needed to come up with a workable plan, and fast.

Waiting for the other shoe to drop wasn't his style, and the best defense was usually an offense. The only unknowns being who he was going to go on the offense against, how many of them there were, and what they were involved in that he'd drawn their wrath.

CHAPTER 33

Warsaw, Poland

Ian and Jet sipped coffee in a breakfast restaurant down the street from a flat the Mossad had supplied to use as a safe house following the explosion. The other diners were working-class men and women, their uniforms and laborer hands giving them away as such, and Jet and Ian fit in with their haggard features, sleep having eluded them both the prior night after they'd left the hotel and transferred to the flat.

"So you're going back home?" Ian asked after another gulp of his steaming drink.

Jet shrugged. "I don't have a home. How about you?"

"There's nothing else to do here, is there?"

She shook her head. "Not that I can see. Unless you've got a new idea since our target vaporized in front of us."

"This was your play, not mine. But I'll need to talk to the director before I do anything."

"Ah, yes. The new boss." She paused. "Not at all the same as the old boss."

"He's a good guy. Just new at the job. He'll adjust."

"How long have you known him?"

Ian pushed his cup aside. "Long enough."

Jet nodded. "Very good. No need for me to know anything about you. Better that way."

"Likewise. There's a reason the rules are in place."

"I suppose so." She finished her coffee. "How long do you have the crash pad for?"

"As long as I need it."

"Mind if I catch up on my sleep before getting out of town?"

He sighed. "Sure, assuming they don't need it for some reason. I'll make my call shortly. Probably head back this evening unless they want me to stick around."

"What are you going to do about the car?" she asked.

"That's one of the items on my list. Our local guys can deal with it."

Ian had parked the vehicle on a side street around the corner from the flat, which was in a neighborhood where a trashed car wouldn't raise too many eyebrows. He'd torn apart a couple of cardboard cartons he'd filched from a dumpster and propped the material in the windshield cavity, so it looked right at home among the decrepit vehicles that lined the street.

Ian stood and flipped a couple of bills onto the table. "I'll see you back at the place. I'm beat. I'm going to grab a couple of hours of shut-eye before I talk to base."

She nodded. "I'll see you when I get back."

Ian had called and left a message with the duty desk after they'd escaped from the warehouse. That had been a good call on Ian's part, because driving around Warsaw without a windshield and with a hood that looked like a grenade had gone off near it might have aroused attention.

Jet watched him leave, and looked around the diner at the sorry collection of misery that were her fellow customers. She'd hit a dead end after getting close enough to taste victory, and the letdown was massive. Jet now had no options, no leads, no hope to do anything but return to her family and go on the run again, praying that whoever was behind the attempt on her wouldn't be able to find her – which she knew from experience was a fool's errand, since anyone could be found these days with technology and sufficient resources, just as they'd managed to find her in the middle of nowhere on an obscure Greek island.

Which left Jet with the unthinkable. She could either remain separated from her family in the hopes that they wouldn't track Matt and Hannah and use them to get to her, or join them and doom them to an existence of constant imminent danger. Either way, she was screwed, because there was an unknown entity out there unafraid of assassinating the head of the Mossad and coming after her, which meant they would never give up until they'd achieved their objective.

She eyed her cup and nodded when the waitress came by with a coffee pot. She held her finger halfway up the mug, and the woman nodded and poured it half full, showing no interest in Jet, her eyes dull with the resignation of someone who was running out the clock until they died, doing something they hated but unable to find anything better.

Jet could empathize. It had been a while since she'd felt this despondent, and the lack of sleep wasn't helping her mood.

When the woman left, Jet withdrew her burner phone and activated it and dialed Matt's burner cell, anxious to hear his voice. The phone rang four times and then went to voicemail, and her shoulders sagged as she waited for the beep to leave her message.

"Hey. I thought we had something, but it went south. Hope you're okay. Keep a sharp eye out. Whoever's out there still is."

Jet hung up and slipped the phone back into her pocket. She was exhausted, and her nerves were frayed, the stress from worrying about her family and hunting down the hunter wearing at her. Jet needed sleep and a plan; continuing to operate on adrenaline and deprivation was a bad idea any way she sliced it.

She took a final pull at her coffee and left the remainder, committed to getting some rest before determining her next step. Racing like a hamster on a wheel would simply deplete her already scarce resources, and right now she needed all she could get.

Jet stood and tossed another bill onto Ian's and then walked slowly to the exit, feeling as low as she ever had. She hoped Matt would listen to her message and leave one of his own soon, but her desire to hear his voice was selfish and not because she had anything optimistic to share.

She exited the restaurant and glanced both ways and then crossed the street and trudged back to the apartment. Her eyes were burning from lack of sleep, her ears still ringing from the explosion, and her skin tender from the blast. Every step she took was leaden and labored, the dull ache that had started just behind her eyes spreading through her skull like a malignancy.

CHAPTER 34

Moscow, Russian Federation

The mood in the boardroom was celebratory, the board members joking with one another. Artem saluted them with a crystal tumbler half full of expensive vodka and offered a toast. The men raised their glasses, and all threw back the liquor with glee, their eyes watering from the high-octane alcohol. Artem took a seat at the head of the table and placed his empty glass in front of him. He scanned their faces before clearing his throat and speaking.

"The Chinese threat has been dealt with in a deniable fashion," he said. "There's no way to trace it back to us, but there's no way they can pretend not to know who was responsible. So they can save face by pretending to not know, while we've delivered a powerful message about accountability and what happens to anyone who crosses the line with us – whatever their position or resources."

"It was a bold move, I'll grant you that. But we don't know what blowback will result from it," Rudolf countered.

"All due respect, that wasn't the point," Artem said.

"I understand the desire to take a victory lap; I'm simply pointing out that this move carries an unknown risk," Rudolf said.

"The objective was to make clear that the consequences to be expected for assassinating one of us are extreme, no matter their standing. Hit a rattlesnake on the head with a stick, you get bitten. Simple. Even for our adversaries to figure out."

Rudolf looked to the others and then back to Artem. "Let's hope it works the way you think. If the Chinese walk away from our joint agreements, we'll be in serious trouble."

"They won't. Zhang took extreme measures. We merely returned the favor. They'll understand the precedent was set by him when he killed Nicolai."

One of the others held his glass up. "Enough of the bickering. I'm out of vodka!"

Everyone laughed, and the men passed the bottle around for the third time, their cheeks flushed and smiles easy. When Artem excused himself, they were laughing good-naturedly, backslapping and ribbing one another over past indiscretions or failures.

He made his way back to his corner office, light-headed from the unexpected late morning alcohol, a smile on his face from how delighted all the board – save Rudolf – had been. So long as he continued to perform and enjoy the sorts of successes he'd demonstrated in just the first days of his leadership, he'd be a lock for permanently heading up one of the most powerful entities in Russia, and Rudolf's sniping would mean nothing.

Artem brushed past his secretary's desk, and his eyes lingered on her gentle curves and ample charms, but then the chirp of one of the cell phones on his desk drew his attention, and he hurried into the office and shut his door behind him. He eyed the phone's screen and activated it as he held it to his ear.

"Yes?"

"I need a favor."

Artem frowned. "We have a business relationship. I pay you. That's the extent of it."

"I'll credit you against future jobs. I'd think you'd be ecstatic after Scotland."

Artem ignored the implicit threat in the mention of the assassination. "You're quickly becoming rich. You don't need favors from me when you can afford whatever you want."

"Just hear me out. I have a problem in Warsaw. I know you're close enough to be able to deal with it in a matter of hours, and time's critical on this one."

Artem lowered his voice. "I'm not in the same business as you."

"I understand that. But I would also imagine that you can snap your fingers and find people who could solve my problem. Whereas I would have to try to locate a dependable group, which could take days I don't have."

"Explain," he snapped.

Artem listened for several minutes, his expression clouding as the voice continued. By the time the caller stopped speaking, his mind was churning.

"So this is really solving a mutual problem," the caller finished.

Artem grunted. "I don't see it that way. I don't have a beef with this woman. It was Nicolai's fight, not mine."

"She may not see it that way. In which case you'll be looking over your shoulder for the rest of your days. And if I were placing bets, I wouldn't wager on your having many of them, given her résumé."

Artem thought for a moment. "Let's say I agree. I can't be active in any way."

"I understand. I can run point. Just give me a liaison, and I'll do the rest."

He exhaled hard. "You ask for much."

"As I deliver. Which you know."

A pause.

"Fine," Artem agreed. "I'll put someone in contact with you shortly."

"Underscore the sensitivity and urgency, please."

"Will do."

Artem disconnected and tossed the phone onto his desk. He was annoyed at the imposition, but reasoned that he could turn the favor owed to his advantage in time. Rudolf was already proving to be a source of irritation, and Artem would no doubt face other situations that could benefit from an…unorthodox…solution, just as had the Chinese problem.

"Keep your friends close…" he murmured, and depressed the button on his office comm line. His secretary answered, and he leaned forward as he spoke.

"Please locate Leonid and have him come to my office immediately."

"Leonid? In security?"

"That's right."

"Yes, sir."

Fifteen minutes later, Leonid was standing in front of Artem's desk, and he again was taken aback at the man's imposing stature. Artem sat forward in his executive chair and locked eyes with the big man.

"I have a sensitive assignment I need some help with. A messy situation a friend's in. Can I depend on your discretion?"

"Of course, sir. You have my word."

"Very well. There's a problem in Poland, and I promised I could source a team to go there and clean it up. Do you have any contacts who could do this?"

Leonid's massive forehead crinkled as he thought. "I'm sure my brother does. I'll ask."

Artem's tone softened. "How's he doing? I heard he's improving."

"Getting better every day, although he's still weak."

"Would you ask who he would use there, and make it happen?"

Leonid nodded. "Budget?"

"Whatever's reasonable. But I don't see any reason to break the bank. You can discuss what's going to be necessary with my friend." He tossed Leonid the burner cell he'd taken the earlier call on. "Just press redial."

"Time frame?" Leonid asked.

"Immediate."

Leonid nodded. "I'll get over to the hospital to talk to my brother, and I'll handle it. You want to be kept in the loop?"

Artem shook his head. "No. I'm very busy. Just let me know how it all turns out. And I don't want you directly involved either, are we clear? You're to act as a facilitator, connecting party A with party B, but no active involvement. We can't take foolish risks where there's no upside." Artem paused. "And Leonid? This meeting never happened, understand? If anything goes wrong or you're ever asked, we never talked."

Leonid examined the phone and then looked at Artem. "Got it. Off the books. I presume you'll authorize someone to get me whatever operational cash we need?"

"Yes. Just let me know the amount." Leonid turned to go, and Artem cleared his throat. "Give my regards to Sergei. I hope he recovers quickly."

"Thank you. That makes two of us."

Leonid left with the phone, and Artem stared at his desktop for a full minute before shifting some papers from one side to the other. The big convict had seemed willing enough, and it might come in handy to create the equivalent of a Praetorian guard for himself as he became more entrenched. His brother, Sergei, had been one of Nicolai's right-hand men, so the family's loyalty wasn't subject to question in spite of the spurious concerns that had followed the airport attack.

He was aware of Leonid's failure in Seychelles, yet he suspected there might have been more to that story than he'd heard. Likewise, the big man hadn't been in charge of Nicolai's Cyprus security, but merely repurposed there at the last minute, so he couldn't be held accountable for failing to protect Nicolai.

Warsaw would be out of both of their hands – all Leonid would do would be to put Artem's friend in touch with whomever Sergei recommended, and let them take it from there. It seemed simple enough, but as Artem knew, the best-laid plans could quickly go sideways, especially when he was unable or unwilling to control every step.

That his "friend" had been willing to impose upon him was a completely different issue, and one that he'd have to deal with in time. Still, he'd run the equation in his head, and having them owe him was net positive, considering the amount of effort he'd be required to put forth. Plus he'd more than double bill for whatever he had to advance to get the team in the air, so in the end he would come out on top no matter how things turned out.

Another winning equation in his continuing string.

CHAPTER 35

Bohinjska Bistrica, Slovenia

Matt parked the Jeep and took the stairs to the lodge two at a time. When he entered, Hannah was in the great room, sitting on the floor with her books, humming to herself. He greeted her and then went to look in on Andrew, who appeared worse for wear.

"We have a problem," Matt said by way of greeting as he entered Andrew's bedroom. "Couldn't make it into town. The police have a car blocking the road, and one of the skinheads is hanging out with them. Doesn't take a genius to see what's going on."

Andrew scowled. "The generator guy finally called back. I asked him about your new friends. All he would say is that they're bad guys – not from around here. Thinks they're Romanian or Bulgarian; everyone avoids them. Apparently, there's eight of them living in a run-down house near here. He's repaired their gas lines and said he saw guns on one of the tables. Small world. Their place is about a quarter kilometer down the road."

Matt shook his head. "Great. So I've somehow gotten into it with the local mafia? Over nothing? So much for keeping my head down."

"If the police are helping them, I can get us a helo or a plane, but we need to make it to wherever it lands without them catching on. And it isn't like there are a ton of flat clearings here."

"You're in no shape to move," Matt observed.

"I'm resilient. I can do it if I have to."

"Be better to avoid it," Matt said. "Our neighbors, huh? Maybe I should do a little recon? See what I'm dealing with?"

Andrew scowled. "Risky, given the cop angle."

"Got any better ideas?"

"I'll make some calls and see how soon I can get us transpo. That's about all I can do right now."

"And then what?"

"We can figure it out once we're in the air. There are plenty of remote locations to choose from in this region. Hungary. Serbia. Montenegro. Albania."

"Once you alert your people about where you are, that opens a whole new can of worms, doesn't it?"

"Sure. But if you have crooked locals working with what sounds like a criminal gang, seems the smart move is not to play."

"No argument. Did the handyman say which direction their house was?"

"On the way into town. Second drive from ours."

"Unbelievable."

Matt left Andrew and retrieved one of the spare magazines for the pistol from his room. He stopped where Hannah was amusing herself, and smiled.

"I'll be back in a shake," he said.

"Again?"

"I have to look at something. You okay here?"

She returned her attention to the books and shrugged. "I guess."

He nodded and made for the door. Outside, he walked down to the road and then crossed to where the trail ran alongside, deeper in the trees. He followed it towards town, pausing periodically to confirm he hadn't missed a drive. When he came to the second one from the lodge, he watched the road for several minutes before jogging across to where a gate barred his entry. Matt followed the barbed-wire fence that delineated the property along the two-lane, and then trotted along the perimeter up the side of the lot until he came to a spot where a tree branch had fallen and flattened one of the wooden fence posts, allowing him to step over the sharp wire onto the grounds.

Fog clung to the moist earth, increasing in density as he pushed farther onto the property. A small creek ran along the periphery, and he skirted it deeper into the woods until he saw the house in the near distance – an ugly deteriorating wood structure badly in need of a coat of paint and some roof repair, judging by the corrugated steel patches that dotted the slopes where the tile had come off. Most of the homes he'd seen in the area were simple but well maintained, with pride of ownership evident in the bright colors and clean landscaping. This, however, looked like it had been all but abandoned.

A trio of older vehicles were parked randomly on a circular gravel area in front of the house, their condition matching that of the building. But no lifted Nissan. So his new friends were out.

Matt's gaze drifted to the motion-detector-activated lights mounted below the roofline. He counted three on just the front façade, cementing his impression that the thugs were doing something sketchy inside. Likely drugs, he thought, from how strung out the ones who'd mad-dog stared him had appeared.

He picked his way closer to the house, using the trees for cover, and was halfway there when he tripped and pitched face forward. Matt landed hard, and it knocked the wind out of him. A white-hot lance of pain shot through his lower ribs on his left side, where his elbow had struck them with his full weight as he'd tried to break the fall. He winced, and his breath hissed through his teeth. He was struggling to recover when the front door of the house flew open, and four men spilled from the doorway, pistols in hand.

Matt glanced at his boots and saw the line of monofilament that had brought him down – a classic low-tech tripwire that had obviously sounded an alarm inside. He rolled away and crawled a half dozen meters from where he'd dropped, but the men were already fanning out and heading towards him. He pushed himself to his feet, ignoring the agony that was his entire left side, and moved deeper into the forest, hoping he could lose the gunmen rather than have to engage.

Shots rang out, and bark tore from a tree trunk a couple of feet from him, making it clear that his hope of evasion was an empty one. He pressed himself against the trunk and waited until he heard branches cracking underfoot, and then darted to another tree, firing six times when he was in the open.

A scream greeted him from one of his pursuers, and he smiled grimly as they shouted to each other in what he assumed was Romanian. The disorganized yelling and their headlong hurtle towards him confirmed they were rank amateurs, and he almost felt sorry for them when he dropped to a crouch and fired three more times from behind the cover of the trunk.

The unmistakable sound of a body collapsing into the brush told him that the odds had been evened more closely with two against one – but two dope-sick punks against an adversary with decades of jungle fighting and specialized combat training. He paused as they took stock of their situation, knowing that it would be a fifty-fifty chance they'd retreat, and was thinking that he might have gotten lucky when the sharp staccato bark of an assault rifle on full automatic shattered the silence from the house, and the brush around him shredded from the undisciplined fire. He waited until the gun's magazine was empty, and spotted a dark figure creeping around to his right, trying to flank him. Matt's pistol bucked in his hand twice, and the gunman dropped with a cry.

The automatic fire began again from the porch with equal efficacy, doing nothing but expending ammo and buying Matt more time for his next move. Then the shooting abruptly stopped, signaling another empty magazine, and Matt darted to where the last gunman he'd shot lay facedown, an ugly exit wound in his upper back staining his black concert T-shirt. Matt waited for another attack, but none came, and after he was sure that the random shooting into the trees was over, he moved away from the house, back to the stream.

He picked up speed once at the water and was half-running by the time he made it to the fence. The gunfight had definitively ended any chance they could remain at the lodge, and now the game would be about how to evade the local police and however many of the skinheads who'd survived, and make it out of the area in one piece.

A trick that would grow more difficult as time passed.

Although because of their location, so far from town, it was possible that the gunfire hadn't been heard by anyone.

A possibility he knew he couldn't rely on.

Andrew's degrading condition only amplified the pressure Matt felt with Hannah in his charge, knowing that there was an actively hostile force hunting them. He had no idea why, but now that he'd killed at least three of them, he'd learned two things: that they were willing to use deadly force without question, and that they had something worth killing over in their lair. The latter would ordinarily have been knowledge he could have used against them with an anonymous call to the police, but because at least some of the force was in bed with them, as evidenced by the roadblock, that was off the table.

He slowed after stepping across the fallen fence and surveyed the forest behind him, listening for sounds of pursuit, silently cursing the tinnitus the gunfire had induced. Matt gently probed his brutalized ribs and grimaced at what could only be fractures, the pain extraordinary despite the relative toughness of the rib cage. He knew from years of nursing broken bones that there was nothing he could do about the injury but avoid strain and give it time.

For now, Matt needed to make his way back to the lodge and figure out how to get out of Slovenia with Hannah and Andrew, while not leading anyone trying to track him directly back to the lodge grounds. That meant a more circuitous route home, which equated to more lost time, which would translate into worse odds they would get clear without incident.

All because some punks had decided to pick on the wrong man.

The stupidity of it was mind boggling; but then again, in his experience, criminals tended to be stupid except for the career ones who'd chosen occupations like banker, lawyer, or politician. That anyone involved in something nefarious had tempted fate by moving aggressively against an unknown defied logic, but there he was, injured in the woods after having killed three men he'd never met, for reasons unknown.

He set off back down the hill, but veered in the opposite direction from the lodge, figuring that anyone trying to follow would be able to track him to the road, after which they'd assume he was continuing to town – a bit of subterfuge he hoped would be enough to buy him sufficient breathing room to organize a pickup with Andrew and put the entire Slovenian adventure behind him before the police got involved and a nationwide manhunt started.

Although the one thing he had going for him was that if he was right about the house, then it was unlikely the skinheads would go the official route.

It wasn't much in terms of breaks, but he'd take it and run with it.

And with any luck at all, make it out of another tight spot by the skin of his teeth.

Ignoring the pain from his chest, he increased his pace, cognizant that each passing minute was working against him, the chill that traced its way up his spine persistent in spite of the morning sun shining through the treetops, warming his way.

CHAPTER 36

Warsaw, Poland

Four men wearing nondescript dark clothes and knit caps emptied from a green van with a yellow and red logo of a dancing corncob painted on the side. They split into pairs, one walking down the sidewalk behind the van, the other moving ahead of it in the opposite direction. All were equipped with flesh-colored earbuds and had satchels strapped across their chests, their expressions serious as pallbearers.

The first pair passed a market, and one of the men tapped his earbud and spoke softly. "We're in position."

A voice responded seconds later. "Do you see the car?"

"Affirmative."

"They went out of range about thirty meters down the street, so they have to be in the building beside the furniture store. It's the only residential unit before the next block."

"Roger that. No signs of any surveillance."

"Copy that. Go in hard. No need for subtlety here. In and out, nothing left breathing."

"10-4."

Their employer had tracked the car from the industrial area by tapping into the traffic cameras at the major interchanges, and had then followed its progress to a hotel and then to its current spot, where it had remained immobile for seven hours. A street view search using sat imagery had narrowed down where the driver must have gone, since nobody appeared on the footage from the cross-street camera. Which meant their target had to be in the duplex, and from the graffiti on the windows of the ground-floor unit, that left the upstairs.

Jet turned the corner and strolled towards the flat, the walk having invigorated her and helped clear her head. She'd stopped at a park on the way to watch an old woman feed a flock of pigeons from a worn plastic bag, the stale bread a delicacy for the starving birds. A trio of youths had noisily ridden their skateboards through the pigeons, sending them flapping skyward before returning, and the woman had shouted at them in Polish, her angry exclamation requiring no translation for Jet to understand.

The boys had circled back around for another go at disrupting the feeding, but Jet had blocked them on the narrow concrete path, hands on her hips. When they'd ridden up to her, she'd shaken her head, and something about her demeanor had warned the youths off, albeit with a couple of shouted expletives as they'd ridden away in search of less confrontational amusement. Jet had waited to return to her vantage point until she'd been sure they'd left the park, and smiled at the old woman when she'd said something to her in a grateful tone.

Jet had eyed a pair of young girls, about Hannah's age, as they ran from tree to tree, squealing in delight while their mothers watched from a nearby bench, and she'd felt a pang of longing, the idyllic scene a reminder of how abnormal her life was and how messed up Hannah's childhood had been so far. She'd promised herself repeatedly to find someplace her daughter could grow up in normal surroundings, but circumstances had conspired against her, and here she was in Poland, unsure of what the future might hold, but afraid that whatever it was, it couldn't be good.

Jet had departed the park when the pigeons took to the sky following their meal, and had enjoyed the warmth of the sun on her face as she'd made her way back to the flat, all worries about things she couldn't control temporarily banished in favor of the simple pleasure of a balmy late morning while the world went about its business.

She looked up in preparation to cross the street to the flat, and slowed when a van stopped at the curb in a no-parking zone and disgorged a group of men who had the distinctive look of professionals.

They split up, and two of them walked slowly towards the flat while the others hurried away in the other direction – a classic, round-the-block move right out of the textbooks designed to verify there were no back ways out of the building or surveillance that wasn't obvious from the front.

Jet slid her cell from her pocket and dialed Ian's number, but it went straight to message, indicating he was either on the line or the phone was off. She whispered a curse and tried again, and this time Ian answered with an annoyed tone.

"I can't talk," he snapped. "On the line with HQ."

"There's a team of four on the street, canvasing the area. They look like they mean business."

"What? Stay on the line."

She felt in her pocket for the pistol and the bulky suppressor cylinder, and then Ian was back.

"Where are you?" he asked.

"Down the block. I'm grabbing a seat at the French bakery so I can keep an eye out."

"They look like police?"

"Negative."

"Then…what?"

"Don't know, but you need to get out of there. Is there another way other than through the front door?"

"No."

"What about the roof?"

He hesitated. "I've never been up there."

"Go up. Is there anything you can rig the flat with?"

"Rig?"

"Like a gas stove or heater."

"There's a stove."

She thought for an instant. "Landline in there?"

Another longer pause. "Yes."

"Do you have the number?"

"It's written on the bottom."

"There you go. Turn the gas on in the oven and all the burners, and get to the roof. They look like they're about to go inside. Call me once you're up there."

"How did they...?"

"I'm hoping we can find out. Now hurry."

Jet took a seat at one of the four tables on the sidewalk and ordered a small tea. She pretended to peruse the menu while she looked over the top at the van and the front stoop of the duplex, waiting for the men to make their move.

The pair who'd rounded the block joined their companions in front of the walkup, and one of them ascended the steps and crossed to the doorknob while the rest kept an eye out. Jet sank lower, her face shielded from view by the menu, and after a few seconds dared a peek at the building. The point man had jimmied the door, and the other three were climbing the porch stairs to join him, moving with obvious haste.

Jet's phone vibrated, and she raised it to her ear. "They're in," she said. "Figure sixty seconds to get to the flat, another thirty, tops, for the lock. They got the front open in less than fifteen." She hesitated. "Hang on. Looks like one of them is staying downstairs. Standing guard."

"We're really going to do this?"

"Hope the flat's in a shell company's name, because it's going to get messy." She checked her watch. "Call the landline in forty-five seconds."

"Okay. Here goes nothing."

The line went dead, and Jet slid the phone back into her pocket. The waitress arrived with her tea, and Jet handed her a bill and indicated she could keep the change. Then she reached in and felt for the suppressor. She threaded it one-handed onto the pistol barrel and tossed back half the tea when she was done, counting silently to herself.

The blast shook the street, and twin fireballs blew out the front windows and sent debris flying down onto the sidewalk. Jet stood and crossed to the corner behind the van, narrowly missing being hit by a car that skidded to a stop in the middle of the lane, the driver transfixed by the sight of the flames belching from the building's façade. When she arrived at the van's open driver's side window, she drew her gun and leveled it at the driver's head.

If the man was in any way surprised, he didn't show it, his expression stony, the cigarette in his right hand rock steady.

"Who are you?" she demanded in English and then in Russian, but the man's face didn't change except for his eyes drifting down to her pistol and then back to Jet.

He shrugged, and then the sound of shooting echoed along the street. Jet dared a sidelong glance and spotted Ian clutching his side, firing at the lookout, who was crouched on the sidewalk a third of the way to where the van was parked, shooting back. Two of Ian's rounds thwacked into the lookout's abdomen as another of the shooter's slugs hit Ian in the chest, and both men collapsed, blood drenching the concrete around them.

Jet was turning back towards the driver when he raised a Glock. She blew his throat out with a point-blank shot, spackling the interior of the cab with bloody gore and sending a crimson aortal geyser across the windshield. The man dropped the gun and clutched at his ruined throat as he slumped in his seat, his lifeblood pulsing from him with every stuttering contraction of his heart.

"Damn," Jet exclaimed, and then ran to where the lookout lay and kicked his gun into the gutter before racing to Ian, who was fighting for breath.

He grinned as he looked at her with unfocused eyes, his teeth stained crimson with his blood, and he coughed up a small river of it.

"Don't try to talk," she said, kneeling by his side.

"I'm…done…" he managed, and then coughed up more blood and drew in a labored gasp that ended with a wet gurgle. His eyes fluttered closed, and he stiffened and lay still as the building burned behind him.

Jet waited to see whether anyone made it out of the inferno, and when nobody did, returned to the dead lookout and frisked him. She found his wallet and pocketed it, removed her phone and took a photo of his face, and then did the same with the driver, who'd bled out in short order. Jet opened the door and dragged him from the vehicle and then climbed behind the wheel and drove off, leaving his body for the rats.

She drove for ten minutes and then dumped the van in a vacant lot on the outskirts of town, after wiping it down so there were no prints to process. Once she'd put sufficient distance between herself and the van, she stopped and took stock. She had a change of clothes in her backpack, and she ducked into a doorway, shrugged out of her pants and shirt, and donned clean ones that weren't blood-soaked before continuing on, no destination in mind, her exhaustion replaced by adrenaline jitters and a sinking feeling in her gut.

Jet eventually found a café and took a seat inside and ordered coffee and a fruit bowl. When the server had gone to process her order, she went to the bathroom and rummaged through the wallets, expecting nothing given the professionalism of the team. Other than two hundred euros apiece and Polish driver's licenses that looked forged to her trained eye, the only other clue was a scrap of brown paper with the safe house address scrawled on it.

In Cyrillic script.

Which wasn't used in Poland.

Her heart skipped as she processed the implications, and then she dumped the wallets sans the IDs and the money and walked back to her table, eyes on a television mounted above the cash register. The burning mass of the flat was being featured in a live TV broadcast that also cut away to the corpses covered by tarps. What she could glean was being described as an organized crime battle gone wrong.

Her drink came, and she sipped it as she collected her thoughts. Then she dialed Noah's private line. When he answered, she spoke softly, eyes roaming around the empty café.

"The operation went sideways. Your man didn't make it," she said.

"What? How?"

"A wet team attacked your safe house. Might want to think about how they knew about it."

"Good lord…"

"Ian was a good agent. Died in the line of duty."

Noah sighed. "Which unfortunately will go unremarked, as you know."

"See to it that his family gets his full pension."

Noah hesitated. "I sense there's more. Who's responsible for this? Can't be the bomber. Ian told me he's dead."

"He is. This must be another actor. I'm going to send you some photos of two of the hit team – the driver and one of the gunmen. Run it through the database and let me know what you find out. I trust I can send it the usual way?"

"Write this down. I have a private encrypted email box."

He gave her the address, and she nodded to herself. "I suspect they're Russian. Could be freelancers, but maybe not. I need to get out of Warsaw immediately. Can you help?"

"Are you compromised?"

"Negative, but I have no idea who knows what at this point. In light of all the fireworks, it seems foolhardy to stay in one place for long."

"Agreed. What do you need?"

"A reliable way out of the country would be good. Maybe to Lithuania? It's only a few hundred miles."

"Let me see what I can arrange. I presume your papers will withstand scrutiny?"

"It's always better if I fly below the radar so there's no record of me coming or going."

"Understood. Keep your phone on."

"Will do."

CHAPTER 37

St. Andrews, Scotland

A black Rolls Royce limousine pulled up outside the coroner's office, and a diminutive Asian man got out of the back and walked to the front entrance. A Vauxhall Combo-e Life stopped behind it, and three muscular Asians in black suits stepped out and followed him at a respectful distance, scanning the surroundings with calm detachment before taking up station on either side of the door. The small man entered the building and walked to the counter, where a heavyset woman with bluish hair was munching on a meat pie. She placed it on a polystyrene tray and looked over her spectacles at him.

"Yes? May I help you?" she asked.

"I'm here to see my brother," he said in good English. "Lun Zhang. He passed away recently, and I was told he was being kept here?"

"Your name?"

"Bai Zhang."

"ID, please," she said, waggling sausage fingers at him, her tone conveying annoyed disinterest.

Bai handed her his passport and waited as she studied it like it was holy scripture. After a long pause, she picked up a phone on the counter and spoke into it.

"Glen? We've got a situation. A gentleman is here about his brother's remains." She listened for a moment. "Zhang. The Chinaman." Another pause, and she set the phone back on the counter and indicated a row of metal chairs against the far wall. "Have a seat, and someone will be with you shortly," she said.

"And my passport?" Bai asked.

"In good time," she said dismissively, and went back to eating, their interaction clearly at an end.

Bai sat where instructed, his expression conveying nothing, and after five minutes checked his watch and approached the counter again. "Will someone be with me soon? I'm afraid I'm on a schedule."

"Dr. Fenway will be out as soon as he's able. He's probably conducting an examination," she said, clearly put out by his question.

"Any idea how long?"

"I'm afraid not. He doesn't consult me with these things."

Bai returned to his seat and busied himself with his phone. Twenty minutes later, a tall, lanky man in his fifties, thinning brown hair askew, emerged from a pair of steel double doors at the back of the room, his blue smock and matching trousers announcing him as staff.

"Mr. Zhang, is it?" he asked as he approached where Bai was seated.

Bai stood and bowed slightly. "Yes."

Fenway motioned to the double doors. "Please, this way. My office is a mess. I hope you'll forgive me."

Bai followed the doctor through the doors into a cluttered office, where he sat before an industrial desk with an old computer monitor on it, the surface strewn with paperwork. Fenway sat in a swivel chair behind it, and steepled his fingers as he eyed Bai.

"I'm afraid I have bad news," he began.

"Yes, I know he's dead," Bai said. "I'm just here to arrange to pick up his remains."

"No, that's not it. I mean, yes, quite, but I'm afraid we can't release the body."

Bai looked confused. "I don't understand."

Fenway sighed heavily. "Your brother's corpse is evidence at this stage. Additionally, it's under a biohazard hold."

"Well, release it. We have a right to give him a proper funeral and put him to rest. I came all the way from China to get him."

"I sympathize, but I'm afraid my hands are tied. He was poisoned. Hemlock. As such, his remains are toxic. They'll require special handling."

"Fair enough. Just tell me what is necessary, and I will arrange for it, as I said before. I'm not planning to carry him to the plane myself."

"The best I can do is notify you when the police have released the body. And I'll consult with customs on what's required to export a biohazard corpse. Quite frankly, in thirty years of work, I've never had to do so."

"I'm prepared to cooperate however you indicate; however, I'm only in England for a short period and need to get this handled."

"As I said, it's not up to me. The police are still investigating your brother's murder, and until they say they're finished, the body must remain here. I'm terribly sorry. I understand how troubling this must be."

Bai rose and fixed Fenway with a cold stare. "You have no idea how troubling it is. None at all. I've flown halfway around the world to deal with this in person, and you're telling me there's nothing you can do? It's outrageous."

"If you'd like to speak to the investigating detective or the captain…"

"I want my brother's body. That's all. A simple request."

"Yes. All I can say is that I'll see what I can do, but nothing in these cases moves quickly."

Fenway escorted Bai back to the waiting area, and when the doctor had returned to his office, Bai glared at the portly woman. "My passport. Now," he said, steel in his tone.

She swallowed hard and fumbled with the papers in front of her and retrieved it from beneath a folder and handed it to him. "Here you are," she said.

"You people are horrible," Bai said. "If you were in my country, you'd be scrubbing toilets or worse."

The woman glowered at him. "Well, we're not in your country, are we? And if you make any trouble, you'll wish you'd never showed your face here."

Bai stalked from the building and made for the limousine. He stopped at the curb and motioned for his men to join him, and spoke in quiet tones for several minutes before climbing back into the car, his features dark as the gathering clouds.

CHAPTER 38

Warsaw, Poland

Jet was seated by a children's play area at a local mall, to all appearances a young mother going about her innocent business of killing time by shopping. Her phone vibrated, and she answered it quickly. Noah's voice was uncharacteristically tense.

"There's a prop plane at Warsaw Modlin Airport," he said. "Private aviation terminal. Sky Charters. Pilot name Werner Zeiss. He's ready whenever you are."

"Destination?"

"He says that Riga, Latvia, is easier to get in and out of than Vilnius. And has more options if you need to fly somewhere else."

"Fine. I don't really care. Anything on the photos I sent?"

"We got a hit, but we need more time."

"How long will it take to get to Riga?"

"Couple of hours. Maybe a bit more. Not sure how fast the plane is."

"Have whatever you've got waiting for me when I touch down. Do you have any assets there?"

"None I'd trust with this."

She thought for a moment. "At least you're being honest."

"Ian was my friend. I have no idea what you've gotten yourself into, but now it's no longer just your problem."

"Are you forgetting that the director was murdered in cold blood by whoever the bomber was working for?"

"You're assuming the attack was connected."

"Really? You're going to play this that way?" She bit back the insult that was rising in her throat. "It's a reasonable inference given the timing, wouldn't you say? Or do you think it's coincidence that someone blew up the warehouse, and then we were attacked less than twelve hours later?"

"We don't know the bomber didn't blow up the warehouse. Trigger it somehow. Dead man switch."

"There were security cameras there. I'd bet hard money someone was monitoring those, and when they saw the fight, they eliminated any evidence. Burro included."

"I'm not saying you're wrong. Just that there's nothing conclusive."

"Welcome to the real world. By the time the desk jockeys have all their t's crossed and i's dotted, it's too late. Someone triggering the explosives at the warehouse is the only thing that makes sense. The bomber was in no condition to do anything, much less commit suicide."

"He could have had a trigger on him. Did you search him?"

Jet exhaled in frustration. "No. He was badly wounded. I don't buy that he killed himself."

"And I can't rule it out."

"I'm headed to the airport. Werner. Private aviation terminal. Just do as I ask, please. We're losing time."

"I'll see what I can come up with."

Jet hung up and looked around the mall. If the police were looking for her, bus or train stations were the likeliest places, not a shopping mall. She had no reason to believe they were, but you could wind up dead if you assumed, and she had no interest in joining the body count this adventure was racking up.

She hefted her backpack and walked to the exit. Once outside, she headed down the street to where a couple of taxis were parked, their drivers smoking and drinking coffee near a bronze statue of some uniformed dignitary from a bygone era. Jet approached them and greeted them in Russian. One of the men looked her up and down and gave her an oily smile before responding in rough Russian.

"*Da?*"

"I want to go to a shop near Modlin airport," she said.

He named a price, and she nodded agreement. He grinned at his companion, dropped his cigarette to the pavement, and ground it out with his boot.

"We go now," he said, and led her to one of the cars. He opened the rear door, and she tossed her backpack in and climbed in beside it. The driver circled around and slid behind the wheel, started the engine, and then twisted to look at her over his shoulder.

"Cash, *da*?"

"*Da*."

The car lurched forward, and Jet settled into the back seat, relieved to be leaving Poland, and hopefully all the ugly memories she'd accumulated in the last twenty-four hours, behind. She watched as the city transitioned into forested land and then freshly plowed fields as far as the eye could see before the highway crossed the Vistula River and the airport swam into view.

Jet leaned forward and spoke slowly in Russian. "I think I want to go to the airport. Changed my mind."

"Airport? *Da*."

She had the driver drop her off in front of the departure terminal, and waited until he drove away before walking to the end of the terminal and activating her navigation software to see how far she was from the private aviation area. It turned out to be about one kilometer, and she set out towards it, the breeze fresh and the temperature refreshingly crisp.

When she arrived, she walked up to a young woman at a computer screen and asked in Russian for Sky Charters. The clerk frowned and pointed at a long hangar and went back to whatever she was doing, uninterested in her. Jet exited the building and crossed to the hangar, where there were a dozen older single-engine planes parked close together. A tall man with long gray hair cinched into a tight ponytail watched her approach, and nodded to her when she was within earshot.

"Werner Zeiss?" she asked.

He patted the Bonanza he was working on. "English, Russian, Polish, or German?"

"English is fine," she said.

"I was told to expect one passenger. I'm guessing you're it?"

"Correct."

He pointed at a door in the corner. "Might want to use the bathroom before we take off. Flight can seem a lot longer when you have to go."

"Good advice. How soon can we be in the air?"

"That it for luggage?" he asked, eyeing her backpack.

"Yes."

"Then as soon as you're done in there. That work for you?"

"It does."

She used the bathroom, and when she came out, Werner was closing up a hatch.

"We've got full fuel, not that we'll need it. Climb aboard and buckle up. This your first time in a small plane?"

She shook her head. "I know the drill."

"Good. Shouldn't be any surprises. Weather shows mostly clear, scattered clouds, twenty-knot crosswind in Riga, so a little dicey on landing, but nothing this old bird can't handle."

"Then let's get going."

"You got papers? Just want to be straight about what I'm walking into."

Jet nodded. "I do. But I'd rather not have to show them."

"Might have to, but it isn't like they're all that efficient, so it'll likely be a clerk giving them a glance."

"Hope so."

After a short wait they were airborne, climbing at a couple of thousand feet per minute. Jet watched as the airport disappeared behind them, and once they were at cruising altitude, closed her eyes, the monotonous drone of the engine a single-note lullaby that put her to sleep within moments, her troubles left far below, if only briefly.

CHAPTER 39

Bohinjska Bistrica, Slovenia

Matt emerged from the brush near the lodge drive, sweat beading his brow from creating false trails to confuse anyone trying to track him. He'd expected to hear sirens from arriving police, but nothing had marred the bucolic silence save the occasional hum of tires on the road and the roar of a big truck engine air-braking on the grade. Matt glanced down the pavement, and when he saw nothing, jogged across it, grimacing with each jarring footfall as his ribs protested the jostling.

He would have to tape them when he had a chance, but right now his impetus was to get packed and move before a full-scale manhunt was mounted by the gang's conspirators on the police force. He had no doubt that he'd stumbled onto some sort of drug or human trafficking enterprise, which would mean sufficient money to co-opt the cops anywhere in the world, but especially in Slovenia, where things were tough and cash hard to come by.

Matt made it to the front stoop and paused, breathing heavily. When he'd caught his breath, he opened the front door and smiled at Hannah, who leapt to her feet and threw herself at him, nearly knocking him down the porch steps in the process.

"You're back!" she exclaimed excitedly.

"I am, honey. But I have to pack our things, so I'm going to ask you to help me by gathering your stuff in your room and putting it in your bag. I'll meet you back here in a few minutes, okay?"

"Everything?" she asked.

"Yes. We're going on a trip."

She pouted. "We just got here."

"I know. But we can't stay."

Her nose crinkled. "That's okay. I don't like it here."

"I know, right? There's nothing to do."

"It's boring."

"Which is why we're getting out of here. Now go pack your stuff."

"Okay."

Hannah ran off, leaving her coloring books on the floor, and Matt walked down the hall to Andrew's room and tapped on the door. He entered and frowned at how flushed the sick man looked. Andrew coughed, and Matt shook his head at the ominous sound.

"You're worse," Matt stated flatly.

"I won't be running any marathons," Andrew said. He eyed Matt's disheveled attire and coughed again. "What happened to you?"

Matt gave him the abridged version of his gunfight. When he was done, Andrew's frown was ominous.

"I reached a charter company that can have a plane waiting at Lesce Airport in a couple of hours. Lear 60 outfitted for air ambulance work."

"How far is that?"

"Maybe twelve miles."

"We have to assume the highway's going to be watched."

"There are a lot of smaller back roads. We can make it."

"That's great. I broke half my ribs. Can't wait to bounce along a logging road for a few hours."

"Not my first choice either. But it is what it is."

"I can help you pack once I'm done."

"I'll have to take you up on that, I'm afraid. Thankfully I don't have much," Andrew said, and then suffered another coughing fit.

"I'll be back in a few. Make the call whenever you're able."

Andrew waved him away as he coughed, and Matt softly pulled the door half closed and walked to his room. He sat on the bed and emptied his pistol's magazine to count the remaining rounds, and then reloaded it and moved to the dresser, where the other spare was, along with his meager clothing inventory. He removed the shirts and placed them on his bed and then crossed to the closet and got his bag. He quickly filled it with his possessions and then did a final walk-around of the room to ensure he hadn't missed anything.

Nicu followed the intruder to the drive and waited until he disappeared to pick his way along the edge. He flattened himself against a tree when he spotted the man standing on the porch, gazing out at the grounds, and removed a handheld from his pocket and keyed it on.

"I trailed the bastard. He's at a big place down the road from us."

"Just him?" Stefan asked.

"Him and a little girl. That's it."

"Cristi's winged, but he's okay. Tell us where you are, and we'll hook up and take him down."

Nicu shook his head. "It's just them. I don't want to lose the time if he's getting ready to run. That's what I'd do. I can take them myself."

"He killed three of us, Nicu. Just wait."

"Grab one of the trucks and find someplace to wait down the road, to the east. If something goes wrong, it's up to you to finish it."

"You sure? I think it's a bad–"

Nicu cut him off. "I don't pay you to think. Do as I say. I'll touch base once I've offed them."

Matt was finishing up his packing when Hannah cried out from the front room.

"What is it?" Matt yelled, and ran to see what had happened. When he made it down the hall, he found himself staring at an older skinhead holding a pistol to the little girl's temple.

"American," Nicu observed, his English heavily accented.

"She's five. Leave her be," Matt said, his gun trained on Nicu.

"A shame. So young. You should have thought of that before you went to war with us." Nicu inclined his head at Matt's pistol. "Toss that or she dies."

Matt slung the gun onto the sofa and took a step to the side with his hands raised.

"I have no idea what you're talking about," he said.

"Who are you with? DEA? A little far from your usual beat, aren't you?"

"I'm not with anyone. We're here for vacation."

Nicu cocked the hammer on his gun. "Over by the window, away from the couch."

Matt walked slowly to the window by the front door. "Now what?"

"Now you tell me the truth or the little girl gets one in the leg. Every lie will get another bullet. And I've got a lot of rounds."

"She's not involved. Let her go, and I'll tell you whatever you want to know."

Nicu's smile was that of a moray eel. "You're on vacation with a gun, and just so happen to shoot it out with my men at our place? Hell of a coincidence, no?" He shook his head. "Last chance. Start talking."

"Okay." Matt sighed. "I'm CIA. Working with the DEA. They know all about your business, so there's no point in doing anything stupid. You kill me or the girl, and there will be a hundred agents here in no time."

Nicu regarded Matt for a long moment. "What exactly do you know?"

"Drugs. And they suspect arms and human trafficking."

"And they sent you? One man? Please," Nicu spat.

"We have others in town. We rented this place because of its proximity to yours. I was supposed to do deep cover. Try to make friends with some of your men. But that didn't work out."

"So you decided to rush us? That makes no sense."

"I was reconnoitering. I wasn't supposed to engage. Your tripwire changed that." Matt shrugged. "But it doesn't change the fact that you're blown, and anything you do to us will be repaid in spades by my partners."

Nicu snorted. "You tell a convincing story. But it's nonsense. You're out here alone. I want to know why." He moved the pistol barrel down Hannah's back and grinned again. "I'm thinking one round and she never walks again. What do you think? I told you not to lie. Looks like you didn't believe me."

Matt's eyes narrowed to slits. "You hurt her and I'll kill you."

Nicu laughed. "You're in no position to kill anyone."

A shot rang out, and a hole appeared in the center of Nicu's chest. He stared down in disbelief, and then a second shot punched through his forehead, and he fell backwards against the log wall.

Hannah sobbed and ran to Matt, who leaned down and hugged her tight. He looked over his shoulder at Andrew, who was leaning against one of the hallway walls, a Walther PPK hanging loosely in his right hand.

"Rather unsavory chap, wasn't he?" Andrew said, and coughed.

"Thanks," Matt said.

"This is probably our cue to leave, don't you think?"

Matt nodded. "I'd say so. Let me drag this garbage out where he won't stink up the place, and then I'll help you load up. Can you watch Hannah for me?"

"Of course. But make it fast, would you? I feel decidedly under the weather."

"Not a bad shot, considering," Matt observed as he walked to the sofa to retrieve his gun.

Andrew coughed again. When he recovered, he waved his pistol nonchalantly. "I could never stand bullies."

"Me neither. I'll be back in a few."

"I'm not going anywhere," he said, and then slid down the wall with a moan. Matt barely made it to him in time to catch him before his head slammed against the floor, and he grimaced in pain at his ribs from the sudden movement and strain.

"Hannah? Honey? Get one of the cushions from the couch, would you? Uncle Andrew needs to rest a little."

Hannah was still sobbing, but did as asked, and when Andrew was attended to, Matt straightened and put his hands on her shoulders.

"Sweetheart? Stay here with Andrew and make sure he's okay. Can you do that for me?"

She nodded, and Matt's heart twinged. God only knew the toll this sort of trauma would take on the little girl.

"He was a bad man," she said.

"Yes, he was. But you're safe now."

Hannah nodded wordlessly again, and padded to where Andrew was wheezing on the floor and sat beside him.

"Hurry back," she said, and rubbed her tears away with the back of her arm, her expression one that would haunt Matt for the rest of his days.

Chapter 40

Riga, Latvia

Jet was relieved to be waved through immigration after landing at Spilve Airport in Riga; the official safeguarding the borders was old and reeked of stale tobacco and a high-octane liquid lunch. Customs was a different officer, this one short and plump, with a network of ruptured capillaries painting his cheeks and a cauliflower nose deformed by rhinophyma. He probed her backpack disinterestedly, seemingly disappointed she wasn't carrying several kilos of cocaine, and grunted as he handed it back to her, the ceremony abruptly over.

She'd spent the flight asleep and had only awakened when Werner had called out to her as they'd begun their descent, yet she felt only slightly rested from the two-hour nap. Now, on solid ground, she walked out of the small building that served as the private terminal and blinked at the overcast sky. The horizon stretched flat and gray, and the still air was perfumed by the exhaust of departing commercial airliners.

Jet found a quiet section of wall to lean against and called Noah's number. When he answered, he sounded irritated.

"I'm on the ground," she reported.

"Not for long. We dug up everything we could on your two faces, and both of them were known mercenaries. Russian mercs, to be specific."

"I could have told you that. Question is who contracted them, and how did they find us?"

"That's where it gets a bit trickier. As to who contracted them, we were able to have our Moscow station pay an unannounced visit to their agent. Like most of these groups, they use middlemen to handle the money and vet the clients. Anyway, this one didn't want to talk, but in the end he was forthcoming. Turns out a name from your past was involved."

"Who?"

"A man the agent knows as Sergei. We have him in the database as the former security chief of your old friend Nicolai."

"He's in a coma. The director was keeping tabs on him. So that's impossible."

"I know. But we checked, and it seems he's now conscious. Happened in just the last few days."

Jet digested the news. "And the first thing he did was send a wet team to Warsaw to take me out? No way." She thought for a moment. "And what's his connection to the bomber? The timing of the attack and our tracking him down was no coincidence. And there's no chance he was behind the attempt on me or the director. Not only is there no motive, but it's pretty tough to do from a coma."

"I agree. We're checking on an angle now, but we're waiting for confirmation."

"What angle?"

"Sergei has a brother. Who recently died in prison. Only the agent indicated that it was Sergei's brother who contacted him, not Sergei. We're waiting on a photograph, but it's possible the brother is still alive."

"Faked his death?"

The silence on the line was deafening. "Apparently there are no new ideas."

Jet had to give him that. "But to what end?"

"That's what we're trying to ascertain. One break – using the agent's account information, we were able to trace the deposit for the sanction. The money came from one of Nicolai's shell companies."

She looked around at the empty field that fronted on the airport grounds as she thought. "Nicolai had the money and the connections to handle the brother's death and resurrection. What's the brother's background?"

"That's where it gets interesting. Special forces. History of violence. Multiple arrests for assault, but prosecutions dropped, which could have been his brother's doing. They finally put him away for murder in their equivalent of a super-max prison. Life without parole. I'm speculating, but with Sergei out of the picture, it could be that Nicolai needed someone deniable who could carry out his dirty work for him. Someone who owed him for getting him out of prison. Someone whose loyalty was unquestioned due to the familial connection. Sergei's considerable hospital bills have all been paid by Nicolai's group."

She didn't have to ask how he knew that. Mossad was legendary for its contacts in the financial world, and there was no bank secrecy for the organization when it needed information.

"What's the brother's name?"

"Leonid. His stats are impressive. I'll send them to you along with everything else. He's huge and apparently all muscle."

"Sounds like I'm going to Moscow."

"There are plenty of flights out of Riga. It's a short flight, but it'll give us more time to see what we can learn about the brother. Let me know when you land, and I can have our Moscow desk supply you with whatever you need. I agree that the attack that killed Ian has to be connected to the ones on you and the director, so if you can get something out of the brother, we can continue down the rabbit hole and see where it leads."

"I'll need a kit. The usual. Gun, spares, suppressor, local cash."

"You'll have it. I'll arrange a rendezvous for you once you're in Russia. I'm presuming you can make it through customs without being flagged?"

"Shouldn't be a problem," she said, her new face and papers having served her well so far.

"Good luck, then. Call me when you're on the ground."

"Will do."

Jet switched the phone off and walked back to the private terminal. She approached the concierge and gave her a tired smile.

"I need a taxi to take me to the big airport. Is it far?" she asked in Russian.

"Oh, no. On the other side of the city. Maybe…eight kilometers," the woman answered in kind.

"How can I get a car?"

"I can call you one. Takes about ten, fifteen minutes for one to arrive, if that isn't a problem."

"That would be amazing. I don't mind waiting."

The woman placed the call, and Jet busied herself with checking on flights to Moscow. When the woman hung up, Jet looked over her phone at her.

"A car's on its way," the woman said. "You can wait by the door."

"Thanks again."

Jet scrolled through possible departures and saw that there was an Aeroflot flight that left in two and a half hours. That would give Jet plenty of time to get to the airport, buy a ticket, and grab something to eat before boarding.

"Perfect," she muttered, and saved the page, the new lead raising her spirits at the prospect of discovering why she was being targeted by a dead man's organization, and unravelling the connection between the director's assassination and Nicolai's group. She'd boarded the prop job with no hopes, and now she was going to be on an airliner, winging its way to a city she knew well, and with which she had a tangled and sordid history.

If anything justified springing for a first-class seat, this qualified, she reasoned, and peered outside at the road, anxious for the taxi to arrive.

CHAPTER 41

Bohinjska Bistrica, Slovenia

Stefan and Cristi sat in their SUV, watching the road from town, on edge ever since being ordered to do so by Nicu. Stefan had tried reaching him multiple times on the handheld to try to talk him out of moving on the lodge alone, but he'd ignore the transmissions, which was typical for him. Nobody told Nicu what to do, and those who persisted tended to meet brutal ends.

Cristi yawned and adjusted the bandage on his wounded arm. "How long are we supposed to sit here?"

"Until we get called back, or the Jeep comes this way. You heard Nicu."

"We're going to have to move the shop. We both know that. After the fight, and now this…"

"That's Nicu's call."

"Nicu's going to get us all killed. There's only us and him left. You think he cares whether we make it or not? Nicu only cares about Nicu," Cristi said.

Stefan glowered at him. "That's a good way to wind up dead. Keep flapping your mouth and see what happens. No story's going to help you then…"

"We haven't heard from him for an hour, at least. He could be dead. The guy he's after managed to kill five of us in a matter of a day or so. And Nicu thinks he can take him? It's nuts."

"Nicu is Nicu," Stefan said, as though that settled the matter.

"What if he never answers? What then? You thought about that?"

"He will."

"But what if he doesn't? What if he called this one wrong?"

"Then we do what we have to do."

The brothers sat in silence for several minutes, and then Stefan slipped a packet of cigarettes from his pocket and offered one to Cristi, who took it wordlessly and lit it with a disposable lighter, which he passed to Stefan. They cracked the windows and smoked, and Cristi was reaching for the radio dial when Stefan slapped his hand away.

"You'll run the battery down," he warned.

"So start the engine. This sucks."

Stefan shook his head. "How much ice you figure we have at the house?"

"Maybe…I don't know. A hundred fifty kilos?"

"That's what, about six million euros wholesale?"

Cristi shook his head. "More like four and change. But street value's more like fifteen for our shit."

"Nicu's making a fortune, isn't he?" Stefan said.

"We're not doing so bad."

Stefan was framing a response when a Jeep streaked past them, heading away from town. He grabbed his brother's arm and then reached for the ignition, but Cristi stopped him.

"That's not him. That Jeep's black," he said.

"You see the paint job? He must have sprayed it himself. It's him."

Cristi turned to Stefan. "What if it is? Nicu isn't answering. Maybe you should try him again and let him decide whether it is or not."

Stefan's eyes narrowed. "Not a terrible idea. He didn't say we should go after every Jeep that came by, did he?"

"Nope."

Stefan raised the handheld to his lips. "Nicu, come in. A black Jeep just went past us. Not sure if it's him or not. What do you want us to do?"

They waited, the radio in Stefan's hand humming quietly, but got no response. Stefan tried again, but nothing.

Cristi eyed his brother. "He's not gonna answer, dude. No way he would have let the guy escape if he was still alive."

Stefan nodded slowly. "If we're wrong…"

"You said it yourself. We've got six mil of crystal at the house, and a head start before the cops get around to checking in for their cut. What are we doing sitting here, waiting for a dead man? I mean, how stupid are we?"

"Where would we go?"

"There's those guys in Trieste. We could unload it at a discount, and they can handle shipping it out."

"They're more dangerous than Nicu."

"If they think it's a onetime deal, sure. But we tell them we took over for Nicu, and they'll be dealing with us from now on. Regular shipments, every two weeks, just like before."

"Nicu stopped dealing with them for a reason."

"Which is why they'll do backflips to get a channel open again. They may be nuts, but they like money, just like everyone else."

"Or we could unload it retail." Stefan gazed into the distance. "Might be worth setting up a network to move it. We'd never have to work again."

Cristi nodded. "So what are we doing sitting here? Start the car and let's do this."

"You'd better hope you're right about Nicu. There's no going back from this."

"Whoever that dude in the Jeep is, he single-handedly took out everyone. You seriously want to tackle that? Whether he's secret police or Romanian narcs or something else, you want to face off with him?"

Stefan thought and then twisted the key in the ignition. "Time to get rich, bro."

"Damn right."

CHAPTER 42

Moscow, Russian Federation

Nicolai's headquarters were buzzing with activity, even as many of the staff were leaving for lunch, the news of their Chinese adversary's untimely demise having percolated through the ranks and energized them. A palpable sense of excitement charged the air like ozone after a lightning storm, and Artem nodded and smiled warmly at the workers he passed, happy to bask in the triumphant glow while it lasted.

Rudolf and the rest of the board were nowhere in evidence, which was a strong positive from his perspective. The last thing he needed was resentful supervisors looking over his shoulder, waiting to pounce on any misstep, real or imagined. His morning had been filled with short meetings with Nicolai's closest subordinates, dealing with logistical issues that were an inevitable consequence of a lack of definitive leadership.

He finished his last conference and informed his secretary that he was going to be out for the rest of the day, and then called for his driver to be ready downstairs in the subterranean parking area. His family was waiting for him at the corporate-owned dacha outside Moscow, and he saw no reason not to start his weekend early and beat the traffic that would be flooding out of the city after lunch. Unlike London, cars clogged the arteries in the expansive city, and he was loath to crawl at walking speed for hours when he could whiz out ahead of the working class who had no other choice.

Artem had finished stuffing folders into his briefcase when his intercom buzzed like an angry bee. He thumbed it to life and leaned over the speaker.

"What is it?"

"You have someone here who says they need to see you immediately. Leonid."

"Ah. Yes. Send him in."

The intercom squawked, and Artem looked up as Leonid's massive form entered his suite. Artem sat behind his desk when he saw the big Russian's expression, and motioned for him to do the same. Leonid lowered himself into a chair that seemed like a toy contrasted against his size, and Artem raised an eyebrow as he regarded him.

"Well?"

"Bad news. The team got taken out."

Artem's eyes widened. "How many?"

"Five total."

"How can that be?"

"I'm just telling you what I've been told by the local contact."

"No possible blowback?" Artem asked.

Leonid shook his head. "None. You have no connection to them."

"But you do."

"Yes, but dead men tell no tales. Isn't that the expression?" Leonid paused. "We're completely insulated."

"Was it anything we did? Some deficiency on our end?"

Leonid shook his head. "They were seasoned men. Our involvement ended when they landed there."

"Christ."

"Sorry to be the messenger."

Artem sighed. "That's okay." He stood. "I need to make some calls. Have you spoken to anyone about this?"

"No."

"Not even your brother?"

"No. He's in no shape, and he has his own battles to fight."

"Very well, then. That's all for now."

"You have my number if you need anything."

"I'm headed to the dacha, so unlikely until Monday at the earliest. Go spend time with Sergei. I'm sure he'll appreciate it."

"Thank you. Have a good weekend."

Leonid rose and left, and Artem called out to him as he was crossing the threshold. "Close the door."

Leonid obeyed, and Artem opened his briefcase and removed a scrambled cell phone. He powered it up and saw there were two messages, but when he listened, there was just a dial tone both times. He dialed a number, and the call picked up on the first ring.

"You have news? I've been calling."

"It didn't go as planned," Artem said.

"I was afraid of that. I lost all contact with the group shortly after they went in."

"Look, I did what I could. I got you men. But that's as far as I can go. You're on your own from here."

"I understand. And you have a credit on my side of the ledger. I won't forget that."

"See that you don't. And there can't be any repercussions, understand? We never spoke."

"I get it. You'll be left out of this from here." A pause. "I can't help but wonder what went wrong, though. It was perfect. Who knew about this on your side?"

"Don't even go down that road," Artem warned. "I had one liaison, and he wasn't involved after they boarded the plane. You were the only one in contact with them. This is on you. If something went off the rails, it wasn't from our end."

He hung up, fuming over the discussion. He'd done a favor his gut had told him he shouldn't have, and now he was being accused of somehow compromising the operation. Artem crossed to the wet bar and poured himself a few shots of vodka in a highball glass, dropped a single ice cube into it from the undercounter fridge, and took a long pull, swishing the fiery liquor around in his mouth before swallowing it. The burn warmed his throat and diaphragm, and he finished the drink in moments and replaced the tumbler on the bar, his attitude sufficiently adjusted so he could concentrate on what mattered – his weekend with his family at Nicolai's luxurious company dacha.

Artem added two more files to his briefcase as well as the encrypted cell and closed it with a loud snap of latches. He glanced up at the wall clock and made a mental note to have the office redecorated – Nicolai might have been a genius empire builder, but he had the taste of a peasant, and Artem was surprised the office didn't feature a stuffed bear or hunting trophies staring down at him from the ghastly wood-paneled walls. Artem favored Scandinavian minimalism, monochromatic with clean lines, and the heavy furniture and dark mahogany everything felt oppressive and hackneyed.

He left the office and walked down the corridor to the elevator, the lingering ennui from the troubling phone call fading with each meter he put between himself and his desk. By the time the steel doors whispered open with a snick, the alcohol had banished all but residual annoyance, replaced by optimism over a future with nearly unlimited opportunity.

CHAPTER 43

Moscow, Russian Federation

Jet filed off the plane and down the jetway among the first of the passengers and then down a flight of stairs to customs and immigration. After a forty-five-minute wait in a long line, she was able to make it past both with no issues, and once outside, dialed Noah and paced in the arrivals area while the line rang.

"You made it," Noah answered, his voice soft.

"Yes. Can you talk?"

"Give me a second. I'll call you right back."

Jet hung up, and five minutes later, Noah was back.

"I had Moscow station assemble a standard kit for you. Phone, gun, ammo, magazines, stun gun, zip ties, combat knife, two thousand euros' worth of rubles. They can meet you wherever you like. Are you at the airport?"

"Yes."

"Take a taxi to Gorky Park, and an operative will be waiting for you at the main portal in an hour. She'll be wearing a green jacket." Noah paused. "You know where I'm talking about? A massive faux-Roman structure?"

"I know it. What about the intel on Leonid?"

"She'll have that as well. I've told her to extend you every professional courtesy. She has a car, which might come in handy."

"That didn't work out so well for the last operative, did it?" Jet asked rhetorically.

"I mean support. Take it or leave it. You can play this however you like."

"Who does she think she's meeting?"

"Just an agent. No other details. Her name's Olga. Thirty-three, dark hair, half Arab."

"Got it. I'll be there."

"Anything else you need, call. We have good resources there."

"Good to hear," Jet said, and didn't point out that she'd been to Moscow multiple times since leaving the Mossad in order to carry out personal sanctions, with no complications.

She disconnected and approached a money-changing kiosk and converted a hundred euros to rubles before she made her way back outside in search of a ride.

The line at the taxi stand was mercifully short, and she was seated in a car with a typically abrasive Moscow cab driver within minutes, his truculence when she told him her destination only matched by his lack of interest in any sensible driving precautions or rules of the road.

The drive took nearly an hour, and when she stepped out at Gorky Park, the afternoon crowds were dispersing, and most of the pedestrians were leaving the grounds. Jet strolled to where the cream-colored Doric columns soared heavenward, supporting an imposing flat roof framed by massive towers adorned with the Soviet-era hammer and sickle, and scanned the area for Olga – no doubt an operational moniker, as was her Sylvie alias. She checked her watch impatiently and pretended to be engrossed with her phone while looking over the small screen at the crowd, her nerves frayed, exerting considerable effort to remain outwardly calm as time slipped by.

Jet was about to call Noah and demand to know what the hell was going on when a woman wearing a green down-filled jacket and rolling a small black Tumi carry-on bag behind her appeared from inside the park and walked to the far tower. Jet watched the traffic coming and going for three minutes, and when she was sure there were no threats, paced over to where the woman was standing.

"Olga, I presume?"

The woman glanced around. "That's right."

"Our mutual friend indicated you have something for me?"

"You want it now, or do you need a lift somewhere?"

"I'd like to review whatever you were given."

"You can do so in the car if you like. Or we can find a café, and you can read it there."

"Is it in the bag?"

"Yes."

"How far away are you parked?"

"A two-minute walk."

"Let's go."

Jet accompanied Olga to a battered Lada that was at least thirty years old, its paint so faded it was difficult to determine the original color, the windshield cracked, the bumpers bent from countless parking attempts gone wrong. The interior was no better, and Jet tossed her backpack onto the rear seat while Olga removed a folder from the carry-on and handed it to Jet in the passenger seat, and then set the bag in back beside Jet's things.

Jet read quickly, and by the time Olga had slid behind the wheel, she'd completed her scan of the dossier.

"Do you know where Luchnikov Pereulok is?" Jet asked.

"Yes."

Jet gave her the address. "See how fast you can get us there. I'll jump in back and inventory the kit."

Jet threw the door open and wedged herself into the small rear bench seat, and Olga navigated through rush-hour traffic. The pistol was a well-used Russian Makarov 9mm that Jet was more than familiar with, and the two spare magazines of ammo were standard issue, as was the clunky suppressor. The stun gun was the usual variety issued to police around the world, and the combat knife was razor sharp, its wicked blade gleaming with a thin skin of oil. Jet pocketed the pistol, suppressor, and stun gun, slid the two magazines into her back pockets, and paused to examine the tie wraps and the phone before doing the same with them.

Nicolai's headquarters were housed in an obsidian glass tower, and Jet instructed Olga to wait down the street, where they could watch the entrance. If the Mossad intel on Sergei's brother was correct, he would be at the headquarters until late. Jet usually discounted information obtained from personnel like doormen and maintenance crew, but she had no choice but to rely on it now in the hopes of catching a glimpse of the man, who, according to the report, was the size of a horse and wouldn't be difficult to pick out of a crowd.

They sat quietly, watching the staff departing the building as the sky darkened with clouds. Jet checked the time every fifteen minutes, doing her best to be patient, but she was on edge from lack of sleep and the events of the last two days. She couldn't help but yawn frequently, and Olga eyed her with concern before speaking.

"If you want, I can spell you. Just show me whoever it is you're looking for, and I can watch for them," she volunteered.

"No. Thanks, but I need to stay alert. I'm only going to get one chance at this."

"Okay. I'm right here if you change your mind."

"I won't."

The number of people leaving had slowed to a trickle when a huge man in a long black overcoat, a knit cap on his head, stepped from the entrance and hailed a taxi. He crammed himself into the car, and Jet turned to Olga.

"That's our boy. Follow them, but don't make it obvious," she said.

Olga slammed the ancient Lada into gear and took off after the taxi, leaving sufficient cars between it and the cab so it wouldn't be detected. After eight minutes of wending through late rush-hour traffic, the taxi rolled to a stop in front of a medical clinic with a discreet green cross over the door and a brass plaque beside it. Leonid stepped from the car and bounded up the stairs, moving surprisingly nimbly for a man of his bulk, and disappeared inside.

"What's the play?" Olga asked.

"Not a lot I can do around a bunch of people. We know where he is. We wait until he leaves, and track him from here," Jet said. "I need to get him alone so we can have a nice chat."

Olga nodded and switched the ignition off. "What if he stays all night?"

Jet shrugged. "Then we'll have sore backs by tomorrow."

Two hours later, Leonid exited the facility and walked briskly down the street. Olga started the car, and Jet put a hand on her arm. "Wait until he turns a corner. We don't want to give it away now."

"He doesn't seem that situationally aware."

"Never underestimate a target. Looks to be more of a blunt instrument than a scalpel. But still dangerous," Jet said.

He crossed the street at the next intersection and rounded the building, and Jet nodded.

"Go."

Olga eased the car forward and, at the junction, made a left just in time to see Leonid entering another taxi. Olga slowed and allowed the cab to take off, and they followed at a prudent distance until they arrived at a Soviet-era apartment block on the outskirts of the city, its exterior drab gray concrete, its architecture mid-century gulag. Leonid got out of the taxi and made for the entrance, and Jet leapt out and called to Olga.

"Wait here."

Jet trotted to the entryway and, once inside, watched the floor indicator as the elevator groaned its way to the third level and stopped there. She waited until enough time had passed so she was sure it wasn't continuing up, and then raced up the stairs to the third-floor landing and cracked the fire door open.

Leonid stood down the hall, fiddling with a set of keys, his expression one of focused concentration. Jet slipped from the doorway and walked towards him, phone in one hand as though reading. He looked up and went back to trying for the right key, found it and slid it into the lock, and then did a double take as she neared him.

The Taser barbs stank into his massive back, and he stiffened and dropped to the ground, slamming his head against the cement wall in the process. Jet leaned over him and confirmed the head blow had knocked him out, and then quickly secured his wrists. She reached up and turned the key and, when the door swung open, dragged the big man by his feet until he was in the darkened apartment hallway. She locked the door behind her and dragged him the rest of the way into a modest living room, leaned him up with his back against the wall facing a large window that looked onto the street, lowered the blinds, and switched on the lights.

The place looked like it had never been lived in, with only a chair, coffee table, and sofa in the space, and a cheap two-person dining table pushed up against a wall opposite a simple kitchenette. Jet went into the bedroom and performed a quick search and found a pistol and several spare magazines, a cardboard box of fifty rounds, two passports in different names, and ten thousand euros and a stack of high-denomination ruble notes stuffed into a toolbox in a drawer beneath some T-shirts and underwear.

She returned to the living area, and Leonid was stirring, the effects of the stun gun less on a man of his size than typical, but the head blow likely concussive. Blood streamed down the back of his skull, and she regarded him without pity, waiting for him to fully regain consciousness.

Three minutes later, his eyelids fluttered and opened. "Who…" he groaned.

Jet stared unblinking at him. "You were sent to eliminate me in Seychelles. By Nicolai."

"You." He closed his eyes. "You almost killed my brother."

"Whatever. You sent a team to Warsaw to finish the job."

His eyes snapped open. "*You*…were the…target?"

Jet considered his genuine surprise. "Who ordered the hit?"

"I don't…know."

Jet's expression hardened. "You often send hit teams just for giggles?"

"It… I did it for the boss."

"The boss," Jet repeated.

"The new boss. Artem Gerdt."

"Why would this new boss want me dead?"

"I…don't know."

"Then what good are you to me? Why let you live?" she asked.

"I can…tell you where…he is." Leonid closed his eyes again. "You can…ask him yourself."

Jet cocked an eyebrow. "You'll give him up just like that?"

Leonid inhaled heavily. "It's just a job."

"What about the bombings? Why did he have the director killed?"

Leonid cracked one eye open. "What…are you…talking about?"

"You and this Artem hired the bomber. El Burro," she stated flatly.

"I… I don't…understand."

"I'm losing patience. I know about the bomber."

Leonid shook his head slightly and grimaced in pain at the effort. "Not me."

"Either you or your boss. They're connected."

"Take it up…with him. I'm out."

"You said you know where he is?"

"Dacha. It's in the woods, outside the city." He named an address.

She memorized it. "Security?" she asked.

"Some. I don't deal with it."

Jet eyed him. "If you're lying about any of this, I'm going to pay your brother a visit, and I'll be the last thing he ever sees."

"Leave him…out of this."

"Sure. You try to kill me and my family on the island, but your family's off-limits. Sounds completely reasonable."

She walked to the window and pushed one of the blinds aside to look down on the street, and was turning back towards Leonid when he vaulted to his feet and rushed her, his face contorted in fury. Jet was shocked by the speed with which the huge man had moved, and barely managed to dodge out of his path at the last instant.

Leonid tried to adjust his headlong rush, but it was too late. His momentum carried him headlong through the window, and he uttered a strangled scream when it shattered and he plunged toward the sidewalk below, enshrouded in the blinds. When he struck the pavement, Jet winced at the wet thwack, knowing what it meant without looking.

His intent to take her with him had been obvious, and she shook her head at how close he'd come to succeeding. The fatigue had slowed her reflexes, and she made a mental note to stay sharp when she paid the big man's boss a visit. She entered the address Leonid had given her into her phone's map program. It was sixty-two kilometers from the city, well off the highway on a country road. If they were lucky, they could be there in less than an hour.

Jet made her way downstairs and back to the car, and Olga was accelerating around the corner when the first ululating of sirens reached them from afar, and then the street behind them strobed with colored emergency lights as a police car swung into view.

"Any complications?" Olga asked once they were clear.

"Nothing I couldn't handle. But I've got an address for your nav software. I hope you've got a full tank of gas. You might wind up needing it."

Jet dialed Noah's number and, when he answered, spoke quickly. "I need anything you can get on Artem Gerdt. The new head of Nicolai's group. A photo, bio, whatever."

"How soon do you need it?"

"Yesterday."

Noah hesitated. "I'll do my best. Leave your phone on."

"Time's of the essence."

"You suspect he's behind the director's murder?"

"I intend to find out. Get me whatever you can."

"Will do."

CHAPTER 44

St. Andrews, Scotland

Night had fallen, and the fog was rolling in, seeping through the trees and blanketing the grass with white so dense it seemed impenetrable. The few streetlights struggled in vain to illuminate the main arteries, and traffic slowed to a crawl, only a few vehicles being foolhardy enough to brave the conditions.

A pair of headlights crept along the road that skirted the golf course, shuddering occasionally from speed bumps strategically stationed along the way, and turned onto a smaller tributary at the end of which sat the coroner's office. The vehicle coasted to a stop at the curb near the rear of the building, and a trio of dark figures emerged and made their way to the back exit, where one shattered the exterior lamp that lit the driveway with a small length of pipe while another moved to the door and knelt in front of it. The third figure stood by watching the street, pressed flat against the wall.

When the lock gave way, the men entered the darkened building and strode down the corridor to the holding room, where the corpses were stored in refrigerated stainless steel drawers designed to hold one body per slot. The men spread out, flashlights in hand, and scouted for a list of the drawers' contents, to no avail. After several minutes, one of the men's cell phones rang. He answered it, listened, and then called to the others in a hoarse whisper.

"We're running out of time. There's a silent alarm, and a call just went out on the police frequency. We'll have to find him by opening the vaults. We have maybe ten minutes."

"There can't be that many here. Town's not that big."

"True. But a lot of old people. Start on that side. I'll start here."

The group began opening the drawer doors and sliding the bodies out so they could see the faces, and within moments one of them alerted the others.

"Here he is."

They gathered around the corpse on the shelf, and one of the men removed a bundle from his backpack and unfolded a black body bag. All of them donned heavy rubber gloves and N-95 masks and went to work moving Lun's body into the bag. When they finished, they zipped up the sack, and one of them checked the time.

"Six minutes. Let's get out of here."

After closing the drawer door, the men carried their grisly burden from the room and retraced their steps down the hall. At the rear exit, they set the bag down, and the lead man cracked the door open and peered out. He scanned the grounds and then twisted to whisper to the others.

"You can't see three meters in front of you. No point in stealth."

They hefted Lun and pushed through the door at a trot, covering the fifteen meters to the waiting van in seconds. The lead man opened the rear cargo door, and they unceremoniously heaved the bag inside and then piled in while the lead man hurried to the driver's seat.

The engine started on the first try, and the van leapt forward through the thick fog. Headlights approached on the main road, and the driver spun the wheel, sending the van careening in a precarious turn, its running lights off, the night dark around it. He used the emergency brake to slow when the van teetered on two wheels and almost tipped, avoiding activating the brake lights. When the vehicle straightened, he gave the accelerator tentative pressure and increased the speed until the headlights swung down the street towards the coroner's office, at which point he slowed again, squinting at the faint outline of the curb he could barely see.

Once he was confident they were far enough away, he switched on the lights and accelerated again, but maintained a sensible speed for the limited visibility. One of the men in the back spoke softly over the sound of the engine.

"They'll think it was a false alarm. There's no sign of any entry. It'll be tomorrow before they figure out anything's missing."

"Assuming they bother to look. Could be weeks unless they have a reason to check all the drawers."

"Either way, it doesn't matter. We'll be in the air within the hour, and at that point they can't prove, or do, anything. The boss was clear on that."

The driver placed a call on his cell and spoke in a neutral tone, his Cantonese crisp.

"On approach to the airport. Should be there in fifteen, tops. Have the gate open so we can drive directly to the plane."

"Any wrinkles?"

"None. Went perfectly."

"Well done. See you when you get here. The boss is on board."

"Perfect. Have the ice ready."

They'd planned for everything and had twenty kilos of ice waiting to keep Lun's corpse from decomposing on the trip to China. It wasn't a perfect solution, but it was good enough, and their master would be more than happy that they had been successful. His brother would get the funeral that befitted a dignitary of his prominence, and all would be well in the world – with the matter of dealing with his poisoner a different problem for another day.

CHAPTER 45

Moscow, Russian Federation

The bright lights of Moscow faded in the rearview mirror as Olga followed the main highway west for twenty-two kilometers before taking a turnoff that veered into dense woods. The road's rough condition wasn't ameliorated by the battered Lada's antique suspension, and the little square car jittered and bounced along the two-lane strip of badly worn pavement, the engine groaning like a hobo in a dumpster. Jet watched the icon on her phone for a reference of how close they were to their target, and when they were within a half kilometer, she turned to Olga.

"Find someplace to pull over where you won't be seen from the road. I'll go the rest on foot."

Olga scanned the brush ahead and shook her head. "I'm not seeing anything. Are you?"

"You may have to just drop me off."

"I'll keep driving. There may be something farther along."

Jet frowned. "We're almost on top of the place."

"Are you sure? There's not much out here."

They drove past a gated driveway, and Olga took her foot off the gas. Jet grabbed her arm. "Keep going. Don't slow down. If they have cameras, it will look suspicious."

Olga did as Jet demanded and maintained her speed. Thirty seconds went by, and the trees cleared where a brook ran beneath a bridge. Jet pointed to the far side.

"There," she said. "You can see a track where cars have pulled off the road. Probably a spot where kids make out, but it'll do."

Olga pulled onto the trail and drove fifteen meters to a clearing by the water.

"Kill the lights and wait for me to get back," Jet said, and shouldered her pack. "Monitor your phone in case I get into a jam and need something."

"Will do."

Jet considered her. "You armed?"

"Of course. And I was top of my class in marksmanship."

"Good to know," Jet said. "Don't move unless you hear from me – or the sun comes up, in which case you can assume something went wrong."

"Got it," Olga said. Jet shut the door and looked around, the moon's reflection on the water a ghostly white in the gloom, and listened for several seconds before moving to the bridge and sprinting across. Once on the other side, she pressed into the forest and, when she was out of sight from the road, picked her way toward the villa.

Her phone vibrated in her pocket, and she answered with a whisper.

"Yes?"

"I'm sending a photograph from his London office site," Noah said. "He's an attorney, registered with the British Bar, and currently in Russia. Forty-two years old. Married, one son, ten years old. Six foot, hundred and seventy-eight pounds. Bilingual. Specialty is international business and contract law. Not much else. Want his address in London?"

"No, just the photo will be fine."

"Stand by."

The call ended, and a moment later the phone pinged softly. She opened the image and eyed the photograph of a relatively handsome man with dark hair and high cheekbones, wearing a conservative suit and tie – typically British understatement, she thought. She committed the face to memory and then switched the phone off lest it distract her at a critical time.

Jet moved cautiously between the trees. As her eyes adjusted to the gloom, she could make out a faint glimmer of amber light in the near distance ahead. Given the dearth of homes in the area, that had to be the dacha, and she slowed further, wary of twisting an ankle or tripping over a fallen branch in the darkness this close to her target.

A few minutes later, she came to a perimeter wall with electric fencing running along the top. That presented a challenge, but one she could overcome. She skirted the wall until she arrived at a tree that suited her purposes, and removed her belt and used it to help her shimmy up the trunk to the thick lower branches. There, she tested the largest that protruded over the fence with her weight, and when it held, pulled herself along it, hanging upside down, and then dropped onto the dacha grounds from above.

Jet landed and rolled and then froze in a crouch as she surveilled the surroundings. The house was to her right, and she could make out a guard sitting by the front door, armed with what looked like a shotgun. A glance to her left revealed another man down by the gate, also with a long gun, but no others in evidence.

Jet straightened and moved along the wall, grateful that it wasn't illuminated except by whatever ambient glow reflected from the dacha. The two-story structure's upstairs windows were dark, with the only light coming from the downstairs, seeping through the curtains. She stole towards the back of the house, staying with the wall, and stopped at the sight of another guard seated by the back door, a Kalashnikov leaning against the house, a cigarette smoldering in his hand as he read something on his phone.

She'd expected security, and was somewhat relieved that there were only three gunmen guarding the house. The most difficult part would be neutralizing the last guard, which was always the case, assuming they were in radio contact, which was a given. While she wanted to begin taking them out, experience dictated that she wait and confirm their reporting schedule so she could understand how much time she'd have between check-ins, so instead of moving on the nearest guard, she resigned herself to watching and waiting from a safe distance – far enough away that she would have some warning if there was a fourth floater patrolling the compound.

Jet found a clump of brush and lay on her stomach, watching from the safety of the cover as the rear door guard finished his cigarette. Jet had started her watch timer when she'd spotted him, and lay motionless as minutes ticked by. Almost a half hour later, the man stood, stretched, and then held his hand to his ear and spoke, laughing in response to something before heading inside. He was back in a minute, and Jet intuited that his zipping his pants meant he'd taken a bathroom break after a routine check-in. He yawned, sat down, and looked around, and then tapped another cigarette from a pack and lit it, the flare of the match momentarily blinding in the dark.

Jet watched as he smoked, again busy on his phone, his body language relaxed, the duty easy in the absence of danger.

A mistake she hoped the other guards were also making.

Because given the timing, she had at least thirty minutes to take them out and locate the lawyer, and she had no intention of wasting any time. They were all as good as dead and simply didn't realize it yet.

But they would soon enough. Jet had no intentions of taking prisoners or offering any sort of mercy. These men were protecting her enemy, which made them nothing but collateral damage. They'd known the risks going in, and were about to pay the ultimate price for guarding a predator who she was sure would show her no compassion were the tables turned.

Jet drew a deep breath and rose and then was in motion, her running gait as graceful as a panther's as she covered the ground to her first target, who had no idea that his stay on the planet was about to come to an abrupt and unexpected end.

CHAPTER 46

Outskirts of Moscow, Russian Federation

The bodyguard chuckled at a TikTok video of a bear dancing a jig while a young woman twerked in the foreground in time with the music, the visual as amusing as it was absurd. He was about to swipe to the next frame of mindless entertainment when the world went white and then black, and his dying breath caught in his throat.

Jet pulled out the blade of the survival knife from where she'd driven it through his ear into his brain, and wiped it clean on the guard's jacket before leaning him back in the seat and pulling the earbud free. She followed the curled flesh-colored cord down into his shirt and removed the small rectangular transmitter from his shirt pocket before stepping back and inserting the nub into her ear. Jet slid the transmitter into her bra and regarded the dead man, whose eyes were open in permanent surprise, as though in wonder at how unexpectedly his life and all his concerns had blinked out like one of his matches in a sudden gust of wind.

She stepped away and crept along the side of the expansive home to where the guard at the front door was seated, listening to music at a low volume from the phone in his lap. He looked up in shock as she materialized from the darkness, and when her little pistol popped once, extinguishing him with a round through his left eye, the phone tumbled to the patio with a clatter. Jet caught the dead man before he fell to the granite, and sat him up in the chair, his head slumped forward as though asleep. She placed the phone back in his lap and darted away as her earbud crackled to life and a male voice called out over the comm line.

"What was that, Misha? You drop that damned noisemaker again?" the voice asked.

Jet was running towards the gate, sticking to the shadows, when the voice spoke again.

"Misha? Come on. Answer. I'm not kidding."

She stopped ten meters from the gate and stood motionless, anticipating the inevitable check on the front door gunman – the recently departed Misha. She didn't have long to wait in the darkness. The gate guard strode purposefully toward the entryway, AK-47 at the ready. She allowed him to pass her position on the way to the house, and then terminated him with a point-blank shot to the back of the skull, dropping him like a bag of wet sand, dead before he hit the cobblestone drive.

She dragged the dead man into the gloom and then returned to the front door, which was locked. Jet trotted to the back of the dacha and found that door unlocked, as expected by the guard's bathroom break. She eased it open, grimacing at the creak of hinges, and stepped inside, the rustic stone floor pale gray in the dim light.

Her rubber boot soles were nearly silent as she glided along the hallway to where a light burned in one of the rooms to her left – the source of the glow she'd seen from the perimeter wall. She edged to a pair of white French doors and peeked around through the glass panes at where Artem was sitting in a black and red silk bathrobe at a desk, intently studying a multicolored graph on a large monitor, a floor lamp gleaming off highly polished cherry wood walls, a Brahms piano concerto drifting softly from a pair of small bookcase speakers.

She pushed one of the doors open and entered. Artem started at the sound and spun his chair around, eyes wide in surprise at the apparition of Jet in head-to-toe black, the pistol in her hand as menacing as her expression.

"Wha–" he exclaimed, and she held a finger to her lips, the gun trained on him.

"Shhh. We don't want to make any more noise than necessary," she said, her tone hushed.

Artem swallowed hard, and his Adam's apple bobbed several times.

She noted that both hands gripped the armrests of his chair and his knuckles were white; good signs that he was fully aware of the danger he was in.

He nodded slightly and tried again. "Who sent you? Rudolf?"

She looked at him curiously. "I have no idea who Rudolf is. Nobody sent me. You should know who I am. You've tried to have me killed enough times."

He appeared genuinely puzzled. "What are you talking about?"

"I'll ask the questions," she said, and indicated a yellow sofa to one side of the desk. "Sit there."

"I don't understand."

She exhaled heavily. "Sit on the couch, or I'll blow your head off. Clear enough? And keep your hands where I can see them."

"I'm unarmed. You've made some kind of horrible mistake," he insisted.

"Last time," she said, squinting down the pistol at him. "Go to the sofa, or you die where you sit."

"All right," he said, raising his arms by his sides, palms facing her. "Don't shoot. I'm doing exactly as you say." He walked to the couch and lowered himself onto it, hands up. Jet moved to one of the heavy leather barrel chairs and sat facing him.

"There. That wasn't so hard. Now we can have a nice talk. Let's start with why you want to kill me."

"I don't want to. I don't know who you are. I swear. I don't know who you're looking for, but I'm an attorney, not some mobster. You've got the wrong place."

Her smile was glacial. "The bomber. El Burro. You hired him to take me out in Greece. He almost succeeded. No more lies."

"I've never heard of any bomber, nor anything in Greece. I'm telling the truth." He blinked rapidly. "How did you make it past my bodyguards?"

She regarded him. "I almost believe you. You're very convincing."

"Because it's the truth. I have nothing to hide."

She looked around the office. "A lawyer in a multimillion-dollar dacha with a private security detachment…who has nothing to hide.

You have to admit, a tough story to sell with a straight face."

"It's true. The place belongs to the company I work for. They let me use it when I'm in Russia. I'm not from here. I live in London. I'm really not whoever you're looking for. You have the wrong man."

"That's funny. Leonid told me you ordered him to send a wet team to Warsaw to take me out. Hard to doubt what ended up being a deathbed confession."

Artem's gaze locked with hers. "That's what all of this is about?" He sighed. "I knew I shouldn't have done her that favor. I knew it."

"What are you talking about?" Jet demanded, her emerald eyes flashing angrily.

"The woman. I've used her for security work. She called and said she needed contacts in Poland, and knew my company has people all over the world. She said it was an emergency. So I had Leonid ask his brother for someone, and then I passed the contact off to her. I swear I had no idea what she was planning or who you are. I still don't. And I don't want to know. As far as I'm concerned, you were never here."

Jet considered his words. "You say this was a woman?"

"Yes. I've never met her. We only do business over the phone. But I can give you her information. I have it all. Phone number, address, the works."

"How do you know her?"

"I told you – she does security work. She's ex-Mossad. Knows everyone, to hear her talk. She contacted me and pitched her services. Impressive and very professional. I pay her in bitcoin."

Jet eyed him. "She said she's ex-Mossad?"

"That's right. Her name's Nabila. I'll give you everything I have on her – she doesn't know I sourced her address, but I did through a private detective so I would know who I was dealing with if she screwed us." He swallowed dryly. "I had no idea what she's up to. If she tried to hurt you, I'm not involved. I swear on a stack of Bibles. All I did was pass on a contact. That's it."

"And how exactly do you know how to find a hit squad on short notice?"

"Leonid's brother. He's been in the security business for years. For the company. I understand those types go with the territory." He paused. "You…you said Leonid's dead?"

"Correct. He didn't seem to like you much."

Artem shook his head. "He hardly knows me. I just met him a few days ago. He was a holdover from prior management."

Jet smirked. "Who also wanted me dead. Nicolai. Real piece of work."

"I'm the corporate attorney. I push paper. I don't take out hits on people. That isn't me."

"Where's all the info on this Nabila? Sounds like I need to…visit with her."

"I can print it out for you. I swear I'm not involved except as a client. We have no other relationship. None."

Jet gestured to the computer with the gun. "Move slowly to your PC and print it."

Artem walked as though in slow motion, tapped in a few commands, and then his printer whirred and hummed. When it was done, he removed a piece of paper and held it up. "Where do you want this?"

"Back on the sofa. Put it on the coffee table here."

"And then?"

"And then we'll see."

"I've told you everything I know. Full disclosure. Total cooperation. I'm not your enemy. I don't even know who you are," he said as he placed the document on the table and sat.

Jet leaned forward and scooped up the paper, removed her phone, switched it on, and took a photo of it. She replaced the phone in her pocket and was forming a thought when she detected movement at the door.

A little boy's voice called from the hall. "Papa? Who's there?"

Jet slid the gun down between her thigh and the side of the chair as the door opened and the boy's head popped in. He saw Jet, and his forehead crinkled in puzzlement. Artem cleared his throat.

"Go back to bed. I've got a guest. Work."

"I…had a bad dream."

"I'll be up shortly. Go back to sleep and wait for me."

The boy nodded at Jet and then pulled the door closed behind him as he left. Artem's eyes moistened, and he fixed Jet with a frightened stare.

"Don't hurt my family. Please. Whatever you do, let them be."

She exhaled and stood. "If I find out anything you've told me is a lie, I'll find you, and it will be scorched earth, do you understand? If you call Nabila to warn her, you and your family are dead. There is nowhere you can go where I won't get you." She hesitated. "I should shoot you just on principle, but for your son's sake, I won't. That's the only reason. You've associated with a murderer, and you helped her almost kill me. I'll never forget that. You're one itchy trigger finger away from meeting your maker, and it's because I feel sorry for a boy who would grow up without a father that I'm sparing you. But there's a limit to my compassion. If I were you, I'd contact someone to take care of your guards' bodies. Don't call the police. You do, I'll know about it, and you'll have signed your family's death warrants. Am I crystal clear?"

"Nobody will ever know what happened tonight. You have my word."

"Stay on the couch for ten minutes, and then go kiss your boy. Then clean up this mess. And pray you never see me again, because if so, it'll be the last thing you ever do."

Artem nodded, the color drained from his face. "I understand."

Jet slipped out of the home office and hurried to the back door and then bolted down the drive, the frigid air invigorating as she made for the front gate, conflicted over the mercy she'd shown Artem but sure in her core it had been the right call. There was no way she could kill him in cold blood and have his son discover his corpse. She believed his story, even if she felt he was holding some details back, and if it was mostly true, he'd done nothing other than make a bad decision on whom to help. That wasn't a capital crime in her book.

A vision of Hannah flitted through her mind, and she smiled slightly as she sprinted down the cobblestones.

No, definitely not a capital crime.

At least not tonight.

CHAPTER 47

Outskirts of Moscow, Russian Federation

Jet arrived at the bridge, breathing heavily from the flat-out run from the perimeter wall. The Lada was still parked where she'd left it, the windows fogged from the warmth of Olga's breath. She approached the car and rapped on the driver's side window, and Olga rolled it down and looked at her.

"How long will it take to get to Bulgaria from here?" Jet asked.

"Bulgaria? At this time of night? No idea. There will be flights tomorrow, but unlikely now."

"Damn."

Olga eyed her. "Noah called and wanted an update. He instructed me to have you call when you returned. What happened?"

"I learned what I needed to know," Jet said. "Give me a minute," she ordered, and walked out of earshot and dialed Noah's number. He answered within seconds.

"Well?" Noah asked.

"There was security. I neutralized them and got to the target. I interrogated him, and it's more complicated than I initially believed."

"Explain," Noah demanded.

"He claims to have no knowledge of the bombings, and I believe him."

"Why?"

"He has a young son at the house. I threatened to kill his family. He wasn't lying. I've interrogated countless subjects."

"So you bought his story," Noah said. "If not him, then who?"

"Remember Nabila? She disappeared when the director suspected her of selling intel?"

The silence on the line stretched for ten seconds. When Noah spoke, his voice was taut as razor wire.

"Nabila's behind this? She killed the director?"

"Apparently she's opened up shop in Eastern Europe and is advertising her services. The lawyer wouldn't go into detail what those services are, but you can guess. And she's sharing that she's ex-Mossad. So yes, I think she bore a hell of a grudge against the director – and me, for exposing her treason. It perfectly explains why she went after both of us." Jet paused. "That, and it probably didn't hurt her murder-for-hire business that she could point to the assassination of the Mossad director and claim responsibility. I imagine that would send her credibility, and her price, into the stratosphere." Jet hesitated. "I have her whereabouts. I need to get to Sofia, Bulgaria, as soon as possible. Can you get me a jet?"

Another long pause from Noah. "I have to say no. This information changes everything. Surely you can see that. Nabila is an agency problem, and her murdering the director makes her doubly so. We're going to have to take it from here. I can't have you involved any longer. I'm sorry. But you know we're very good at what we do, and she's going to have to pay for her crimes. I'll need you to send me everything you have on her, and I'll take care of the rest."

"Nobody's going to be as efficient as I will. By now you have to know that."

"Your kind of efficiency isn't required for this. She's a traitor to Israel and a murderer. We have to deal with her, not some vigilante or covert strike. I can't agree to your participation any longer."

"And if I refuse to send you the info, and go after her myself?"

"Then our relationship is over, and you'll be considered an enemy of the state. I'd consider very carefully what that means, both to you and your daughter. You know we have a long reach." He paused. "And if for some reason she evades you, that would be on you – we'd have to hold you responsible for allowing the worst traitor in our history to escape."

"I don't respond well to threats."

"It isn't a threat. I'm the director now. You've delivered information that requires that I act in the most official possible manner – not just for you, but to avert an escalation in Palestine that would kill God knows how many innocents due to the prime minister's insistence that the bombings were their work. So I can't keep this secret. Please understand, this isn't personal. It has nothing to do with your expertise or performance. Mossad needs to clean up its own mess. And if you cooperate, I'll happily reciprocate. Anything you need. Safe passage for you and your family. Access to our resources. Money. Whatever."

"I don't need your money."

"The offer's there. But I absolutely need the information. Every moment you delay increases the chance that she gets away. That should be obvious."

Jet's instinct was to refuse, but she took a few moments to think through the ramifications of doing so. If Noah was going to go after her with the full weight of the agency, then Nabila didn't stand a chance, and her threat to Jet and her family would be extinguished. In the end, while Jet might have enjoyed personally destroying the woman, Jet's main priority was her daughter and Matt, not a personal vendetta. If the outcome was going to be the same either way, then Jet had no real reason, other than ego, to make an enemy out of Noah over Nabila.

And making decisions based on ego wasn't a recipe for success.

Jet relented with a sigh. "Fine. I'll send you a photo. But don't delay. I'm prepared to get on a plane as soon as you can get one here if you're short of qualified operatives."

"That won't be necessary. For her, I'll pull out all the stops." Noah took an audible breath. "I know this is hard for you, but it's for the best."

"I want your word that you'll make her pay. No mercy."

"You have it. And I owe you a big one."

"Stand by for the photo. Tell Olga to take me to the best hotel in Moscow so I can get some rest. You're paying."

"Deal."

CHAPTER 48

Sofia, Bulgaria

Inside the French bistro across the boulevard from the main square, the lights dimmed and the music faded to a soft murmur, signaling closing time. The last of the diners finished their drinks and paid their checks, leaving a lone woman seated near the bar, waiting for change, her wineglass empty. The server arrived with a sheaf of bills, set them in front of her, and gave her a courtesy smile.

"All finished?" the waitress asked.

"Yes, thank you," Nabila responded, and collected her money after counting out a generous tip.

She rose and slung her purse over her shoulder, and allowed the server to escort her to the front door. Out on the sidewalk she glanced around and then set off toward the flat she'd rented, only a few short blocks from the city center, her mind turning over alternatives now that her gambit in Poland had gone awry.

Nabila wasn't surprised that Jet had turned out to be harder to kill than the director, but even so, she'd been shocked by her resilience, as well as the speed with which she'd managed to track the bomber. Nabila had hacked the server that controlled the bomber's warehouse's security cameras and detonators as a necessary precautionary measure – after the disaster in Morocco, she couldn't leave anything to chance, which had proven fortuitous when Jet and a helper had appeared in Warsaw and moved on El Burro. The bomber hadn't been aware that she'd taken over his systems, which was just as well, since he'd become expendable once his sloppiness had allowed Jet to track him to Poland. Still, it had been nothing more than bad luck, a split-second trick of fate that the explosion hadn't ended Jet once and for all, and now Nabila had to contend with an enemy who was as capable as any she'd encountered, having evaded the bomb in Greece, then in Warsaw, and then an entire Spetsnaz wet squad – although that group had been incompetent, as far as Nabila could tell, going in heavy before verifying the target was in place.

The street was empty except for a few late-night revelers on their way to the next club and an old drunk seated on a dirty cardboard square, humming to himself, the bottle beside him nearly empty. Nabila gave the derelict a wide berth, but something about him briefly drew her eyes as she passed.

The clothes were tattered, filthy, the man's hair long and unkempt…

So what was it that had drawn her attention?

She'd reached the corner when it hit her.

His shoes. They were as dirty as the rest of him, but the soles, the undersides, were white, like new. As though he'd been made up by a theatrical team, but they hadn't considered the bottom of his shoes.

Her pulse increased, and she rounded the corner, senses on full alert. It could have been nothing, too much wine and jumping at shadows. Could have been a panhandler who'd figured out that he could make far more as a beggar than working an office job and had contrived a suitable persona to engender maximum reward. Or he could have been the genuine article and had just been gifted, or had stolen or found, a new pair of Adidas.

There were any number of innocent and plausible explanations.

Or it could be that she'd been blown. That somehow, someone had tracked her and was mounting a surveillance operation.

She took a deep breath and shook off the premonition as a function of nerves. Nobody knew her location, much less that she dined at the little restaurant a few times a week, or that she'd leased a vacation rental for six weeks under an alias, paying cash. All of her business was conducted over burner cell phones or via the web. Her contractors operated the same way – payment was made in crypto, contact was maintained via anonymous servers, clients were either referrals from trusted customers or had been selected by Nabila as promising candidates. As she'd done with the Russian when it had become apparent he'd be moving up in Nicolai's organization. He'd initially been uninterested in her offer, but had relented and given her a chance to prove her abilities with the Siberian, and after that, with the faux attack in London to seal his credibility with the board. When she'd arranged to take Lun out for him, that had established their relationship as one with a unique bond – but even so, she hadn't told him where she was based, and had interjected red herrings about her whereabouts, just in case.

Nabila increased her pace, hugging her long black wool coat around herself, the wind suddenly colder, with more bite, than moments before. A young man on a moped rode past her on the street, the flapping end of his red scarf trailing behind him like a dragon's tail, and she relaxed somewhat. Her imagination was probably playing tricks on her, with enemies lurking in every doorway and lying in wait behind every dumpster.

She'd chosen Bulgaria because it was largely safe, had sufficient infrastructure to be comfortable, but hadn't deployed the surveillance hardware that much of Europe now had, with cameras logging every move and a cashless society tracking the population's behavior. It was still a decade behind in that respect, which made it perfectly suited for her purposes, where she could blend in without raising any eyebrows and wouldn't trigger any alarms the Mossad might have in place for her apprehension after her abrupt disappearance from Israel.

Nabil had been forced to reinvent herself when she'd fled, her finances limited and her prospects bleak. She'd elected to hang out a shingle as a specialty facilitator, thanks to her background in the dark world of clandestine dirty deeds, knowing that, like prostitution, the business of killing never went out of style, and there was always someone plotting the downfall of a rival or an enemy or a romantic entanglement gone wrong. From her Mossad days she had a long list of contractors who would do anything for a price, so it had just been a matter of establishing her bonafides with a few clients with sufficient financial resources to keep her busy, and her new career had taken off, her credibility boosted in no small part by her claim to having eliminated the head of the Mossad.

Jet was a different matter and was proving to be a thorn in her side; but Nabila knew that she had an Achilles' heel – her daughter. Nabila could afford to be endlessly patient about terminating Jet for her role in Nabila's downfall, and could back-burner any actions until she'd grown so powerful she could be assured success. After the Warsaw comedy of errors, that was what she'd decided to do, and she'd stick with her plan until such time as she was ready to pounce. Jet would eventually let down her guard, whether it was a month or a year from now, and when she did, Nabila would be waiting to strike.

She had almost talked herself into believing that any threat was in her head when she heard distant footsteps behind her; two sets, by the sound of it. She increased her speed slightly and listened intently as the footsteps behind her matched her pace, which confirmed that someone was in fact tailing her, and it wasn't her imagination at all.

Nabila cut down an alley that stretched behind her apartment building, and broke into a run, throwing caution to the wind as she bolted for the far end. She was nearly at the next street when she landed awkwardly in a puddle, and her ankle shrieked pain up her leg. Nabila gasped and tried a cautious step. Her leg nearly buckled, and she leaned against the nearest wall for support as she limped toward the light at the end of the alley, wincing at the agony that radiated with each step.

When she reached the street, a dark sedan screeched to the curb, blocking her way, and two men jumped out and approached her. One held up a wallet with a badge that glinted in the streetlight, and Nabila's heart skipped a beat at the realization that this wasn't an assassination, but rather was something more benign – something that held the promise of survival.

"Yes?" she demanded.

"Nabila Ergovy? You're under arrest for violation of the Espionage Act, among other things."

She blinked at the officer, who'd used her alias, not her real last name. So they didn't know as much as they might have. Another positive, slim as it was.

"I'm sorry – there must be some mistake," she said. "I ran because I thought someone was trying to mug me…or worse. I haven't done anything."

"Save it for the judge," the officer said. "I'll apprise you of your rights on the way to the station."

Nabila shrugged, apparently defeated, but inwardly wondering why her contacts with the police hadn't warned her of this. She paid them handsomely, Bulgaria being a country where everyone was corruptible for a price, which implied that her apprehension had been ordered at the highest level, with the beat cops being kept in the dark.

Problematic but not fatal, she thought as she held out her wrists for the officer to cuff.

"You're making a mistake," she insisted. "I've done nothing. Whatever you think, it's wrong."

"I'm sure it will all get sorted out at the station. And I'd advise you not to say anything more. You'll get your chance soon enough."

Nabila bit back the angry retort that rose in her throat, and instead remained silent, trying to grasp what could have gone so badly wrong that her foolproof anonymity had been breached, and who might be behind it. She'd left no trail to follow, her flat had nothing incriminating in it, and her phone and computer were secured with unhackable protection; so whatever this was, there was no proof of any wrongdoing on her part.

A thought that gave her slim comfort as she was forced into the back of the sedan, although the mention of the Espionage Act had her mind racing, the implication anything but good.

CHAPTER 49

Ljubljana, Slovenia

Matt rolled over and squinted at a ray of early morning sun that seeped between the hotel room blinds, and rolled off the mattress and onto his feet. He glanced over at where Hannah was asleep in the bed beside his, her mouth half open, snoring softly. Matt grabbed his cell from the bedside nightstand and trundled to the bathroom, pulled the door softly closed behind him, and switched on the light.

The reflection that stared back at him was puffy and unshaven, with bleary red eyes. He checked the time and saw that he'd been asleep for five and a half hours after a difficult trip that had culminated in Andrew being admitted to a hospital straight from the airport, his breathing progressively worse as they'd driven the back roads from the lodge. They'd aborted their planned trip to Austria, as his situation degraded after a few minutes in the air, and had set down at the capital city for a medical emergency, with an ambulance waiting on the tarmac.

Matt dialed Jet's burner, and to his relief, she answered.

"You have no idea how happy I am to hear your voice," she said.

"I'm glad I didn't wake you up," Matt said.

"Yeah, it's been a long one. Where are you?"

"Still in Slovenia. But Ljubljana. Andrew took a major turn for the worse, and we had some complications where we were."

"Anything…serious?" she asked.

"Nothing I couldn't deal with. But he's in a bad way. We just got in from the hospital a few hours ago. The doctors say his lungs are completely clogged. Double pneumonia. And they're testing for cancer. So…yeah."

"That's awful. How's Hannah taking it?"

A pause. "She misses her mother. So do I." He swallowed dryly. "Where are you?"

"Russia. But I'll be on the first plane to Slovenia this morning. Assuming it's safe to come."

"It is. Nothing related to your thing has happened here."

"And the…complications…aren't an issue?"

"Pretty sure not. But I don't have any burning desire to stay in Slovenia any longer than necessary."

"You fine with leaving Andrew on his own?"

"There's nothing we can do for him in the hospital. Let me know when your plane arrives, and I'll meet you at the airport. Maybe we can pick something off the monitor and just go."

"I'm game for whatever."

"How about your situation?"

"I'll tell you all about it when I land," Jet said, reluctant to discuss anything on the phone, even though it was secure.

"Fair enough. I can't wait to see you."

"Me too. I'll call when I know more." She paused. "You sound worked. Go back to sleep. You're never awake this early."

"For good reason."

"See you soon."

Matt terminated the call and looked around the squalid bathroom of the mediocre hotel he'd checked into. It would do for a night, but he was growing weary of a life on the run, and the idea of finding somewhere they could settle down and lead peaceful lives had never been more attractive. Hopefully Jet had resolved her problem, and they could disappear for good. The world was certainly a big enough place, and they only needed to find somewhere they could assimilate, where nobody would ask questions, and they could live in relative safety without having to look over their shoulders constantly.

If for no other reason than so Hannah could have a shot at a normal childhood and could put the various traumas of her short life behind her.

Matt wasn't worried about the police looking for them. The ringleader Andrew had shot was buried in a shallow grave off the lodge grounds and, with winter coming, would likely stay undiscovered for months, if not years. By which time they'd be well clear of the country, assuming anyone particularly cared about a drug-dealing lowlife getting whacked, which Matt had a hard time imagining.

The net effect on Hannah was more troubling to Matt than any longshot possibility of a law enforcement response to a den of cockroaches being cleaned out. The look on her face after Andrew had gunned the miscreant down, and her lack of response on the mad dash down the mountain road with Andrew gasping for breath in the back, haunted him, and he knew that he and Jet would have a battle on their hands trying to help her make sense of it all.

A fight for another day, he reasoned, and switched the ringer off and padded back to his bed to snatch a few more hours of sleep before reality slammed him in the head with a brick.

CHAPTER 50

Sofia, Bulgaria

Noah stepped from the plane onto the tarmac and waited for his assistant, Levi, to join him, and then walked to a waiting sedan flanked by a pair of unmarked police cars with emergency lights on their grilles strobing silently. The embassy driver wordlessly drove from the airport grounds, and the convoy arrived at the main jail twenty minutes later.

A trio of uniformed officers waited for them at the main entrance, their expressions as wooden as their posture, and Noah felt a tingle of anxiety creep along his limbs as he climbed from the car with Levi in tow. When they reached the officers, Noah nodded to the eldest, who offered his hand.

"Captain Borekoff, at your service," the Bulgarian said in passable English.

"Nice to meet you," Noah said, shaking the captain's hand.

"I wish it were under better circumstances."

Noah frowned. "I'm not sure I understand. We've got all the paperwork to take the prisoner into custody. There's no question about extradition."

The three officers exchanged uncomfortable glances, and Borekoff shifted from foot to foot.

"That's not the issue. Perhaps you'd like to step into my office so we can have some privacy?"

Noah frowned. "Is this really necessary? I've got a plane waiting on the runway."

"I think under the circumstances it is."

"I can assure you our documents are in order. Signed by one of your Supreme Court justices this morning."

"I'm sure that's true. Please. This way," Borekoff said, gesturing down the hall.

When they were seated in his office, the captain leaned back in his chair and indicated a pack of cigarettes on his desktop.

"Smoke?" he asked.

"No, thank you."

Borekoff nodded as though an important point had been made, and sighed heavily. "I'm not sure how to say this, so I'll just give it to you straight, is that not the phrase?"

Noah's frown deepened. "I'm not sure what you're talking about."

"This morning, the prisoner was found dead in her cell. She apparently committed suicide. Hung herself with the bedsheet." He hesitated. "I'm sorry. I only found out a few minutes before you arrived."

Noah half stood. "Is this some kind of joke?"

Borekoff shook his head. "I'm afraid not. She was in solitary confinement, and the guard last checked on her at three this morning, when she was sleeping peacefully. But when we went to get her cleaned up for delivery to you, she was dead."

"How the hell could this happen?"

"The guard is going to be disciplined; you have my word on that. A full inquiry is being launched."

Levi cleared his throat. "Do you not have security cameras you monitor the cells with?"

The captain tapped a cigarette from the pack and placed it on the rim of a glass ashtray without lighting it.

"Of course. But there was a problem with them. Some sort of technical malfunction. We're looking into it. This is the first time anything like this has happened."

Noah glowered at the Bulgarian. "That the cameras stopped working, or that you lost an extremely important prisoner to suicide?"

"Well, both. You have no idea how disturbing this is for everyone involved. This can't happen. There are protocols..."

"Yes, I'm sure," Noah spat. He stood, his lips a thin line. "Where is she?"

Borekoff appeared puzzled. "I'm sorry?"

"The prisoner. Her body. Where is it?"

"Well, I believe the coroner has taken her. We're not prepared to store corpses here."

Noah's eyebrows rose. "Already? I thought you just found out?"

"His office is around the corner. If I'd known it would be an issue, we would have kept her here…"

"How do you mount an investigation without a body?"

"With all due respect, it was clear she had hung herself, and was quite dead. Revival efforts failed. She was already cold to the touch when officers entered the cell. The method of death isn't in question, and the coroner will establish the precise time."

Noah stood. "I want to see her."

"Of course. I'll call over and let them know to expect us. Again, I realize no apology is adequate under the circumstances, but I'm truly sorry you had to fly all the way here for nothing."

The captain lifted his phone to his ear, dialed an extension, and then spoke softly in Bulgarian before hanging up and standing. "Please," he said, motioning to the office door, and rounded his desk to open it for the Israelis, both of whom were barely containing their fury. They followed Borekoff to a rear exit and, once out in a large parking lot, made their way to the coroner's office, where a pair of men in white lab coats were waiting with hands folded in front of them.

The taller of the pair spoke in Bulgarian, and then they all trooped inside, where the strong odor of bleach and formaldehyde permeated the hallway, which was colder than the jail by at least ten degrees. The coroners led them into a room where two stainless steel dissection tables stood beneath banks of lights, crossed to where the bodies were stored, and slid one of the corpses from the vault. One of the men pursed his lips as he checked the tag affixed to the end of the steel tray, and then pulled the opaque plastic cover free, revealing a discolored face whose mouth was frozen in a death rictus, distended tongue protruding from between bared teeth.

Levi looked away with a pained expression, but Noah didn't flinch and instead stepped closer and leaned in to inspect the dead woman. After several moments, he straightened and gave Borekoff a frigid stare.

"This isn't Nabila," he said, his tone glacial.

Borekoff blinked rapidly and seemed at a loss for words. He rattled off rapid-fire Bulgarian at the coroners, who answered in hushed tones, their faces blanks.

"I can assure you this is your associate," he began, but Noah cut him off.

"No, it isn't. The photo you sent last night was. This isn't the same woman. If you compare the prints, you'll see."

"You understand that her face is swollen and blue from her death? I'm sure that's where the confusion lies. Of course she doesn't look identical after that."

Noah shook his head emphatically. "No, this isn't the same woman. Look at her ears. They're a different shape than the photo." He snapped his fingers, and Levi withdrew a black-and-white booking photograph from the folder in his hand and presented it to Noah, who glanced at it and passed it to the captain. "You can see they're not the same."

The Bulgarians studied the photo for a half minute. Borekoff handed it back to Noah, his face ashen. "I… I'm at a loss for words," he stammered, and then growled at the coroners, who argued back, their voices collectively rising in volume as the seconds passed.

Noah looked to Levi and shook his head. "We're done here. This is a major international incident. Your government will hear from mine. You have no idea what you've done," he hissed, and turned on his heel and stalked from the room, Levi close behind him, Borekoff playing catch-up as the enraged Mossad chief stormed from the coroner's building and back to the waiting embassy car.

"Please. I'm sure there's an explanation…" Borekoff pleaded, but Noah refused to engage as the driver held the rear door open for him.

Levi followed Noah into the car and glared up at the flustered captain.

"This is a complete outrage," he said, and slammed the door in the Bulgarian's face, leaving him to stand open-mouthed at the curb as the car pulled away.

Noah closed his eyes and allowed a long exhalation to hiss through his teeth before turning to his subordinate, his complexion waxy.

"I should have let her kill Nabila," he said.

Levi blinked in confusion. "I'm sorry? Who?"

Noah waved the question away. "Never mind. Just thinking out loud. Call the section chief and let him know what happened. I want everyone on high alert. If there are any honest cops in this hellhole, I want them looking for her. Probably a waste of time, but we need to at least try."

"How do you think she did it?" Levi asked as he fished his phone from his jacket pocket.

"Money. Anyone can be bought. Guards, officials, whoever. It's always just a matter of price, unless there's a system that really punishes corruption at this scale. Otherwise it's a wrist slap and a firing for incompetence versus a once-in-a-lifetime payday. Which Nabila would know. Probably one of the reasons she chose this place."

Levi connected to the unlisted headquarters number and began speaking in barely audible Hebrew while Noah watched the buildings blur by, the cold rage in his gut robbing him of words, his jaw muscles clenched tight as iron at the thought of how the most murderous traitor in the agency's history had managed an escape worthy of Houdini right under his nose.

Chapter 51

Skopje, North Macedonia

A double-decker Volvo bus groaned to a stop at the Skopje Central Bus Station, and a line of passengers disembarked into a gloomy Macedonian morning, the slate gray sky threatening rain at any moment. A mother clutched the hands of her two children and struggled towards the luggage area, her shoulder bag sliding down her arm and nearly braining one of the little toddlers.

A woman grabbed the strap and offered the mother a kind smile, and the mom muttered a hasty thanks, her kids demanding all of her attention.

Nabila watched them retrieve their bags, and smiled again as the mother read the infants the riot act, and then continued down the platform to the taxi stand, her carry-on rolling alongside her with everything she owned in it. She inhaled the humid air with deep appreciation and then continued to the cabs, eager to be rid of buses and trains, already booked into an apartment for a week courtesy of the bus station wireless and a vacation rental website that was happy to exchange a fraction of a crypto token for a stay, no questions asked. She checked the address on her phone and looked around for a café where she could get a meal and a cup of roast, one chapter closed as another opened, no worse the wear for her ordeal if a half million euros poorer – but that was what emergency funds were for, after all, and a necessary cost of doing business.

She spied a yellow sign with a pastry and a cup of coffee on it across the street and beelined for it, the exercise invigorating after being cooped up on the bus for five hours, the adrenaline in her system having prevented her from sleeping until after she'd cleared customs using one of her three passports, the future a blank slate for her to paint however she wished.

And in Nabila's mind's eye, her hellscape artistic creation would be brutally rendered in the blood of her enemies.

Whose fatal mistake had been failing to put a bullet in her instead of having her arrested.

Which they would come to recognize too late.

But for now, she would hunker down, rally her resources, and plot a revenge that would only end with the last of the anguished screams of those who'd sought to destroy her. Because Nabila was at war with them, and in war she would offer no quarter, nor expect it.

They'd underestimated her, and it would cost them everything.

She would see to that.

About the Author

Featured in *The Wall Street Journal*, *The Times*, and *The Chicago Tribune*, Russell Blake is *The NY Times* and *USA Today* bestselling author of well over fifty novels, including *Fatal Exchange*, *Fatal Deception*, *The Geronimo Breach*, *Zero Sum*, The *Assassin* series, *The Delphi Chronicle* trilogy, *The Voynich Cypher*, *Silver Justice*, the *JET* series, *Upon a Pale Horse*, the *BLACK* series, *Deadly Calm*, *Ramsey's Gold*, *Emerald Buddha*, The *Day After Never* series, *The Goddess Legacy*, *A Girl Apart*, *A Girl Betrayed*, and *Quantum Synapse.*

Non-fiction includes the international bestseller *An Angel With Fur* (animal biography), *How To Sell A Gazillion eBooks In No Time* (even if drunk, high or incarcerated), a parody of all things writing-related, and *Expat Secrets of Mexico.*

Blake is co-author of *The Eye of Heaven* and *The Solomon Curse*, with legendary author Clive Cussler. Blake's novel *King of Swords* has been translated into German, *The Voynich Cypher* into Bulgarian, and his JET novels into Spanish, German, and Czech.

Blake writes under the moniker R.E. Blake in the NA/YA/Contemporary Romance genres. Novels include *Less Than Nothing*, *More Than Anything*, and *Best Of Everything.*

Having resided in Mexico for a dozen years, Blake enjoys his dogs, fishing, boating, tequila and writing, while battling world domination by clowns. His thoughts, such as they are, can be found at his blog: RussellBlake.com

Visit RussellBlake.com for updates

or subscribe to: RussellBlake.com/contact/mailing-list

Books by Russell Blake

Thrillers

FATAL EXCHANGE
FATAL DECEPTION
THE GERONIMO BREACH
ZERO SUM
THE DELPHI CHRONICLE TRILOGY
THE VOYNICH CYPHER
SILVER JUSTICE
UPON A PALE HORSE
DEADLY CALM
RAMSEY'S GOLD
EMERALD BUDDHA
THE GODDESS LEGACY
A GIRL APART
A GIRL BETRAYED
QUANTUM SYNAPSE

The Assassin Series

KING OF SWORDS
NIGHT OF THE ASSASSIN
RETURN OF THE ASSASSIN
REVENGE OF THE ASSASSIN
BLOOD OF THE ASSASSIN
REQUIEM FOR THE ASSASSIN
RAGE OF THE ASSASSIN

The Day After Never Series

THE DAY AFTER NEVER – BLOOD HONOR
THE DAY AFTER NEVER – PURGATORY ROAD
THE DAY AFTER NEVER – COVENANT
THE DAY AFTER NEVER – RETRIBUTION
THE DAY AFTER NEVER – INSURRECTION
THE DAY AFTER NEVER – PERDITION
THE DAY AFTER NEVER – HAVOC
THE DAY AFTER NEVER – LEGION
THE DAY AFTER NEVER – NEMESIS
THE DAY AFTER NEVER – RUBICON
THE DAY AFTER NEVER – REMEDY

Books by Russell Blake

Co-authored with Clive Cussler
THE EYE OF HEAVEN
THE SOLOMON CURSE

The JET Series
JET
JET II – BETRAYAL
JET III – VENGEANCE
JET IV – RECKONING
JET V – LEGACY
JET VI – JUSTICE
JET VII – SANCTUARY
JET VIII – SURVIVAL
JET IX – ESCAPE
JET X – INCARCERATION
JET XI – FORSAKEN
JET XII – ROGUE STATE
JET XIII – RENEGADE
JET XIV – DARK WEB
JET XV – SAHARA
JET XVI – FLIGHT
JET XVII – BODY DOUBLE
JET XVIII – IGNITION
JET – OPS FILES (prequel)
JET – OPS FILES; TERROR ALERT

The BLACK Series
BLACK
BLACK IS BACK
BLACK IS THE NEW BLACK
BLACK TO REALITY
BLACK IN THE BOX

Non Fiction
AN ANGEL WITH FUR
HOW TO SELL A GAZILLION EBOOKS
(while drunk, high or incarcerated)
EXPAT SECRETS OF MEXICO

Made in the USA
Columbia, SC
01 December 2024